KARLMARX.COM

A Love Story

Susan Coll

Simon & Schuster

New York   London   Toronto   Sydney   Singapore

SIMON & SCHUSTER
Rockefeller Center
1230 Avenue of the Americas
New York, NY 10020

SIMON & SCHUSTER and colophon are registered
trademarks of Simon & Schuster, Inc.

Designed by Deirdre Amthor

Manufactured in the United States of America

1   3   5   7   9   10   8   6   4   2

Library of Congress Cataloging-in-Publication Data
ISBN 0-7432-0003-9

To Steve

And to Ally, Emma, and Max

Hegel remarks somewhere that all great world-historic facts and personages appear, so to speak, twice. He forgot to add: the first time as tragedy, the second time as farce.

—Karl Marx

karlmarx.com

Prologue

I will confess at the outset that my interest in political theory stems largely from a crush on a former professor, and has never had much, if anything at all, to do with politics.

While palm trees tilted outside a pink stucco classroom, Louis Schwartz tackled Marxism with a vengeance that would have alarmed Karl himself. He interrupted a lecture on surplus value once to berate a student for bleaching her hair. He threatened to drop another girl's grade from a C to a D if she continued to wear red lipstick. He taught Marx as pure science, forcing us to commit to memory formulas derived from *Capital*:

> Let us assume that the line A B represents the length of the necessary working-time, say 6 hours. If the labour be prolonged 1, 3, or 6 hours beyond A B, we have 3 other lines:
>
> Working-day I.   Working-day II.   Working-day III.
> A-------B--C   A-----B---C   A----B----C
>
> representing 3 different working-days of 7, 9, and 12 hours. The extension B C of the line A B represents the

length of the surplus-labour. As the working-day is A B+B or A C, it varies with the variable quantity B C. Since A B is constant, the ratio of B C to A B can always be calculated. In working-day I, it is 16, in working day II, 36, in working day III, 66 of A B . . .

There was much of this sort of ground to cover before the semester was through: the general formula for capital and the quantitative determination of relative value, not to mention exchange value and surplus value and the fetishism of commodities and the secret thereof.

All of which was vaguely interesting, of course, but it was really Louis Schwartz himself, with his swarthy rock-star good looks, combined improbably with a thick Brooklyn accent, that kept me awake during those early morning lectures.

I was not the only girl hanging on his every word. We dutifully recorded his lectures in our spiral notebooks and braved a few odd, ignorant questions.

The girl who continued to wear red lipstick was especially full of inquiry, her flailing hand constantly vying for Louis Schwartz's attention: "If one use-value is not exchanged for another of the same kind," she asked during a particularly mind-numbing seminar on the twofold character of the labor embodied in commodities, "how do you explain used-car transactions?"

Professor Schwartz seemed delighted with these sorts of questions. Not because they demonstrated any understanding of the subject matter, but because they showed that at least some of us were taking Marx seriously: we needed to master these sorts of details if we were to go off and form our own socialist cooperatives in downtown Los Angeles. Or whatever it was we were meant to do with the blueprints for a communist society when the Berlin Wall was crumbling as we took our notes.

That my parents did not approve of my flirtation with campus communism went without saying. But then it was tough to recall a time when any of my variously fleeting ideologies had earned their praise. Certainly not when, as an eleven-year-old, I had liberated all of the meat in our sub-zero freezer and fed it to the neighbor's dog in a zealous attack of vegetarianism. Nor did they show much enthusiasm when I became enamored of existentialism as a brooding high school junior and took to chain-smoking cigarettes and quoting Sartre at dinner.

At least they had my two older sisters to brag about, who were typically less tiresome. They brought home trophies from their field hockey games to line the mantelpiece, dated well-dressed Gatsby-like boys who were good at sports, and then attended Sarah Lawrence and Vassar, respectively. And to enable children to live such privileged lives was, of course, the very point of my ancestors' many years of struggle.

My family had worked very hard to reach the gilded shores of America, and once settled, became skilled manipulators of the capitalist system. My grandparents had fled from Germany to New Jersey during the war, whereupon they changed their name from Stein to Kennedy and flirted briefly with Catholicism before settling, with some discomfort, into a life of agnostic anti-Semitism. Their oldest son, my father, subsequently moved to Maryland, married a woman named Bunny Rosen who was all too happy to become a Kennedy, and founded the most successful chain of discount department stores in the mid-Atlantic region. He then wrote a book entitled *Bulk Discounting,* which confounded many people, including myself, by remaining on the best-seller list for nearly a decade.

All this at least partly explained my need to temporarily escape to California, if not my attraction to a radical bearded professor.

The college had seen fit to pair me with a roommate who was in every way my opposite. Devon was exquisitely blond, beautiful, petite, and from an enviably repressed family in San Marino. In contrast I would probably be described as ordinary were it not for my long, chaotic dark hair, which was usually so incorrigible as to be worthy of remark. I was also several inches taller than I wished to be. Perhaps due to years of unrelenting suggestions from my mother about ways to self-improve, I had grown to feel more awkward and unattractive than really necessary. Devon intuitively sensed my plight and took pity. She brought me back doggie bags from her dates with fellow premeds, understanding that one didn't go out for a lot of surf and turf dinners when hanging out with Marxists. She harbored no illusions about changing the world; she planned only to become skilled at taking expensive images of it as a radiologist.

While Devon met the love of her life playing Frisbee in the quad during her senior year, none of my college romances went much further than the odd one-night stand.

On an emotional level, no relationship went any further than the one with Louis Schwartz, which admittedly did not go very far at all. He happened to be married, for one thing. I was only one of many groupies, considering the number of girls who turned up most Friday nights when we assembled at a local bar, ordered bottle after bottle of cheap red wine, and talked about the plight of migrant farmworkers.

Still, I had reason to believe there was something between us. There had been that time, for example, when he invited me to his house, and we worked together late into the night strategizing about how to best orchestrate a campus boycott of grapes. His wife was out of town, and our thighs had brushed together as we sat side by side on the leather couch, squeezing lime into our Mexican beer. When we finally parted, he had kissed me once on each cheek, and then—in what quickly became the most reflected-upon kiss in human history—I thought his lips touched mine, if only for a second.

One agonizing month later, I boldly presented myself at the door to his smoky, paper-strewn office and asked if we could talk. He seemed vaguely annoyed—it was not official office hours, and he claimed to have been in the middle of composing our midterm exam—but he motioned for me to come in. I took a seat in a creaky folding chair underneath a poster of Che Guevara and put my backpack on my lap. I quickly lost my nerve and felt very small and stupid and wished I were back in my dorm room. I began to speak, nonetheless. I don't remember my choice of words, exactly, but I pretty much declared myself to be in love with him.

As I spoke I started to cry, understanding intuitively what he was about to say.

I wiped my nose on my sleeve and tried to look composed. He appeared to be mildly bemused, and took a few long, hard drags on his cigarette before responding. He tried to be polite. He said that he found me "not unlovely."

He scratched his beard and thought some more.

"Your father is the Karl Marx of retail," he continued, "and this explains many things." I was unsure of whether any of this was meant as compliment, and had been unaware that he knew I was my father's daughter.

The phone on his desk began to ring, and I excused myself, anxious to flee his presence. I had no idea at the time that I would never see him again.

The next day, while pondering his riddle at the library, ravaging the stacks in search of Karl Marx's views on bulk discounting, unconfirmed reports that Louis Schwartz had died began to circulate through the tiny campus. I ran from the library and found a small group of attractive girls gathered outside the building that housed his office, peering through the ground-floor window in disbelief. His black leather jacket was still draped behind his empty swivel chair, suspended in time like the music left blaring on the car radio after a wreck.

And so began the flurry of unconfirmed rumors. One version of events had him accidentally walking through the plate-glass window outside the dining hall, a story partially corroborated by a pool of blood and shards of glass (later attributed to the previous night's fraternity party). The rumor with the most cache—the one that was later confirmed with some small variations—was that he had been hit by a truck driven by inebriated migrant farmworkers while crossing Los Feliz Boulevard against the light. He had, some said, been holding the hand of the girl with the red lipstick.

While I had gotten the answer I wasn't looking for about our lack of a future together, other questions remained. What the fuck was Professor Schwartz talking about, for example? Why was my father the Karl Marx of retail? What did he mean by "not unlovely"? Was not unlovely more linguistically akin to lovely, or not lovely?

In the months and then the years that followed I continued to weave my way through a maze of undergraduate courses, from political theory since aristotle to advanced seminars on being and time. I later wound up at the London School of Economics, where studying political philosophy was still considered worthwhile. Eventually I landed at Columbia University, where I hoped to earn my Ph.D. I was, I suppose, thrashing about like a just-caught fish, searching not for water but for context; for some body of work, some set of principals, that might give purpose to the spiritually empty but materially entitled childhood I had spent charging meals at country clubs and loitering in shopping malls. This is all post-facto conjecture, of course. At the time I was mostly operating on the romantic notion that studying political theory, and Marxism in particular, would bring me somehow closer to the dead professor I had once found so attractive.

Although I had always done reasonably well, earning A's on exams and writing compelling essays that were often rewarded with departmental distinction there was a level at which I was really just winging my way through school without truly learning anything. This caught up with me when it came time to write my dissertation, and I began to seriously flounder. The idea of pulling together a treatise that would present some novel idea to the world and simultaneously herald my arrival as an official political theorist (and thereby justify some seven years of higher education at an expense I dared not calculate) was suddenly and completely paralyzing. It forced me to contemplate questions such as what, exactly, was my niche in this dying field of Marxist scholarship, and more to the point, what did I intend to do after finally earning my degree? Suffice it to say I was not the only one posing this latter question.

At first I considered working on an analysis of the transition from a socialist to a consumer economy in the former Soviet Union, but I felt that I was in over my head, being more of a theorist than an economist-type person. Instead I chose to analyze Marxism in relation to Mao, but after a full year of contemplation I decided that not only was my topic a bit dense, but I would probably need to learn something about China, first. Three years passed, during which time I managed to fill five shoe boxes with index cards, purchase hundreds of dollars worth of thick academic tomes, and embark on three failed relationships. Somewhere during that period, my father stopped sending me a monthly stipend, forcing me to explore a secondary career as one of the most highly educated waitresses in America.

Then, while browsing in a used-book store in Soho one day, I stumbled onto a biography of Eleanor Marx, Karl Marx's youngest daughter. Curiously, in all of my many years of scholarship, I had never paused to consider the idea that Karl Marx might have had a family. I was intrigued by the blurb on the back of the book that described Eleanor as having grown up, quite literally, beside the thickening manuscript of *Das Kapital*. The blurb also alluded to her troubled personal life, including a long-term relationship with a married man. A relationship that apparently led to her suicide.

My head may have been mostly awash with abstract ideas, but I considered myself walking evidence that the little personal things in life (e.g., like a crush on a professor) tended to dictate events in the larger sphere (e.g., my costly education). Perhaps, then, there was some way to shed light on Marx, and on Marxism (and on the state of the world at the dawn of this new century!) by figuring out how and why Karl Marx's daughter might have killed herself. I was certain I had found my subject, at last, though it was a struggle to convey the idea convincingly.

My doctorate advisor, a scowling, frustrated little man named Ira who had been unable to find a publisher for his own opus on Kant, was not enthusiastic.

"You can't simply string a bunch of biographical material together and call it a dissertation," he said, not unreasonably.

Ira worked out of a cramped studio apartment on the upper Upper West Side, and his earthy wife (replete with loopy earrings and Birkenstocks) and a menacing-looking brown dog the size of a small pony were invariably present during our meetings, listening in, witnesses to my cumulative failures.

"The point of a dissertation is not simply to rehash history, but to come up with something new," he continued, while his wife pretended to be busy with a crossword puzzle. "You should think of your thesis as science project," he advised. "You should do the theoretical equivalent of discovering a cure for AIDS. You should find a new planet, so to speak, or identify a new form of mold. At the very least, you ought to set out to unearth previously unknown documents. Spend a year in Europe or something. Go dig through archives, search for old letters."

I looked at him blankly. "I was thinking of something along the lines of showing how the personal is political," I declared after a few minutes of awkward silence.

"Oh," he said, struggling to be constructive. "Do you mean that you want to demonstrate how Eleanor, as a daughter, influenced the role of the female in Marxist literature . . . or affected socialist thinking on birth control and population growth or . . ."

"No, not really," I interrupted. "But those are terrific ideas. . . . I'm really much more interested in the family-life aspect. In how Karl Marx might have been as a father and consequently how that might have affected Eleanor's life choices and give insight into why she fell for a man who was a jerk. I mean, I might also want to consider the ancillary question of why smart women fall for bad men," I added, thinking out loud.

Ira began to scowl again, and reminded me that I was working toward my doctorate in political theory, not pop psychology. Still, he kept trying: "Perhaps what you want to do is *deconstruct* Eleanor Marx. I mean, I suppose you could view her as a marginalized figure in nineteenth-century literature," he said tentatively.

"Yes, exactly!" I had no real grasp of what he meant but was anxious to end the conversation already. I had made it a point to avoid all classes on deconstruction, and refused to even consider enrolling in courses I considered trendy, such as anything with a reference to postmodernism in its catalogue description.

We went on to have a vague discussion about time frames and deadlines and interim status reports.

I said goodbye to his wife; the dog grabbed on to my pocketbook and I dragged him with me to the elevator, trying to remain calm.

At about this same time, I received a phone call from Lisa, my best friend, and idol, from graduate school. We had first met in a seminar on socialist literature in post-colonial India. I had admired her shoes, and she sent me to Bloomingdales, where I found them on sale. She had a sort of magnetism, a sort of designer political theorist aura that I sought to emulate. She always dressed in black, wore her silky long hair in a gravity-defying construct held together with what looked like twigs, and was fashionably pale. She was also very smart. Not to mention competent and directed.

Impressionable as I was, I wanted to *be* her. The next best thing was to be her friend, a position I enjoyed but which ultimately cast me into the humiliating state of perpetual jealousy. Not only did she manage to finish her dissertation without incident, but she married Roger, a popular classmate of ours who seemed both her physical and intellectual equal. They had a baby and moved to Washington, D.C., about a year later where she found an actual job in the actual field of political theory. She worked for a fledgling consulting firm called the Institute of Thought and had landed the job at roughly the same time I began my stint at Julio's Greek Diner.

"Great news," she said, after we caught up on things like her son's many preschool achievements. "I'm hiring you!"

"I'm not hireable," I protested. "I've finally figured out what I'm doing on my dissertation and I'm totally immersed in it now." This was only a partial lie: I had, in fact, read two biographies of Eleanor Marx and had even drafted the first few pages of my introduction, which was arguably the most progress I had made in years. "Besides," I added, "You know I couldn't possibly live in Washington. My parents are there and they would drive me insane."

"Oh Ella," she insisted, "it's just for a while. Three months or so. You'll make tons of money—it pays really generously—and you're the perfect person. We need a Marxist."

"*I'm not a Marxist,*" I insisted, not for the first time.

I launched a series of small related protests, but Lisa prevailed, as she always did. The project she had in mind for me would neatly parallel my dissertation, she urged, even though I had not yet actually described my latest topic to her. And sometimes, when one is stuck, she added politely, her voice growing small, a change of scenery can help. I bristled at her words but had to privately acknowledge their truth. I *was* stuck, repeatedly seduced by new beginnings, both of the academic and romantic varieties, that ultimately led nowhere.

Even if I was stuck, the more urgent problem was that I was broke. I tried to avoid asking for help from my parents. Their checks came with an inflated emotional price tag and I found it preferable to live off leftovers from the Greek diner. I supplemented my diet with Top Ramen soup, alternating flavors for variety.

Reluctantly, I packed up a few belongings and illegally sublet my student-subsidized apartment. I bailed my battered car out of the impound lot; threw Eeyore, my cat, into the backseat; and drove down the New Jersey Turnpike, toward Washington. My father, although he couldn't abide handing me hard cash to stay in New York, nonetheless agreed to put me up in a furnished apartment in a building he owned on Connecticut Avenue. I then prepared to check myself in for a financially rewarding and intellectually motivating stint at the Institute of Thought.

So one might have reasonably chosen to absolve Louis Schwartz and my expensive liberal arts education on the charges of having corrupted my mind. My life was not, on the surface anyway, a complete disaster. I did not, for example, go off to fight other people's armed revolutions in the developing world. Instead, I had landed my first job somewhere in the vicinity of my field of study.

But I was about to learn the hard way that some theories are better left unpracticed. That not everything you learn in books is true. That sometimes stuff just happens, and it is not always helpful to analyze that stuff to death. One day, for example, you might glimpse a man at a door—a man in a scarf and an overcoat, perhaps—and before the wisps of smoke from the end of his Camel have evaporated into the afternoon sunlight you might have fallen painfully, inexplicably, in love.

Chapter 1

My first day on the job, Carmen, the Institute of Thought's haggard Peruvian cleaning lady and apparently my only colleague, instructed me to spend the morning deciphering and realphabetizing a personnel directory for the Embassy of the Kyrgyz Republic. A software glitch had caused most consonants to be replaced by exclamation points, except for certain d's which became transposed with b's. "Kyrgyzstan," for example, had been rendered "!y!!y!!!a!"

Lisa had been unexpectedly detained, Carmen explained, and would arrive after lunch to give me my official mandate.

The morning was long and dull. It had not occurred to me to bring anything to eat. I considered searching for a coffee shop, but was not sure about office procedure. Did I get a lunch break? Did I have to tell anyone I was leaving? Would I run into the Colonel, whom I had not yet met, but was known to me as the founder of the Institute of Thought, and so far as I could tell through eavesdropped conversation, had spent the morning entertaining a steady stream of interior decorators?

Paralyzed by hunger and fear, and wondering how long it would take to dehydrate, I sat inert in the damp basement office of a Georgetown mansion fantasizing about tuna melts.

Lisa finally arrived around two o'clock. I stood to hug her and knew right away that something was wrong. Usually the very picture of composure, on that particular day she looked as if she had come unglued. Not only was her hair unkempt and graying at the roots, but instead of black she wore a yellow sweater with red embroidered tulips. She had also put on a fair amount of weight since I had last seen her.

"We need to talk," she said simply.

"Yes, we do," I agreed. "I'm not really clear on what I'm supposed to be doing," I confessed, staring longingly at the paper cup in her hand. "Is that coffee?"

"Sorry," she said, tossing the cup in the trash. "It was orange juice, but it's all gone. . . . Listen, Ella, I think I should let you know that I've made sort of a radical decision."

Lisa began to pace around the tiny office—a claustrophobic, windowless room made even smaller by the mounds of outdated academic journals and unopened junk mail that littered every corner. An oversize white desk stained with coffee rings took up most of the room, which looked like it had last been painted some time in the early 1930s. Seemingly irrelevant newspaper clippings, such as one on the arrest of the Unabomber, hung on the walls in place of artwork.

Lisa began to describe the revelation she had had while reading *The Wall Street Journal* on the bus that morning, in which a front-page article claimed to identify a new trend in America. "We've all been operating under the wrong assumptions, apparently," she said breathlessly and without evident irony. "Women do *not* want to have it all. What women want is to blaze a path toward a more balanced lifestyle."

I sensed where this was going, and knew right then that I had been duped.

"No, this is good!" she insisted, reading the skepticism on my face. Lisa paused mid-monologue to trace her finger along a crack in the plaster, which led to a small puddle on the floor.

"It must have seeped in from last night's rain," I offered.

"Oh that's nothing," Lisa explained. "It floods in here every time it rains . . . " She continued her soliloquy, weaving in the themes of motherhood and apple pie—or brownies or cookies or something—and the fact that Hayden, her two-year-old, was growing up so quickly. Somewhere in the midst of these effusions, she happened to mention that she was pregnant.

I tried to picture Hayden. Mostly he seemed to toddle about in smelly diapers interrupting conversations and demanding things. I could not really imagine it was possible for him to grow up too quickly. But that was not the point. The point was that Lisa had misled me.

"Are you trying to tell me that you just figured out that you're pregnant this morning?" I nearly screamed. "Coincidental with some life-altering article in *The Wall Street Journal?* Which conveniently coincides with my arrival here in Washington?" Perhaps I was angrier than circumstances demanded; it made no fundamental difference whether we worked together or not, as I would still earn some quick cash. But I was suddenly reminded of other small betrayals, such as the time she had insisted we sign up for a weekend seminar on the exploitation of athletes in organized sports, and she had dropped out, had obtained a full refund, even, without telling me. Or the night I sat alone, holding a table in the packed Chinese-Cuban restaurant on Seventy-eigth and Broadway for nearly an hour, before giving in to the realization that she had stood me up.

"You wouldn't understand, Ella," she said defensively. "I mean, there's just got to be more to life than work. I want to be there for my kids. I want to watch them grow up. I want to go their soccer practices and be involved in their schools and I want to cook nice nourishing meals."

She said all of this with the insistent tone of a religious convert, as if she had just embraced Jesus Christ the Lord.

"Have you talked to Roger about this?" I asked. Surely Roger—who had put his own political theory career on hold for a while in order to practice the art of mortgage banking—could talk some sense into her.

"Yes. He said whatever makes me happy makes him happy." I stifled the urge to laugh at this banal display of spousal support.

"But you can't do this," I pleaded. "I mean, I'm only here because of you, and I don't even know what you need me for, and besides, I need to get back to my dissertation." I paused as the door slammed upstairs, sending tremors through the walls, and I heard the Colonel shout to Carmen that she should not let that particular crook of a decorator back in his house ever again.

"Not to mention that the Colonel guy gives me the creeps," I added.

"Speaking of which," said Lisa, "he said to meet him upstairs in five minutes. He wants to talk about the transition."

"The *transition?* . . . I really can't believe you've done this to me. Didn't he understand I would be here just temporarily?"

I pulled a hairbrush from my bag and paused to unsnarl the frayed tampon that had become entangled in the bristles. The prospect of a meeting in the upstairs residential quarters of his home made me as anxious as the man himself. Lisa made no effort to reply.

Although I had not yet officially met the Colonel, I had read about him. He had allegedly earned his nickname back when he had been Chief Librarian of the Library of Congress. Some said the name stuck on account of his uncanny resemblance to Marlon Brando portraying Colonel Kurtz in the film *Apocalypse Now*. Others said it had to do with his temper, and his iron-fisted rule of the library, evidenced by a story that had landed on the front pages of both *The Washington Post* and *The New York Times* several days running.

According to the stories, the Colonel was asked to resign following allegations by two employees that he had thrown books at them. Both of the alleged victims had had especially bad news to deliver. A woman named Maria Jimenez drew the short straw in her department and was deputed to tell the Colonel—who had somehow failed to receive or take note of the fourteen memos she claimed to have sent to him on the subject—that the library basement had flooded, and that countless documents, including a recently acquired and lavishly expensive collection of Islamic manuscripts, were, as she tried put it gently, "a bit wet."

A man named Joe Witzen, in turn, had knocked on the Colonel's door, according to the newspapers, planted himself squarely on one of the antique Persian rugs, and boldly delivered the news that the new computer system—the one that cost millions to install and contained the entire catalogue of fiction—had crashed.

Civil suits were discussed, assault charges contemplated. And when someone leaked these details during a particularly slow news cycle, the story won heavy play for a week, spawning related feature stories on how to cope with temperamental bosses and the hidden hazards of the white-collar workplace. But then the whole imbroglio just faded away. There was some speculation that the Colonel had made private reparations to the employees involved, but apparently neither Jimenez nor Witzen was willing to discuss the matter further.

Shortly thereafter, the Colonel had cleared his desk out at the library and come home. He ordered a bronzed plaque for his front door and proclaimed his residence to be the center of a new enterprise that would help Washington embassies and think tanks advocate the thinking of lofty thoughts.

Lisa had been the first employee at the Institute of Thought. She had lasted slightly longer than a year. I was, evidently, about to become the second.

The Colonel motioned for us to sit in any of the several Queen Anne chairs positioned randomly throughout his living room. Each was draped with mismatched fabric samples. This grandiose room, like the office downstairs, looked as though it were in some state of flux, as if the Colonel were in the middle of moving, or preparing to leave on vacation, or had just moments ago returned from a round-the-world journey.

I sat uncomfortably in the chair across from him, putting the blue-and-gold-striped swatch of fabric on my lap, and was momentarily distracted by the odd way in which the Colonel's shiny head refracted a beam of afternoon sunlight, sending it bouncing toward the chandelier.

I glanced around the room, searching for clues to the Colonel's private life. Lisa had briefly told me that he claimed to have lived in an African village for several years, had toured the world with the rock group U2, and had once played minor league baseball for a triple-A team in the Cleveland farm system. He wore expensive suits and bow ties spotted with ducks and geese and hunting dogs as though he were the descendant of landed Virginia gentry, but as nouveau money detects nouveau money, I thought I recognized a Ralph Lauren–like fabrication of this upper-class aura.

I also knew that, while chief librarian, the Colonel was forever getting himself in trouble with his radical agendas. He had managed to alienate just about every relevant member of Congress, many if not most of whom thought that government money should not be squandered on exhibits celebrating unsavory historical figures. Two exhibits that had been planned by the Colonel, one on Adolf Hitler and one on suicidal writers, had both been canceled amid great congressional outrage.

"Lisa tells me you will be replacing her," he said, crossing one crisply pressed trouser leg over the other.

I thought of several caustic replies, but only managed to mumble something about having to get back to my dissertation in a few weeks.

"Did she tell you about the project?" he asked.

"No," I said truthfully. "I mean, I know there is some project you have in mind for me, but so far I've only been working on the Kyrgyz directory."

"Ah, that catastrophe. . . . Well then, let me fill you in . . . " He paused to ring a porcelain bell next to his chair, and Carmen came scurrying into the room. "*Tres* coffees, Carmen, *por favor,*" he said. "You do drink coffee, don't you . . . Ally?"

"Ella," I corrected him. "Yes. With milk, please." And a corned beef sandwich, I thought silently.

"None for me, thanks," said Lisa. "The doctor told me to cut out caffeine for a few months."

"Right. Of course," he said, clearing his throat. I sensed he was uncomfortable with such intimate biological disclosures. "Well, this is good timing, then, Ella," he continued. "We have a client, you see. We've had a client before, of course—the Kyrgyz—but this is a big client, well, one with big money anyway, and big ideas."

"I see," I replied nervously. "Who is the client?"

"They call themselves Neoclassicists for Universal Thought and Study," he said. "I think they might be Russian."

"N . . . U . . . S," I said aloud.

"Yes," he said. "That hadn't actually occurred to me."

"What do they do?" I asked. "The name sounds a bit vague."

"No, they're quite focused, actually. What they want is to get people to rethink Marx. Lisa said you were a Marxist, and might be uniquely qualified to help on such a subject."

"*I'm not a Marxist,*" I whined. "But I am working on my doctorate in political theory . . . and, admittedly I do know a bit about Marxism."

"Well, what our friends at NUTS, as you call them, have in mind, is putting a new face on Marx. They believe he was a misunderstood man. They want to give him a human face, if you will . . . "

"Yes," I said with enthusiasm. "In fact, I was just beginning to research Marx's family life, for my dissertation—"

"That's great, Carmen," he interrupted. "Yes, put the coffee right here . . . *no, not there,* how can Ella reach it if you put it over there?"

"It's fine, I'll manage. Thank you, Carmen . . . "

"Now the first step that these NUTS people are interested in, of course, is fund-raising. And we came up with the idea for a mail-order catalogue. . . .

"I was thinking that we should call it Karl Marx Unplugged," he announced while joining the uneven strands of an impressive paper-clip chain.

"What, the catalogue?"

"Yes, Karl Marx *Unplugged*," he repeated, playing with the emphasis of the words. "What do you think, Lisa?" he asked.

"I think it's overused," she replied without hesitation.

"Do you really think so?" he asked uneasily. "I mean, aside from Nirvana Unplugged and 10,000 Maniacs Unplugged and Pearl Jam Unplugged . . . wait a minute, was there a Pearl Jam Unplugged? In any event, everything seems to be either un-plugged or low-fat. So why not Karl Marx?"

I looked at Lisa wearily, hoping he would not seek my opinion, mostly because he was confusing me. I wrestled silently with the issue and decided I would vote for "unplugged" if asked, simply to be compliant.

The Colonel suddenly shifted his focus to Lisa, urging her to stay on at the institute, which I could only take as a reflection of my failure to have impressed him thus far.

She was leaving him high and dry in a moment of crisis, he said. The grant was huge, the project crucial to the institute's reputation.

"Can't you find a nanny?" he asked. "Or how about one of those au pair–type people I keep reading about in the news? Or a good boarding school?"

Lisa simply reiterated her determination. She was planning to give nothing more than a few weeks' notice, she said, and minus accumulated sick leave and unused vacation days, she made it clear that she was already pretty much out the door.

The Colonel looked as if he had just tasted something rotten, and he looked to me for help.

"Take some time to think about this," I urged Lisa, my voice revealing a lack of conviction. I had just remembered another little incident involving overdue library books borrowed on my card. It had seemed inconsequential at the time, but now it counted as admissible evidence in my mounting case against her. The accumulating memories made me so angry with her that I no longer cared if she stayed or not. I might have said as much aloud had the Colonel not abruptly changed the subject again.

"The first step, Miss Kennedy, is to brainstorm on ideas for the catalogue. We basically want to mass market Karl Marx. Make him accessible. You know, refrigerator magnets, coffee mugs, umbrellas. He's been totally underexploited, in my view."

"And this would be an actual catalogue?" I asked. "Like that you get in the mail, like Pottery Barn?"

"That's right," he said. "This is a big job. You need to not only liaise with manufacturers, but you'll then need to design the catalogue. There's some design program on the computer that you can use . . . PageMaker or something. You can figure it out. . . . You'll also need to come up with a mailing list. Maybe we could rent some lists, like find out who subscribes to the *New Republic,* or the *American Spectator.*"

"But those aren't exactly left-wing journals," I offered.

"It doesn't matter. Those are smartish people. Thinking, literate people, and they'll be into smartish catalogues. At the same time I would like—or should I say the NUTS people would like—to get a website going."

"A website?" I asked incredulously. Clearly Lisa had not informed him that I was the only person of my generation without a single entrepreneurial impulse.

"A Karl Marx website, that links . . . is that the right word? . . . that somehow connects up to NUTS and to the catalogue, of course, so that people can buy their merchandise directly through the computer. And naturally this would be the perfect opportunity to create a website for the institute."

"I don't think I'm the right person," I said. "I have no computer experience. I don't even have e-mail."

"You're young and smart, and Lisa has recommended you so highly," he replied. "I'm sure you'll figure it out."

The doorbell rang, providing a welcome interlude; I was about to cry.

We all sat frozen while the bell rang a second time.

"Carmen!" the Colonel yelled, but his summons went unanswered. We could hear the sound of the vacuum running upstairs.

"I'll get it," I offered, the fabric sample floating to the floor as I rose from my chair.

It took me a minute to figure out how to turn the heavy bolts on the front door, but I eventually opened it and there he was—Nigel Lark, as I would come to know him.

"Um, hullo," he said, startled. I detected a charming British accent slightly muffled by confusion. "I, um, I think I must have got it wrong," he said, pointing to the plaque. "I'm looking for the Institute of *Avian* Thought."

"Oh," I said, stating the obvious, "this is just the Institute of Thought . . . not of avian thought in particular."

I thought he was the most beautiful man I had ever seen, though he was disheveled in an adorably Hugh Grant–ish, absent-minded professor sort of way.

He wore a heavy overcoat and a nubby wool scarf even though it was early spring and already unseasonably warm. He had curly dark hair and sported a few days' worth of stubble.

"I'm really sorry," I said, not sure why I was apologizing.

"No, no . . . it's quite my fault. How ridiculous of me . . . I misread the sign. I think I'm looking for the place across the street," he said, pointing to a Victorian town house with a plaque on the door.

"Common mistake," I said.

He started to leave, though it did seem to me that he hesitated. I tried to think of something clever to say to keep him from going, to no avail. I watched him walk away, and then closed the door, returning to the miserable scene in the living room.

"Well?" said the Colonel expectantly, when I returned.

"It was just some lost soul at the door," I replied, unaware of the accuracy of my description.

"We've only got about six weeks to get the catalogue designed and in the mail," the Colonel said. "That's why I'm urging Lisa to stay on at least until this is through. But the woman seems to have made up her mind."

He looked at Lisa again, his eyes pleading for a change of heart, but she simply shook her head. I didn't say a word. My anger had turned to ice; I'd practically forgotten she was in the room.

"To recap, then," he continued, "the souvenirs need to be ordered, the catalogue needs to be designed, a mailing list needs to be generated, and then there's the website . . . you should have plenty of time."

"I'm not really sure this is going to work," I began, sipping from my dainty china cup of lukewarm coffee. "I have to confess that I didn't really understand the nature of the job, you see . . . I've just begun work on my dissertation . . . " Even as I protested, however, I had to confess to feeling a little surge of excitement. I was no longer a waitress! I could actually call myself a political theorist, if anyone ever thought to ask.

"Did I mention that we'll also need some slogans?" he asked. "To put on our souvenirs."

My face must have betrayed bewildered alarm.

"I once heard some congressman or other quoting Mao a few years back," he continued. "'A dinner party is not a revolution,' he said . . . or wait . . . was it the other way around? I can never get this story right. . . . That's why we have you, Ella, to keep us on track."

I tried to respond but nothing came out of my mouth.

"Anyway, whatever it is he said, I found it inspiring all the same," he went on. "We need to bring Karl Marx alive in the same way this guy did Mao: I want people in America walking around speaking in Marxisms. You know, 'Workers of the world, unite,' that sort of thing, only more relevant and less threatening."

"Sure," I said. My mind was drifting back to that man at the door. I was wondering about the Institute of Avian Thought. I was thinking birds. Birds of the world, unite!

"And by the way, I'll need to talk to you about health insurance," he said.

"Well, I hadn't expected that . . . I mean, I could use health insurance, but I don't think I'll qualify. I'm one of those temporary contract employees, if you know what I mean. I'll only be here a few weeks."

"I'm shopping for a good plan," he continued, oblivious. "And I've been interviewing my decorators about *their* plans. Let me know if you have any thoughts on the subject. I'll try to get some papers for you to sign in the next week.

"And did Lisa tell you about the other little perk?"

"I'm not sure." I hesitated.

"A health club membership. You can use my club. But you have to pretend to be my wife."

"That's great," I said. "Really . . . thanks. But I'm not that into fitness, so much . . . "

As I wove my way back to my office through the maze of furniture and down the dark stairwell, I was finally visited by a relevant slogan: Our leader is mad.

He will drag us down with him, clutching tight to our Karl Marx umbrellas while the water pours in through the walls. We will all become wet. And then, unplugged.

I sat in the basement like a prisoner, listening to footsteps overhead. After half an hour or so, I heard the door open and close, followed by silence. As best I could determine, Lisa had departed with the Colonel, leaving behind one clueless protégée, as well as her jacket and a singularly inspiring edition of *The Wall Street Journal.*

Carmen later passed through the office holding a pile of neatly pressed boxer shorts, and informed me that she didn't know where Lisa had gone, but the Colonel had flown to New York to visit furniture showrooms, and wouldn't return until the following evening.

I was essentially back where I started, with nothing much to do. Was I was supposed to begin working on the catalogue? And if so, how?

I flicked on the computer and managed to find the PageMaker program that the Colonel had mentioned, but I couldn't seem to make any text appear on the page. Twenty minutes later, I had succeeded only in creating countless pagelike rectangles, one on top of the other. When I tried to move them, the screen went blank. I decided to begin exploring the Internet, thinking this might be useful if I was really going to design a web page. But that, too, proved impossible; the computer had no modem.

I sat around for a while and split the split ends of my hair and rummaged through the desk drawers, which were empty save for a few random office supplies and some loose change and canceled stamps. Leaving seemed like the most sensible thing to do, but I was reluctant to disappear midafternoon, given that it was my first day on the job, and Carmen was still hovering about, periodically stopping in to chat.

I needed to look busy. I was already beginning to panic about finding the time to work on my dissertation, given the open-ended mandate of my new job, plus I still hadn't given any thought to the whole business of deconstruction. But there was a bright side of sorts: I was alone in a room with a computer. I pulled my notebook out of my bag and figured I might as well refine the first small bit of my dissertation. I hoped the Colonel wouldn't mind if

I used his computer for the occasional personal thing. I could always blame it on first real job syndrome—not knowing the protocol. In any event, he wouldn't really have to know.

Karl's Carbuncles. Eleanor was about four when she first became aware of her father's carbuncles. They were hard to miss; his body was covered with random but recurring abscesses. He told her they were self-inflicted wounds, but it was years before she understood what he might have meant.

"My illness always comes from my head," he wrote to his friend, Friedrich Engels. But no amount of self-awarenesscould will the wounds away. Nor did any of the conventional treatments employed alleviate his enormous boils. Marx had the doctors lance the wounds, and on the many occasions when he couldn't afford to pay their bills, he slashed at the carbuncles himself with a rusty razor. He took innumerable trips to the sea, as doctors were then convinced that salty ocean air could cure all ills. He swallowed arsenic as prescribed, but then gave it up; the poison aggravated his liver and besides, he said, it only made him stupid.

He would hold the bourgeoisie responsible for his carbuncles, he joked. That is, if they—the bourgeoisie and not the infernal carbuncles—lasted long enough to blame.

Indeed, the bourgeoisie was still alive and well in 1866, when Karl was copying over the manuscript of the first volume of *Das Kapital.*

The completion of the book coincided nicely with his youngest daughter's eleventh birthday. The two had grown up together, the manuscript thickening day by day as Eleanor played beside her father, tugging on his coattails—she sometimes even harnessed him to his chair and whipped him, pretending he was the horse in her game of coach—while he scribbled on, oblivious.

At the time, however, Karl had a few other things on his mind beside celebration. He lived in a home of perpetual crisis. Of the six children born to the Marxes only three survived. Three girls, at that. As he put the finishing touches on his manuscript, Eleanor was battling the measles, and her sister Jenny was still weak with diphtheria. Mrs. Marx's once beautiful face had been ravaged by smallpox, and Marx himself was stricken with recurrent liver pain and toothaches and a host of respiratory problems.

There were also financial woes: rent, for example, was in such serious arrears that on one occasion the landlord held a pistol to Marx's head, demanding cash. So many of the Marxes' possessions were in hock that careful planning was required before leaving the house during any given season: a wristwatch might need to be exchanged for a pair of shoes, for example, or a candlestick for a coat, should the weather turn cold.

"Never, I think," Marx once quipped, "was money written about under such a shortage of it."

In any event, he enjoyed discussing his physical ailments, and spared Engels few details in the intimate letters that Eleanor watched him write:

This is a perfidious Christian sickness. When I received your letter, I congratulated myself on the healing of old wounds, but the same evening a big furuncle broke out on the left side of my chest under the neck and an antipodal one on my back. . . . A few days later, another carbuncle erupted on my right leg, right under the place to which Goethe refers: And when he has no posterior, how can the nobleman sit? This is now the most

*painful of the known abscesses that I have ever had,
and I hope it will finally be the end of the series . . . you
should be informed that a new furuncle has broken out
on my back, and the one on my chest is only beginning
to mend, so that like a true Lazarus . . . I am attacked
simultaneously on all sides.*

And there are many more letters to this effect. While
there were many happy childhood memories for
Eleanor—of picnics on Hampstead Heath with Engels
and her father; of riding on top of Karl's shoulders
with purple flowers in her hair; of poetry readings and
Shakespeare recitations in the garden—there was always a backdrop of angst.

Of ugly oozing open wounds that could not be contained.

Silly as it was, I couldn't help but feel slightly envious of
Eleanor. No one had recited Shakespeare in our garden, unless
perhaps the Guatemalan gardener had been riding around on the
lawn mower, quoting Othello in Spanish. Nor were there rides on
my father's shoulders—he'd complained of a bad back ever since
he pulled a muscle picking me up in an elevator once, when I was
four. And the only purple flowers in our backyard—irises that
bloomed in spring—were not to be touched, let alone picked.

Still, I paused for a moment before shutting down the computer
and packing up my things. I did not mean to be ungrateful. My
parents certainly had an appreciation of some of the finer things in
life. There were no poetry readings in our garden, but we did
travel frequently to New York to attend Broadway musicals. And
there were many many books in our house, even if just about all of
them were the various international editions of *Bulk Discounting.*

Next time I visited my parents I would pump them for details
about my early years. I would inquire about the circumstances in

which my father wrote, though it was hard to envision him doing anything quite so cerebral. I had images of him from childhood, but they were of a man pacing around the room, shouting orders into a telephone, negotiating contracts on the golf course, or wandering around a Value Giant store inspecting things. I had always imagined, as an adult, this was what he did while calculating the subtleties involved when discounting things in bulk.

I resolved to rethink Bunny and Morton. To change those memories. To better them, and give us all a second shot at being enviably dramatic people.

Chapter 2

He was an ornithologist. Between jobs and between countries, in an overall state of transition, but hopeful that things would sort themselves out soon.

"I had a feeling we'd meet again," Nigel said in his seductively lilting voice. He was leaning against a blossoming dogwood tree outside the Colonel's house, and I had to keep myself from trembling at the realization that he was waiting for me. The heavy coat was slung over his arm, and he carried a fat bundle of papers. I realized then that he was somewhat older than me—perhaps by as much as ten years—and looked even more rumpled, though no less adorable, than he had earlier in the day.

"Yes, I had that feeling, too," I replied, relieved that the spark had not been a figment of my imagination, as most of my sparks turned out to be.

"I know this will seem odd, but I have something I'd like to give you," he said, setting his papers down on the lawn and rummaging through his coat pockets. He produced a set of keys, several pencils, a handkerchief, a pack of cigarettes, and a metro fare card before pulling out three tarnished gold bangles. I watched him in amused disbelief, feeling slightly giddy.

"I've been carrying these around for a while," he said in a tone more full of fact than sentiment. "I think you should have them."

I slipped the bracelets on my wrist and jangled them. "They're beautiful," I lied. They might be once I spruced them up with a little polish, I figured. Already I had a million questions for this man with unexplained treasures in his pocket but I was so hungry I could barely think. "I'm absolutely starving," I explained. "Will you have dinner with me?"

"Dinner?" He glanced at his watch. "But it's not even six o'clock."

"I don't care. I haven't eaten a thing all day." Without waiting for a response I took his arm, as if we were already lovers, and led him toward the shops on Wisconsin Avenue.

I am still baffled by what enabled me to do that. On that first day I was a very different self with Nigel—confident and aggressive, possibly even witty. I had never truly been in love before then, and I felt as if I could see the future.

Or perhaps more accurately, just a sliver of it.

The only sure thing I learned about Nigel that night was that he had a thing about birds.

He had originally come to America on a speaking tour organized by the Audubon Society, he explained. He had been asked to lecture on the use of mechanical birds in fieldwork, a subject with which he became familiar during his recent stint in New Guinea. He had originally gone to the island to study birds of paradise, he said, but had found himself distracted by the bowerbirds, instead.

"I've never even heard of a bowerbird," I confessed as I devoured a well-done ten-ounce sirloin smeared in mustard. "Never mind a *mechanical* bowerbird."

He grew pleasantly animated and pulled the pack of unfiltered Camels from his pocket. An elderly couple at the next table began to cough profusely and in unison as Nigel struck the match, attracting the attention of another patron, who appeared to be a law student busily adorning his Property casebook with a light blue highlighter. The student stood up and walked to our table and announced loudly that smoking was not allowed, citing some city ordinance for emphasis, and Nigel apologized and crushed his cigarette into the saucer of his coffee cup and kept on talking, unfazed.

"There are at least eighteen different species of bowerbirds," he continued, "and eleven of those live in New Guinea. Actually, the first bower was discovered in the mid-1800s—"

I interrupted him and said that was sort of a coincidence—not a terribly profound coincidence, but an interesting one all the same—since that was roughly the era that I was studying for my dissertation.

Nigel didn't seem terribly impressed by the parallel—in fact he didn't even pause to ask me what dissertation—and he went on to explain that male bowerbirds were best known for building elaborate structures in order to attract mates. The less attractive the male bird, he said, the more elaborate the bower.

I flagged the waitress down and asked for coffee and some cherry pie with vanilla ice cream and considered ways to change the subject. I wanted to know more about him, and less about the birds. His eyes were a spectacular profusion of colors, with green specks layered on blue, atop the deepest brown I had ever seen. I couldn't stop staring.

As he spoke, I found myself possessed by strange, disturbing urges. I wanted to climb across the table and seduce him, but another part of my desire was entirely cerebral. I wanted to study him. I wanted to turn him inside out, to read the labels in his clothing, to rummage through his wallet, to examine his dental work, to smell his underarms, to understand the sum of the pieces that made him instantly and inexplicably desirable to me.

"Do you ever eat?" I asked, embarrassed at the amount of food I was consuming.

"Yes, but not right now," he replied, and smiled before continuing. It seemed he had information to deliver, and could not relax until he had emptied his notebook. "They build either maypoles or bowers or in some extreme cases, even small but elaborate cottages," he explained, "and then they decorate them. They love anything shiny and colorful. Berries, pebbles, parrot feathers . . . even human objects like coins or keys or hair clips or jewelry. And yet, somewhat surprisingly given their eye for detail, the male birds seemed quite willing to mate with the mechanical birds even if they were not painted with the proper colors—"

I probably should have asked profound follow-up questions but there were really so many other things that I felt the need to know. "What's your favorite color?" I interrupted.

"Hmmm . . . ," he replied. "Haven't given it much thought. Blue, I suppose. There isn't much blue to be found in the rain forest." He went on to explain that bowerbirds were one of the very few species of birds that were not monogamous, and it was only at that point that I noticed the wedding band on his left hand.

It had been threatening to rain all day. The skies had grown progressively darker since lunchtime, and as Nigel described the impressive stick hut built by the Vogelkop bowerbird in the Wandammen mountains of Irian Jaya I saw a flash of lightning through the restaurant window.

The waitress came over with the check, which I insisted on paying given that he had not eaten anything, and the law student gathered his books and left and the elderly couple asked the waitress to ask Nigel to put out the cigarette he had just lit and Nigel finally stopped speaking and reached across the table for my hand and asked me a favor.

"Will you walk me home, Ella?" he said, averting his eyes. "-I've got a thing about the rain, you see . . . a sort of rain phobia."

I laughed, but quickly realized that he was serious. "What do you mean?" I asked.

"I can't really explain it very well. Ever since New Guinea . . .

it seems to attack me personally . . . the rain, that is," he said, growing self-conscious.

I began my descent.

"What do you mean, it *attacks* you?" I asked worriedly. This was certainly something to pay attention to: the man I had just fallen in love with had a potentially disconcerting rain phobia.

"It just . . . it just sort of slashes at me," he said, shrugging his shoulders as if this should suffice as an answer. As if the rain singled him out, slashed at him in particular, and not at everybody else.

"Have you tried, like, a raincoat, or an umbrella?" I offered stupidly.

"Nothing helps. It finds me underneath the largest of umbrellas, even. Under the thickest of raincoats."

"Why?" I asked again, this time more gently, suppressing my alarm. "What happened in New Guinea?"

"Please, let's not talk about it," he said in such a pleading sort of tone that I decided just to let it go. In fact, I might have written him off as a lunatic had I not already fallen into some sort of intoxicating spell due in no small part to the kaleidoscopic eyes and the euphonic delivery of his lines.

I walked him home in the rain and entered his wreck of a one-room apartment in a decidedly ungentrified section of upper Georgetown. He invited me in and I accepted, actively defying everything my mother ever told me about strange men, and, given the presence of his wedding ring, against my better judgment.

We were both drenched. He handed me a dish towel and I wasn't really sure what to do about my dripping clothes and he asked if I would like a cup of tea.

While he put the water on to boil I began to subtly inspect his apartment for signs of a wife. Instead I found a green parrot named Bob, whose messy cage seemed a metaphor for the rest of the place. Nigel's bower was not exactly his best selling point. The furniture was worn and tattered, dirty dishes were beginning to mold on the coffee table, and rainbow pebbles of bird food were ground into the rug. Ashtrays were overflowing, and laundry was seeping out from under the bed.

After a few minutes he brought in a pot of tea and we drank in silence. I studied the face of Winnie-the-Pooh on my chipped mug.

"'How sweet to be a Cloud Floating in the Blue! It makes him very proud To be a little cloud,'" I read aloud.

"'The more he looked inside,'" said Nigel, "'the more Piglet wasn't there.' . . . I think that's terribly profound, don't you?"

"I have a cat named Eeyore," I offered.

"I think I could fall in love with a woman with a cat named Eeyore," he replied.

We kissed, then sipped our tea.

We spent every night together for two weeks, shifting to the more civilized environs of my apartment. Although we shared an easy physical intimacy, I progressed very little on the information-gathering front. I was prepared to devour this man whole. I wanted to hear about his childhood in England and about his favorite teacher and about his first kiss. I wanted to know the history of the small scar on the milky side of his arm. But he seemed reluctant to answer personal questions, and my random sleuthing revealed only that his clothes were mostly from Marks and Spencer; he carried no wallet, but only a bit of loose change and crumpled bills in his pocket; he appeared to have had no dental work whatsoever (in marked contrast to my own multiple crowns and painful root canals); and his underarms smelled deliciously musky.

When I pushed him to be more communicative he replied that he was a man, for god's sake, and a British man at that. Yes, he had a wife, he agreed after my gentle but persistent queries, but the relationship was decidedly over. He'd once had a dalmatian, as well, he volunteered, as if these two details carried equal weight.

His confessions did not suffice; I was intellectually incapable of letting the subject drop. When I was not actively interrogating him, I was torturing myself with questions. Why had his marriage fallen apart? Or *had* it fallen apart, really? And what had happened in New Guinea? I had several images to feed into my already over active imagination: a wife, a dalmatian, and some slashing rain. Not to mention eighteen different species of bower-birds collecting brightly colored objects and mating indiscriminately.

Apart from droning on about birds, or answering my questions with spectacularly unsatisfying replies, Nigel was not much of a talker. I, in turn, overcompensated by chatting relentlessly in an effort to fill in all of the awkward silent gaps.

Questions such as "Wasn't Eeyore looking especially cute curled up on his sweater?" for example, or "Would you like your eggs scrambled or fried?" at least produced a smile and sometimes even a response. But I tried not to mind. I decided his aloofness simply reflected a preoccupation with more important things. He was busy thinking deep thoughts about ornithology and its relationship to the human condition. I should have been busy, myself, thinking deep thoughts about Eleanor Marx, or at least about the Institute of Thought and my Karl Marx mail-order catalogue and web page, but I found that thinking deep thoughts about Nigel was pretty much an all-consuming activity.

There was, after all, no shortage of questions to ponder about what might have happened in New Guinea that left him sort of shattered. Had the wife and dog been with him? Could the dog have attacked the wife, or eaten the birds? Could the birds have attacked the dog and the wife, like in the movie *The Birds?* Then again, perhaps I was going about this all wrong. Maybe there had been a natural disaster, like an earthquake. Or a volcano. But then where would the rain phobia fit in? A monsoon maybe? Did they have monsoons in New Guinea? I would have to find an encyclopedia or something.

And then there was a whole set of questions having to do with vanity. What did his wife look like? Did they ever talk? And what did he see in me? I was not exactly the other-woman type: I had ungodly hair and big feet and boring brown eyes and did not possess the sort of fetching lingerie that might advertise the possibility of a freer, lustier sort of life.

Still, already we had a short history of perfect moments that was hard to contemplate losing. One night we stayed up very late watching a PBS documentary about sea turtles, for example. We were bathed in the television's blue reflection, limbs entwined, and I wanted to freeze time, to stay like that forever.

He knew a thing or two about sea turtles, he said, from a stint working at the London Zoo. I tried to draw him out about the Zoo experience, again to no avail.

Though my larger questions went unanswered, he advertised his commitment in nonverbal ways. After our first three nights together he took the radical step of moving his bird into my apartment.

At the end of the second week he suggested we marry.

I wanted nothing more than to have and to hold this mysterious creature, as a matter of legal principle, for the rest of my life. And yet, at the same time that I was surely in love with everything about him including what I decided to regard as his charming eccentricities—the rumpled blazers, his absorption with birds, his sloppiness, his delicious accent, his crooked right eyebrow that I longed to pluck—I was unexpectedly miserable. I was obsessively trying to figure him out, already worried about how to keep him from going when intuitively I sensed it was best that he leave. On a practical level things were simply moving too quickly and there were complications, mostly having to do with a wife about whom he would not speak.

I jokingly told Nigel that even if I wasn't going to learn all that I needed to know about him, I would let him in on my own secret—I was sprung from the materialist seed of Bunny and Morton Kennedy.

What I really thought was that a noisy dinner with my parents would so completely put him off that he'd bolt from my life, and probably from my country. In any event that was usually the effect my parents had on me: they inspired the very strong urge to flee.

Nigel adored my father for reasons I could not fully determine: he seemed too oblivious to be impressed by the huge faux Tudor house, or by the swimming pool, or even by the three hot tubs, nor did he seem to notice the brand-new shiny red Mercedes on display in the freshly paved circular driveway. I had parked my used Ford Escort just behind my father's car, the rusting dent on the passenger door facing conspicuously onto the street of posh homes.

The affection was startlingly mutual; my father seemed quite taken with Nigel from the moment they shook hands and he heard the British accent. As the predinner cocktail hour wore on and Nigel regaled my folks with a variety of tales from the animal kingdom, he claimed a peculiarly paralyzing hold on them.

At first my mother had sniffed with disapproval—her eyes focused mostly on the frayed lapel of his aged taupe jacket. But just before we sat down for dinner, at the denouement of a moving but convoluted saga about a yellow Labrador retriever befriending a lost Canadian goose, he seemed to win her over, too.

"Did I tell you that I was in the hospital last week?" my mother asked as she gracelessly dropped a slab of teriyaki chicken onto each of the four plates. We were seated around a table that could easily accommodate sixteen people; the maid had the day off, and my parents were unable to figure out how to remove the leaves from the table following the dinner party they had thrown the night before.

"What happened, Mom?" I asked, alarmed. She didn't look unwell, particularly given her recent spa week in California that I suspected was really a euphemism for more cosmetic surgery. With her frosted blond hair pulled back tightly in a ponytail and her svelte body pounded into shape by her personal trainer, she was actually far more fit than I was.

"Well, yes. I was sure I told you. I must admit I was slightly surprised that you didn't call. But I know how busy you are at your Institute of Thought." She made no effort to disguise her sarcasm.

"It's really interesting, Mom," I lied. "We have a huge grant from a prestigious Russian foundation, you know."

I felt vaguely unwell—my cheeks were on fire and I had no real appetite and I was reminded of all those dinners as a child, when I sought in vain to win my parents' approval.

"She's in love with Marx and Lenin and Stalin and Trotsky," my father explained to Nigel. "It's a way to spite her father. By being a communist!" His voice echoed off the cavernous walls as he shouted across the table.

"Dad, please!" I said, embarrassed. "Nigel knows what I do and it has nothing to do with being a communist. I'm a registered Democrat for god's sake."

"Communist, Democrat. It's the same thing, isn't it?" my father asked, winking at me. "The girl spites me by buying retail, too," he continued, assuming for some peculiar reason that Nigel would be his ally in humiliating me.

"Here I offer her a deep discount on anything she needs at Value Giant," he said. "And what does she do? She buys her ladies' underthings at Saks Fifth Avenue, her toilet paper at Sutton Place Gourmet, her shoes at Neiman Marcus . . . "

I felt like I had just been stripped naked before a crowd, or worse, had my American Express statement read before a panel of judges. I did, admittedly, have a love of shopping well. Still, I was about to defend myself, to point out to my father that Value Giant didn't even carry decent women's shoes, when his train of thought suddenly shifted back to my mother's medical woes.

"Your mother had to have a bunion removed," my father said accusingly.

"Isn't that something they can do in a doctor's office these days?" I asked innocently.

"Yes," said my mother. "But I had it done at the hospital. It was just like an operation. They had to use a local anesthetic. And this bunion was the size of a golf ball. You can't imagine the pain. I have to take an antibiotic. If it should get infected—God forbid—they might have to cut off the whole foot. Uncle Andrew's father had to have his whole leg amputated, you know."

"Really? From a bunion?" I asked. It never ceased to amaze me how much pain my mother was willing to suffer silently in the name of beauty—surely tummy tucks and whatever else it was she endured during her periodic disappearances had to be more painful, more dangerous, even, than bunion removals. I looked at Nigel worriedly, But he was mercifully absorbed in his meal.

"It wasn't from a bunion," said my father. "He got gangrene. It was during the war."

"Nigel, would you like more rice? More chicken? How about some salad?" My mother seemed to be finished with the bunion story.

"No, no, Mrs. Kennedy. I'm just fine for the moment. This really is lovely chicken."

My parents both stopped chewing and stared, enchanted. No one had ever complimented my mother on her cooking before. Eating my mother's cooking was simply something we tolerated, like having our teeth cleaned. I dared not tell them about the marriage proposal. My father would probably drop his fork and run directly to the phone to book a caterer.

"If you like the chicken, I can give you a tip," said my father enthusiastically. "The teriyaki sauce is on special. We're selling it in bulk, designed to last you three years. And I can give you a discount on the already discounted size."

I envisioned a vat of teriyaki sauce the size of a Volkswagen in the middle of my tiny kitchen.

"Mr. Kennedy!" Nigel said with what sounded like genuine enthusiasm. "That would be really wonderful. You know I've never even been to a Value Giant. Don't you have to join, first? I've always been afraid they might not let me in, you see."

My parents thought this was another of his charming endearments—self-deprecation. What they failed to realize was that he was probably right. I wasn't sure what to make of Nigel's financial status.

"That's sweet, Nigel," said my mother. "But really, anyone can join. You just have to pay a nominal membership fee. But we can waive that for you, can't we, Morton?"

"Of course," said my father. "In fact, after dinner I'll get you signed up by computer. Is there anything else you need? Pampers are on special, but I don't suppose you need those yet."

Uncomfortable silence from my parents.

"Lisa has quit work," I said, feeling the overwhelming need to change the subject. My parents had met Lisa once, when she first moved to Washington, and they frequently asked about her—and about her husband and her son.

"Would anyone like more chicken?" asked my mother. "Nigel?"

"Lisa has quit work," I repeated, "and they've put me in charge of a really big project."

"That reminds me," said my father, "I saw your librarian guy, Mr. Whatshisname, in the Rockville store yesterday."

"Really?" I asked, trying to picture the Colonel prowling the aisles at Value Giant, twisting the ends of his bow tie. "What was he buying?"

"CDs" said my father. "Lots and lots of CDs. But he also took some teriyaki sauce. I'm telling you, the price is too good to pass up."

"More wine, anyone?" asked my mother.

"So, anyway, this might be a good opportunity for me," I tried again, looking for some small crumb of parental interest in my burgeoning career as a political theorist.

"That reminds me," said my mother, picking up the butter and offering it around the table, "your sister called. She's been promoted to head of pediatrics at the hospital."

"I didn't know you had a sister," said Nigel.

"Ella has two sisters," said my father. "A doctor and a lawyer."

"And they both have kids," said my mother, who, if pulled before a grand jury or a psychotherapist or even a firing squad would insist that none of these comments had anything to do with her feelings about me.

"Very impressive," said Nigel, seeming genuinely impressed. My parents tended to flatten me emotionally, and yet I couldn't help observe that they seemed to bring Nigel alive.

"I've decided to write another book," said my father. "A sort of sequel to *Bulk Discounting.*"

"More chicken, Nigel?" asked my mother.

"For god's sake, why don't you just open his mouth and shove it down his throat, Mother!" The words came from nowhere, and elicited no response. My parents seemed used to my outbursts. I was the difficult daughter. The one without children.

"I don't really want to write the book," my father continued, "but my publisher is breathing down my back."

"But isn't *Bulk Discounting* still on the paperback best-seller list?" asked Nigel.

My father beamed. He loved nothing more than to talk about his success.

"It is. But this publisher is greedy. He says that a sequel will not only sell well in its own right, but will extend *Bulk Discounting*'s run on the best-seller lists."

"So what's the sequel on?"

"Well, we're still thrashing it out," Morton said, pausing to stare at one of his many author photographs scattered around the room. The picture on the back of *Bulk Discounting* had him leaning on a split-rail fence, posing with an Irish setter borrowed from the neighbor down the road. "But they're interested in my views on labor relations. My employees aren't unionized, you see, and they report in surveys that they are unusually satisfied."

"More rice, anyone?" said my mother, sending the bowl in motion around the table.

"One of my methods has been to supplement employee pay with their product of choice. Individual choice. Whatever they may need. As a Christmas bonus, for example, they can take home enough imported virgin olive oil for an entire year. Or, if someone's not a gourmet cook, maybe he'd like motor oil, or paper towels. Or whatever."

"That's fascinating," said Nigel. "Mrs. Kennedy, I will have another slice of that chicken, if you don't mind."

My mother managed to beam at Nigel and glare at me simultaneously.

"I give them what they need," my father said, "and people like that."

"From each according to his abilities to each according to his needs . . ." I said. *My father is the Karl Marx of retail . . .*

All three of them eyed me quizzically, and then decided to ignore me.

"Hey, Dad," I asked. "Where did you write *Bulk Discounting,* anyway?"

"What do you mean?"

"I mean where were you, physically, when you wrote? I have no memory of your writing it. I was just thinking of Eleanor Marx playing in the same room while her father wrote *Das Kapital.*"

"What are you trying to imply? . . . I wrote that book myself. I mean, I had a little help from my researcher, but—"

"I'm not implying anything. I'm just wondering—"

"Morton, relax," my mother interrupted. "She's just asking a simple question. Your father wrote in bed late at night, dear," she said, turning to me. "You were already asleep. Sometimes he wrote at the office, too."

"You know, Mr. Kennedy," Nigel interrupted, "I must confess

that my interest in *Bulk Discounting* is not completely random. I have this idea, you see, I've been working on a play—"

"You have?" I nearly screamed. He had told me so little about himself, and here he was blathering openly to my parents. Maybe this revelation explained it all. He was merely a deep, introverted playwright concerned with life and death and the existence of god, and here I'd been berating him for his inability to make small talk.

"About what?"

"Well," said Nigel, "it's mostly about my fieldwork in New Guinea."

We all stared at him, filled with suspense.

"*And?*" I finally asked.

"Well, it's about birds, of course. And . . . it's about relationships and . . . and also about shopping."

I had the sense that he was making this up as he went along, but my parents were now hanging on his every word.

"And I could see tying in some of the themes of my play to *Bulk Discounting*," he continued while chewing.

"Maybe I could set the entire play inside a Value Giant store."

"Kind of like *No Exit*," I said. But, as usual, no one—not even Nigel, now the self-professed literary man—paid any attention to my pithy observations.

"Would it be a musical?" asked my mother, who had seen *Cats* repeatedly.

"Could be," said Nigel. "Haven't really thought it through that far yet."

My father was ecstatic. "That's brilliant," he said. "I could give you the props. You might need a forklift, or certainly a shopping cart. Or better yet, you could do some kind of alternative theater and actually use one of our larger stores instead of a theater. I'd be happy to supply refreshments. We have a shipment of Chilean wine coming in in gallon-size bottles next week. We could set a few cases aside and use those for opening night."

"Well," laughed Nigel, "slow down, Mr. Kennedy. I need to write the bloody thing first."

"When did you start writing this?" I asked suspiciously.

"Ella, dear, creative minds work in strange ways. Leave the poor man alone," ordered my mother. "You're going to scare him away."

Bunny was never known for subtlety, but this was a tad blatant, even for her.

"I have cheesecake for dessert," she continued. "Would anyone like some cheesecake? Nigel? How about some lovely cheesecake?"

"I'll get it, Mrs. Kennedy," said Nigel, rising, and heading toward the kitchen. "I don't want to see you strain your bunion."

"Oh, please, call me Bunny," my mother gushed.

He squeezed my hand as he left the room and all I could think was that I hadn't a clue as to who this man really was.

"He's fabulous," said my father, simply.

"Ella, dear," my mother whispered, leaning across the table, "have you noticed that he seems to be wearing a wedding ring?"

A Few Impressions of Edward Aveling. "Though no woman seemed able to resist him," wrote George Bernard Shaw of the man whom Eleanor would come to call her husband, "he was short, with the face and eyes of a lizard, and no physical charm except a voice like a euphonium." Shaw was so intrigued that he wrote a play about Aveling, immortalizing him as the scoundrel character Dubedat in *The Doctor's Dilemma*.

When the actress Ellen Terry inquired about Aveling, Shaw's response was to the point: "Shut up your purse, tight . . . " he warned. "His exploits as a borrower have grown into a Homeric legend."

William Morris's daughter, May, concurred with the reptilian comparison, calling Aveling "a little lizard of a man."

Eleanor's best friend, the novelist Olive Schreiner, ran into the couple on their honeymoon and wrote, "I have a fear and a horror of him when I am near. Every time I see him this shrinking grows stronger."

Eleanor had her own view of the man: the worse the reputation, the brighter the merit.

Chapter 3

The deafening squawking of the bird served as my alarm clock Monday morning, some two weeks after the dinner with my parents. I reached for Nigel, but the space beside me was already cold. Typically I was the first one out of bed, but I had stayed up late the previous night buried in the Eleanor biographies, taking notes, responding to an anxiety attack about my dissertation. Despite the many hours I had logged in the past few weeks agonizing about my thesis, I had made no tangible progress in terms of pages produced. This was a problem, particularly as I owed Ira a status report.

Meanwhile, I was struggling to suppress a growing sense of resentment that I had to get up and go to work, while Nigel got to lounge about the apartment all day. On the one hand I recognized that our arrangement was arguably progressive—I earned the money (or at least I would theoretically earn the money when the Colonel paid me), while Nigel stayed home, finding ways to stay occupied.

He claimed to be moving forward on his play, though I had seen no real evidence that any manuscript actually existed, and as with so many other things, he was reluctant to talk about it.

Still, he was there, physically if not emotionally, and almost to a fault. I would open the door after work each day, and there he'd be, leaning against a tree or perched on the stone wall that surrounded the Colonel's property. He would kiss me and hold me tightly, almost desperately, pressed awkwardly against his scratchy wool coat. We would then wander back toward my apartment, picking up something to eat along the way. It was sweet and unspoken. It was the sort of steady companionship I had always envied in others. But it was also a little weird.

Despite my doubts about him, I felt biologically trapped—I had never felt so physically attracted to a man in my all life. Already his scent was imprinted on my brain in an intensely animalistic kind of way that I had never before experienced.

Though I had not previously had any serious, prolonged relationships, I was not completely inexperienced. There had been Matthew, for example. He was a second-year law student at Columbia with whom I had spent a passionate week until he announced that he was allergic to my cat and besides, his girlfriend had just returned from the Peace Corps. And there had been Raj, who had lived across the hall from me and invited me over for occasional meals he prepared with ingredients from the natural foods cooperative he managed on campus. We had spent several months together in what had seemed to me a potentially sustainable relationship until he declared quite suddenly that he was returning to Bombay for a previously arranged marriage.

While things with Nigel felt intrinsically different from the start, I still had the disconcerting sense that I was headed down the wrong path, that I was waiting around for the tragic end, so to speak.

Not only were there the multiple issues of his wedding band, his inability to talk to me about what mattered, and his strange, almost wounded neediness, but I began to suspect that I had hooked up with the ultimate Neanderthal man. It was not that he expected me to take care of him, but rather, I feared, that he was content to live in total squalor.

Meanwhile, as much as I found Bob the bird to be an amusing

pet, the hygienic condition of the birdcage was rapidly becoming one of my chief gripes. Bob seemed incapable of eating anything without flinging half of it through the bars of his cage and onto the floor, much to the delight of both my cat and the rapidly multiplying ant population in the kitchen. He also had the endearing habit of pecking at his bird food like a chicken while laughing, scattering the contents of his purple plastic dish across the room.

I made a conscious decision not to focus on these things. I told myself that life was too short to go around bitching about the inconsequential. I gave myself philosophical pep talks along the lines of *the ends justify the means*. Which in practical terms meant that if I could get this man to stick around long enough to figure him out, I was willing to empty ashtrays for a while.

But the scene in the kitchen that morning came pretty close to shattering my resolve.

"Hey, what's going on?" I asked in as cheerful a tone as I could muster before my first cup of coffee. I wandered into the kitchen wearing one of Nigel's T-shirts, grumbling that it was barely 7 A.M. I was jarred into consciousness rather quickly, however, by the sight of Bob sitting on top of the coffeemaker. The bird seemed to be studying the broken shards of glass that were floating in the thick brown broth, contrasting starkly with the once-white tile floor.

"Just a bit of a mishap," explained Nigel. "Nothing to worry about. Just watch the glass," he said distractedly. He was standing over the birdcage, his head half inside its open door, deep in thought.

"Nigel, what are you doing?" I asked. "It's so early. Are you all right?"

"I'm great, darling. Except that I was looking forward to some coffee, but never mind. I'll just have another cigarette, instead. I had the strangest dream, you see, and in it I had a job . . . and so I got to thinking I'd take a look at yesterday's employment section, only I couldn't find it. But then, I had a brainstorm, and eureka! Here it is. You used it to line the birdcage."

"Yeah, I did. . . . Sorry, it hadn't occurred to me that you'd want it," I apologized pitifully. I had, in fact, cleaned the birdcage Sunday afternoon in a brief attack of domesticity. Nigel pulled the newspaper out and began to turn the pages, dropping more bits of seed on the floor. His enthusiasm quickly waned, however, when he found the entrees under O.

"Not a single fucking job for ornithologists," he said bitterly, slapping the newspaper on the table for emphasis. "You'd think in these enlightened United States of America they might be paying some attention to birds . . . but no. It's all chimpanzees and dolphins . . ."

I looked at this man for a moment—this oddly attractive specimen of a male who had not shaved for a week and had holes in both underarms of his sweater and whose long cigarette ash was dangling precariously over his cereal bowl—and wondered what he was doing in my kitchen. Or rather, technically, in my father's kitchen.

"Why don't you skim through all the ads," I tried helpfully. "You never know where they stick things. Maybe there's something under B for birds. Or R for research."

He made a face and wadded the paper up, tossing it toward the trash bin where it landed a foot short of its destination. He then doused his cigarette in a half-empty glass of orange juice sitting in the sink and lit another.

"I think I'll take a shower now," I said. It was too early for confrontation, and suddenly the Institute of Thought, with Carmen's coffee brewing in the kitchen, began to look like a pretty good place to spend the rest of the day.

Objectively speaking, I had accomplished very little since I'd first set foot in the Institute of Thought.

When I had asked the Colonel for a quick PageMaker tutorial he sheepishly confessed that he had no idea how to so much as turn the computer on. He suggested I buy a couple of computer books—one on PageMaker and one on HTML—which I did, but they were not dumbed down enough for me. Entire text blocks continued to disappear off the page, never to be seen again. I had gone ahead and ordered a modem, but the people on the other end of the dollar-a-minute help line were unable to successfully talk me through the installation process, and the real live computer technician who was supposed to show up had yet to materialize.

The whole situation was embarrassing: I was probably the only person my age who was so computer illiterate as to be unable to hook up a modem, let alone communicate effectively with the tech geek on the other end of the phone. I blamed the problem on the Colonel for having had the poor judgment to hire me, and also for being too cheap to simply trash his antiquated computer and begin anew.

The man was hardly ever around, but on one occasion when I ran into him at the cash machine on the corner during my lunch break, I told him I was not making much progress. At first I was not sure he even knew who I was as it took him so long to reply, but then he shrugged his shoulders and repeated his refrain. "-You're smart," he said. "I know you will figure it out."

Meanwhile, I had not heard back from the NUTS people, though I had faxed an eloquent memo to them introducing myself and outlining a proposal for our Karl Marx Unplugged catalogue.

Aside from untangling the Kyrgyz directory, which had taken nearly two weeks, the only other concrete thing I had done was order 5,000 Karl Marx T-shirts, which were scheduled to arrive any day. I hadn't managed to flag down the Colonel in order to get his authorization, but I was confident that I had negotiated a pretty good deal with the T-shirt vendor who worked the north entrance to the Dupont Circle metro station, and had what looked like a solid little monopoly on Bob Marley paraphernalia.

Before I went any further, however, I felt I needed to talk to the Colonel. I had some questions along the lines of how does the PageMaker program work and when do I get paid?

And since it was practically impossible to get the Colonel's attention—on the rare occasions that he was on the premises, he was usually occupied with either an architect or a landscaper or a representative from one of his teams of leggy designers—it was with a not insurmountable level of guilt that I pulled my notebook from my bag and tried to coax some prose from my scribbled notes.

Hampstead Heath. There was that day, lying on a checkered blanket, sipping hot sugary tea from a silver flask. Her father on one side, Engels on the other, and for a moment anyway, she felt she had the world firmly in her grasp.

The geese had run onto their blanket in search of scraps of food, and all at once it began to rain, and Engels laughed while Karl cursed and she stood up—a small girl, with black ringlets of hair—and began to mimic Hamlet: Mr. Goose, she said, you have my father very much offended.

She had committed several scenes of Shakespeare to memory by the time she was four. Fantasy was an integral part of the Marxes' family life, and it went beyond the one about waiting around stoically for the capitalist system to collapse.

There were nicknames, for example; so many that one needs a glossary to decipher family letters. Karl was called Mohr, or the Moor, on account of his dark complexion. Engels was widely referred to as "the general." Eleanor was known as Tussy.

They played a lot of games. One of the most popular involved writing out a list of qualities one most admired. It was called a "confession," and Eleanor's, at age ten, was telling:

Your favourite virtue   *Truth*
Your favourite virtue in man   *Courage*
Your favourite virtue in woman   *(no answer)*
Your chief characteristic   *Curiosity*
Your idea of happiness   *Champagne*
Your idea of misery   *The toothache*
The vice you excuse most   *Playing the truant*
The vice you detest most   *Eve's Examiner*
Your aversion   *Cold mutton*
Your favourite occupation   *Gymnastics*
Your favourite poet   *Shakespeare*
Your favourite prose writer   *Captain Marryat*
Your favourite hero   *Garibaldi*
Your favourite heroine   *Lady Jane Grey*
Your favourite flower   *All flowers*
Your favourite colour   *White*
Your favourite names   *Percy, Henry, Charles, Edward*
Your favourite maxim and motto   *'Go ahead.'*

Hyppolyte-Prosper-Olivier Lissagary was named neither Percy, Henry, Charles, nor Edward. So it is possible to argue that Karl had nothing but his daughter's own interests in mind when he put his foot down. Revolution was perhaps inevitable. Organic, even. But it was not to begin at home.

"Jenny is most like me," Karl once said of his daughters, but Tussy . . . *is* me." It was not simply that father and daughter looked alike—Eleanor once quipped that she might sue her father for damages for having inherited his nose—but there seemed to be a deep bond between them as well.

Their special connection, however, only made the battle of wills over her first serious boyfriend that much more intense.

Politics aside, Karl Marx was nothing if not a classic Victorian father, and he did not want to see his daughter—the one who was a little bit of him, no less—cavorting with a thirty-four-year-old Frenchman with a reputation as a flamboyant Communard.

In 1873, when Eleanor defied her father's wishes and became engaged at the age of eighteen, Karl proved himself even less well versed in the subtleties of child psychology than in money management, and responded with a simple "no." If he ignored the engagement long enough, he figured, it would eventually go away.

But the engagement persisted for nine long years. And whether or not Karl's interventions can be blamed directly, it was at about this time that Eleanor began to suffer fainting spells, as well as inexplicable aches and pains and nervous twitches. She lost her appetite and ceased to eat for dangerously long periods.

Still, the rift between father and daughter was largely unspoken. It took the form of subtle tension. Both of Eleanor's sisters had married Frenchmen, and both had given birth to a new generation of sickly children. Karl would outlive four of his children, as Jenny died at the age of 38. He was outliving his grandchildren, as well. He seemed to be holding tight to what he had, which was mostly Eleanor.

.   .   .

I had been so completely absorbed in my writing that I bristled at the sound of approaching footsteps. It had been a long time, a couple of years or so, since I'd found myself engaged by a subject, and it made me hopeful that perhaps I might one day actually earn my degree. Granted, I was not really doing what I was supposed to be doing: I had not deconstructed anything, nor had I discovered any new forms of mold, nor had I even posited a thesis. But I was finding out some interesting things about Eleanor's early love life, possibly shedding some light on my own question of why such a smart woman had fallen for reptile.

In any event, I owed Ira that progress report, and despite my dissertation's readily identifiable shortcomings, I needed to write a few more quick chapters, or at least a few quick thoughts about quick chapters, and stuff them in the mail pretty soon. I looked up from the computer and saw my long-suffering colleague, mop in hand.

"Ella, are you all right?" Carmen inquired worriedly. "It is becoming very late, no?"

"Yes, I suppose it is," I agreed, glancing at my watch. It was all of five-thirty, and I usually bolted out the door by five.

"I'm fine. . . . I'm just thinking about my dissertation, that's all. I know I'm moving too slowly and I don't know where I'm headed and I keep forgetting about this deconstruction business," I whined before remembering that I was supposed to at least be pretending to work on the NUTS project. I hoped Carmen was not a spy for the Colonel, though I knew, of course, where her primary allegiance lay and it was certainly not with me.

"What are you doing here?" I asked, fairly certain that she had not been there earlier in the day. She looked tired, and dots of perspiration were visible through her I LOVE MARYLAND sweatshirt, which had a dancing crustacean motif.

"The Colonel called me at home. He said he had an emergency . . . he needs the house spotless by the morning; he's having some big conference of decorators or something like that tomorrow. He also said he needs to see you at five o'clock at some bookstore. The Vaja Bookstore? I think he said something like that."

"Java Books, probably. . . . But it's five-thirty already," I moaned. "Why didn't he call me?"

"He said he tried, but he couldn't remember the office number. He rang the other line, and you didn't answer. . . . Are you having any troubles?" Carmen asked again.

"But I thought I'm not supposed to answer his private line. . . . And no, I'm not having any *troubles*," I said testily. None that was any of her business, anyway.

"Oh, well that's good. Because the Colonel, he is worried about you."

"He's worried about *me?*" I asked, incredulous.

"Yes. He said, 'This Ella person, I think she might be very smart about reading books, but I don't know if she can do this job. She needs to pay attention to the details.' He also said to give you this memo a few days ago. I'm sorry, I forgot. . . ."

She pulled a slightly crumpled sheet of paper from her apron pocket and dropped it on my desk.

My Dear Miss Kennedy,
I'm sorry I have been distracted all week by important
meetings, but I wanted to share a few thoughts with
you:
A. Please remember to use only scratch paper for in-
tra-office work. I have noticed a preponderance of
wasted paper in the trash can.
B. I assume you speak some French, Spanish, and
German. Enough to translate, anyway. It occurs to me
that we should be considering the international angle
for our catalogue.

"He's written me a nice note," I said defensively. "I mean, it doesn't say anything bad, anyway. . . . What exactly did he say about me?" It was humiliating to imagine the Colonel and Carmen upstairs in the kitchen, possibly in cahoots with the decorators, gossiping about me.

"Only that you are unfocused."

"Unfocused? In what way am I unfocused?" I asked, trying not to whine.

"He says he is not sure you will be able to handle the job. He needs someone with a business sense. But he will give you a chance."

I took a deep breath and urged myself to be mature: shouting at the cleaning lady would not be productive. I shut down the computer and put on my jacket, straightening up my desk in silence.

"I wonder if I should try to meet him at this point," I said, thinking about Nigel, who was probably waiting outside. "It's probably too late to bother."

"No, you must go," Carmen said with certainty. "It is important to do as he says. He is not a bad man, but he can be, how do you say in English"—she paused, pointing to her head and drawing imaginary circles with her index finger.

"Crazy?" I offered boldly.

"Yes! Crazy. A little bit cracked, I think is the word, no? Especially when he has the drink . . ."

Java Books Inc., a trendy chain of bookstores featuring nightly poetry slams in its cafés, seemed to be the refuge of those with nothing better to do and no place better to do it. I had spent a great deal of time there, myself.

The only danger of hanging out there was of running into my father, who had recently expressed an interest in buying the entire Java Corporation and merging it with Value Giant.

I looked around the vast store with trepidation. What could the Colonel possibly want from me? How would I ever find him? I'd only actually seen him on a couple of occasions; would I even recognize him?

My questions were quickly answered by glancing in the café: I spied him seated at a corner table with a thick stack of books, drinking some variety of latte with lots of froth and seductive bits of chocolate floating on top. It was hard to say why the man made me so nervous: there was nothing about his appearance that was especially threatening. If anything, his physical shortcomings should have served to make him seem less scary and more approachable: he was completely bald, slightly overweight, and myopic. I guessed he was in his mid-forties, just a few years older than Nigel, but quite his opposite in terms of not inconsequential things such as fastidiousness and cash flow. Apart from the fact that he seemed to be trying too hard to look the part of someone else, with his silly bow ties and expensive suits, he was somehow endearing. Or he might have been endearing had he not invoked in me such feelings of dread.

He invited me to sit, and he flagged down the waitress. Although I was hungry, I asked only for a cup of black coffee.

"What are you reading?" I asked in an attempt at casual conversation.

"*Magic Mountain,*" he replied, making no effort to elaborate. I scanned the books at his elbow, none of which was *Magic Mountain,* but instead appeared to be about ten pounds' worth of kitchen design manuals.

We sat for another moment in uncomfortable silence until he cleared his throat and adjusted the knot in his bow tie and began to speak.

"I had a call from the NUTS people this morning," he said, scooping foam from his cup with a spoon. "They would like to see some sample merchandise and a proof of the catalogue by the end of the week."

"I haven't gotten quite that far, sir . . ." I stammered. "You see, was waiting to hear from you . . . and from them."

"You must learn to work independently, Miss Kennedy. That's what I hired you for. I simply don't have the time for these projects anymore, what with my house . . ."

"Well," I ventured uncertainly, "I did go ahead and order T-shirts. I hope that's all right."

"Without my approval?" he boomed. Others in the café turned and stared at us. He leaned across the table and I instinctively hunched my shoulders, fearful of flying objects, but he was simply reaching for the sugar. He must have realized the effect he had on me because he apologized. "Look, I didn't mean to upset you . . . you need to run these things by me first, that's all."

"I'm sorry, sir, it's just been kind of hard to track you down these last few days. But while I have your attention, I think you should know that I'm having a little trouble with the computer. . . . I don't really know how to use this PageMaker program. I can get it to work all right for a while, but then everything I do just disappears."

"Keep fooling with it," he advised. "You're smart. You'll figure it out. How's the website coming?"

"Well, about the website, sir, you know, as I mentioned before, that we need to go online, and I'm doing everything I can to arrange that, but it takes some doing and I'm beginning to think it might be useful to get a new computer or maybe get someone else to do the web page because I mean, it's a whole field in and of itself, web design and I'm more a political theorist than a computer person." I paused for a quick breath. "Maybe I should take a class or something. Although truthfully it might not be worth the investment because I need to get back to my dissertation pretty soon and—"

The Colonel interrupted. "Oh, you don't need a class. . . . All classes are a colossal waste of time. I have a friend who can help us with the website. Unfortunately he's very ill right now. *Cancer*," he whispered, leaning across the table to utter the secret word. "Still, I'll give him a call. Maybe a little project would help take his mind off his troubles."

We were forced from our seats before the Colonel could elaborate further on his friend's condition, as a small crowd began to take over the café. It was, apparently, time for the poetry slam, and a young South Asian man stood at the microphone and began reading something about revolution while audience members shouted words to the effect that his poem was crap.

"There'll be riots in the streets, they'll be shackled by their feet . . ." were just a few of the words wafting in our direction as the Colonel paid the bill and then rose from the table.

"A poem about revolution," he announced. "The time is ripe, I think."

I nodded my head though I wasn't sure what he meant, exactly—was the time ripe for revolution, or for a poem about revolution, or maybe for a mail-order catalogue about revolution?—and began to follow him through the store, practically jogging to keep up.

"I have something to show you," he said as we ascended two flights on the escalator and passed a wall display of *Bulk Discounting* paperbacks. He dragged me through the children's section and then through the music section. At last he stopped and pointed to a table of pillows on display between the fiction and the political science sections.

I looked at the pillows. They were cute but overpriced. There was a Freud pillow and a Virginia Woolf pillow and Princess Diana pillow.

"Who's this?" I asked, picking up a pillow of a severe-looking bespectacled woman.

"I don't know," said the Colonel. "Janet Reno, maybe."

"Do you really think so?" I asked, studying the hair.

"Look," he said irritably, "you're missing the point."

"I'm sorry," I apologized. "What is the point?"

"What do you suppose the point is, Miss Kennedy?"

"The point must have something to do with the pillows," I said aloud. "The point must be that there are no pillows here of Karl Marx."

"Precisely," he said. "I knew you were smart."

He took my arm and pulled me over to another display. "And look here," he instructed. I studied a pile of bookmarks. There were, in fact, bookmarks celebrating a wide range of literary and political figures, from Salman Rushdie to Ronald Reagan.

"No Karl Marx?" I asked.

"Precisely," he said again. "And you're going to change all that."

"I am?" I asked without much enthusiasm.

"Of course you are, Miss Kennedy," he said, walking toward the political science section. "And you should be proud. It will be a great service to your cerebral little world of political theory. Let me ask you a question. What was the last museum you went to?"

I thought for a minute. I wasn't much of a museum person, though I did venture to the occasional blockbuster exhibit when coerced by friends. "Oh, I know!" I said excitedly. "I saw an exhibit on the Victorians at the Met not too long ago."

"And what did you do after viewing the exhibit?"

"I, um . . . I think I went out for dinner or something," I replied.

"*Before* that. Think hard. Did you visit the gift shop?"

I suppose I had, I confessed, although now I wished I had done something a little less predictable.

"And what did you buy?"

"I bought a few postcards and a pocket-size jigsaw puzzle of a Millais painting," I said. The puzzle had collected dust on my bedside table in New York, a morbid picture of a very dead Ophelia floating in a river with flowers in her hand.

He looked at me, smirking. "You see," he said. "People pretend to visit these highbrow exhibits because they want to seem enlightened. It was the same thing when I worked at the Library of Congress. People want to impress their friends. They want to begin a sentence with 'When I was visiting the Birman Empire exhibit at the library last week . . .' But all they are really after is stuff to bring home with them. Little notebooks with maps on the front. Playing cards and such . . ."

It was hard to argue with him, given the amount of gift-shop junk I had accumulated over the years.

"It was kind of like back when I was a Boy Scout," he explained. "The point was essentially to accumulate stuff, you see. And not just to accumulate stuff, but to accumulate the *most* stuff. Badges and beads and the like."

"I agree that souvenirs are generally popular," I said, trying to absorb the logic of the Boy Scout leap, "but all the same I just can't help but think how contradictory this is to everything Marx stood for."

The Colonel smiled, which only made me more nervous. "I've hired the last remaining Marxist in America. I love it! "

"I'm not a Marxist," I objected. "Just because I believe something to be of interest intellectually does not mean that I am out there advocating revolution."

"Well, what are you advocating, then?" he asked, studying the books on the shelf.

"I'm not advocating anything. I'm just trying to write my dissertation. . . . But, well, I suppose if I was going to advocate anything, it would be only to take another look at Marx. I really do think his work was misinterpreted. I don't think he ever envisioned anything quite like the Soviet Union. I think he was talking more about something like Arthurdale."

"Arthur who?" said the Colonel, picking a slim volume entitled *The Marxist Prophecy* off the shelf.

"I've read that," I said. "Look, on the back it promises to offer a reason to continue to read Marx well into the twenty-first century. But it's totally incomprehensible. One would need to reinvent the whole idea of sentence structure as well as earn several master's degrees in linguistics to even begin to grasp the point."

I then pulled another book off the shelf and began to browse through *The Man Behind the Beard,* which made the loose thesis that the infrequency of Marx's bowel movements had something to do with his need for long-winded economic analysis.

"Do tell me about this Arthur person," said the Colonel.

I was about to answer when I suddenly caught the profile of someone who looked like Nigel riding down the escalator, accompanied by a young woman. He hadn't been waiting for me outside the institute that afternoon, a curious fact that no doubt fueled my paranoia.

My heart started pounding. I told the Colonel I'd be back in a minute. Like a fool, I bounded down the escalator, but when I got to the bottom, the couple had vanished.

I panicked. I felt like an addict in need of a fix. I found a pay phone in the hall behind the café, and called both of our apartments, willing him to answer so that I would know he was home, that the couple on the escalator had been a figment of my imagination. But there was no answer.

I began to wander dejectedly through the giant store, wondering if there were some detox center, some Betty Ford Clinic for people involved in relationships that were bound to end badly.

The Colonel found me eventually; I had wandered into the Books for Idiots section, and in a nearly catatonic state, had picked up primers on deconstruction, Spanish, French, and German. I had so much to learn in such a short time! Why had I avoided learning about deconstruction? Why had I elected to study Latin and ancient Greek? Why did I know nothing about computers? Why had I been born in the wrong century?

The Colonel looked at me worriedly, and I realized he must have thought I had run off in response to something he had said.

"Look, Miss Kennedy . . . I didn't mean to insult you by suggesting you were a Marxist or anything. But I am curious. If you're not a Marxist, why did you spend all those years of school studying Marx? Isn't that a little bit like reading about how the earth is flat, along with a variety of useless theorems to prove the point. Any clever person will be reading about how to trade shares in pharmaceuticals on the Internet. Certainly not about communism—"

"Look," I replied angrily. "I mean, what if I were a scientist who figured out how to build a bomb. Just because I can build it doesn't mean I would advocate using it!"

"Yes," said the Colonel, "but if you don't believe in bombs, you shouldn't be mucking around with them in the first place."

"Well, *you* are," I nearly shouted.

"Yes, but I'm in it for the money. Still, this is quite interesting. You can't possibly think that Marx had nothing to do with what happened in the Soviet Union, in China, in Cuba—"

"But I *do* think that. Marx would never have condoned any of that. What I was trying to say before was that I think Marx was advocating something more like Arthurdale," I said, surprising myself with my boldness. "In order to understand why Marx wanted to create a more just society you have to look at the conditions in which he lived," I said, thinking I should write that down as it sounded like the kind of thing a deconstructionist might say.

"Tell me about Arthurdale."

"Arthurdale was Eleanor Roosevelt's experimental society in West Virginia. She went out of her way to distance herself from radical politics, but it was, I think, very much the sort of thing Marx would have advocated, though it was a bit utopian for him. Maybe even a bit too agrarian. But still, it was a pretty good vision of social democracy."

The Colonel had a huge, possibly patronizing smile on his face. "So what happened to this Arthurdale place?"

"Well, the idea was that the government would buy a huge chunk of farmland, and then build affordable housing and provide good schools and move a lot of unemployed coal miners over there. Then the government would set up an industry and give people jobs. Eleanor herself was involved in everything from selecting the families to buying the plumbing fixtures. It was a brilliant idea."

"And?"

"Well, it didn't work. But it was a brilliant idea."

"Why didn't it work?"

"There were a number of flaws. Things that she didn't see ahead of time. Her heart was in the right place but she wasn't exactly an economist. There was a lot of wasted money. The housing turned out to be a disaster, for instance."

"How so? I'm particularly interested in housing right now, what with my renovation project about to begin."

"Well, for one thing, they ordered up a bunch of prefab Cape Cod cottages, which were designed for summers at the beach, not for winters in Appalachia. The people were literally freezing. So they had to redesign all the houses, which became way too expensive, and then the foundations were the wrong size, and then they had to move the structures away from the original site, after they had already drilled wells . . .

"There were a few other problems, as well. They couldn't get a government industry up and running, for example. There were fears that these sorts of projects would wipe out private industry . . ."

We had wandered toward the front of the store, where the Colonel was sorting through a pile of refrigerator magnets. I couldn't tell if he was still listening, but I continued nonetheless.

"Anyway, things continued to go downhill. General Electric set up a vacuum cleaner assembly plant for a while, but that didn't work out, either. Everything Eleanor tried to get going fell through. The homesteaders had no way to earn a living, you see?"

"Well, I think you've proved your own point," he said.

"What do you mean?"

"That it was a good idea. But it didn't work. Kind of like Marxism. I'm not saying Marx wasn't a brilliant man. He obviously was. But his ideas didn't work."

"But don't you see, Arthurdale was never even given a chance to succeed. People were too afraid. Eleanor was sabotaged!"

"You're totally amazing, Miss Kennedy," he said. I wasn't sure if he was being sarcastic. "You're a walking encyclopedia of bizarre trivia. Do you spend all of your time reading?"

I did, mostly. Well, I had until I'd met Nigel, anyway. Now most of my spare time went into fretting about him. But I didn't reply.

"Listen, Miss Kennedy, this is really awkward, but, well, do you want to get a martini or something?"

A martini? Did people still drink martinis? Actually, maybe they did. I recalled reading somewhere that martinis were popular again, and I briefly considered accepting his invitation, just to taste a martini, and, well, just to see what the Colonel might be like after tasting one himself. But I politely declined, explaining that I had plans, which was not entirely untrue.

I was still shaken by my Nigel sighting, and needed to get home to prove it was not true.

Helene Demuth. Lechen, as she was nicknamed, came to the Marx household when she was twenty-two. She was sent as a gift by the Baroness von West-phalen, who, taking pity on her daughter Jenny, handed Helene her beat-up, half-empty valise along with train fare, and sent her off to Brussels, where Jenny and Karl were living at the time.

Helene was no stranger to travel. At the age of eight she had been employed by a family who abused her, and when she wound up in the Westphalen household three years later she considered the change fortuitous.

Since Helene has left no recorded version of her life, one only has the Marxes story to go by, which paints a fairly glowing picture. Helene, they said, was not so much a maid as a part of their family. She was like a mother to Eleanor, especially since her real mother was often otherwise occupied, either tending to the dying children or scheming up ways in which to keep the family fed and clothed. And as for Karl, one only wishes for more tantalizing details of their relationship—Jenny suspected that when he went padding around the house late at night, his bulky frame flickering in the shadow of the candlelight, he was headed in the general direction of the maid's room. Yet when Helene gave birth, when the baby boy was quietly whisked away and given to a working-class family to raise, the blame was laid tacitly at Engels's doorstep.

And whether one believes that this "like family" business is patronizing, the mere justification of a socialist engaged in one of the oldest and most exploitative of capitalist relationships, there is one detail worth considering: She is buried in the same grave as Karl and Jenny.

Chapter 4

During another unremarkably unproductive day at the institute, I found my mind drifting back to that brief, thigh-brushing interlude with Louis Schwartz, the professor whom I now held responsible for having got me into this particular intellectual muddle.

Why had this man used his tenure to teach Marxist economics as a sort of gospel, particularly in the late 1980s, at a liberal arts college in middle-class America?

And, more important, why had I found Marx so appealing? Or was it simply that I found Louis Schwartz's lectures on German ideology inexplicably arousing, and would today be digging for rocks outside of Cairo had he taught archaeology, instead?

It seemed perfectly natural at the time that we political theorist types went about much of our regular activity in an effort to please the gods of socialism. We had unfurled giant banners of Karl Marx at college rock concerts, for example, assuming instinctively that Marx would approve of loud music and hallucinatory drugs. We belonged to political organizations with names like Democratic Socialist Alliance, and were relentless in our efforts to get the college president fired on account of his dealings with banks that invested in South Africa.

But now I wonder: had Louis Schwartz been a brilliant scholar who chose to study Marx as an exercise in pure thought? My point being, had he not been lucky enough to find gainful employment at a liberal arts college, might he have organized a small militia group and blown up federal buildings, instead?

There were, of course, plenty of people who had not succumbed to Schwartz's charms. There was Len Grezekowski, who sat next to me in class for a while, entertaining himself during Schwartz's lectures by playing a game of silent baseball with Mike Shuster; each time Louis Schwartz used the word "proletariat" the players would advance a base. Each time Louis Schwartz slammed his fist on the table for emphasis they would register a strike. I forget the other subtleties of the game.

There were the heavy drug users, largely self-reliant when it came to the world of ideas. There were also premeds and football players and sorority girls, whom I more or less categorized into one lump of conservatism. And there were also large numbers of people who managed to graduate college unscathed by any ideas whatsoever. In other words, there was no shortage of people who found their stride rather quickly upon graduation, and went on to hold normal jobs and get married and pay property taxes without ever agonizing over historical materialism.

While I made no progress at work that day, I did determine that I was being too passive about my personal life. Viewing my situation from a strictly historical perspective, I was supposed to be too emancipated, too enlightened, to be unraveling over a man. I needed to move forward, and in order to do so, I needed answers to my very simple questions.

Although Nigel never blatantly refused to give me information about himself, he did seem to expertly elude it. Either that or he gave improbably weird answers. When I'd asked him about his whereabouts the previous night, for example, when I thought I saw him at Java Books, he explained that he had been stuck inside a coffee shop, waiting for the rain to pass. It had only been a light rain, but enough to make him lie low for a while, wishing I'd been there to help.

I thought about that for a moment and then asked whether he might have been at Java Books with his wife. He laughed and said the question was absurd. I accepted his answer, chastened. But then, a day later, I found myself emotionally back where I'd started.

We stood before a watercolor rendition of a fiery-billed aracari at the Phillips Collection, holding hands. The Audubon Society was sponsoring this opening night exhibition, and Nigel had been asked to give a brief introduction. He had spoken his two lines of gratitude to the various corporate sponsors quite eloquently and had even dressed for the occasion with a nicely pressed pair of khaki trousers and a new jacket that I had purchased for him using my mother's Macy's credit card. He looked stunning, and I was proud to be with him. I smugly observed that we made a nice couple. In cold, hard Darwinian terms, however, we were markedly uneven. Nigel was a splendid, brightly plumed cockatoo, while I was your run-of-the-mill garden sparrow. Not that it mattered: I considered myself to be too highly educated to care about superficial things like clothes and good looks. I only shopped at Saks, for example, because . . . well, because it was not Value Giant, I supposed. In any event that was one issue I didn't especially want to explore. I felt no need to defend my personal spending habits. The only truly embarrassing thing was that no matter how much money I spent on clothes, I always seemed to look the same.

I pretended to be impressed by the size of the aracari's flame-colored beak, but was really contemplating the proper delivery of my next sentence. In the end, I just blurted it out.

"Nigel," I said bluntly, "what's the story with your wife? Like, where is she, for example?"

"I don't know," he replied flatly.

"What do you mean, *you don't know?*" I didn't mean to sound sarcastic, but a tone of disbelief crept into my voice all the same.

"I mean exactly what I said. *I don't know.*" And with that he deftly changed the subject, presenting me with a small box pulled from his pocket.

"I wanted this to be a special evening," he said. "So let's not get started on all that again. . . . Look, I know this isn't a proper engagement ring, but I wanted you to have it, for now."

I opened the box and was momentarily silenced. Inside was a small silver ring adorned with a heart. It looked about as tacky as the sort of gift an eighth-grade boy might give to a girl he had a crush on, save for the fact that it appeared to possibly be of some quality.

I slipped it on my finger and squeezed his hand. "I think we need to talk, Nigel, before we are actually . . . or um, technically engaged, but I'm really flattered. It's beautiful," I said, trying to sound sincere.

I must have been somewhat convincing because he raised my wrist to his mouth and kissed the back of my hand in the sort of heart-stopping way that happened only in books and movies set in Victorian times. And that was precisely why I loved him: we were meant to be! We were two unconventional relics from a past era, an era full of roses and wine and books and ideas and, well, of birds, as well. The magical spell was quickly broken, however, by the dull intrusion of reality. "Did I tell you about a new study on the mating habits of birds that I read about in the newspaper today?" he asked, still holding my hand.

"No," I said, pulling him toward a wooden carving of a horned lark. The exhibit seemed to have brought together an unusual mix of patrons. There were the artist types with gelled hair and designer eyeglasses, dressed mostly in black; and there were the donor types who vibrated wealth and wore dark business suits; and then, the bird-lover types, clad in varying degrees of eccentric disrepair. "I thought you knew it all already," I said teasingly.

"Well, there's a new study out," he replied, a bit too enthusiastically. "It was written by someone I went to school with, in fact. It turns out that contrary to what we previously thought, only about ten percent of the birds that seemed to mate for life are truly monogamous."

"Great," I said.

Nigel mistook my quip for genuine interest and continued with more distasteful details. "Apparently there's a difference between social monogamy and sexual monogamy," he explained. "Social monogamy is where couples raise their young together, which is of course quite common. But sexual monogamy . . . fidelity, in other words, is quite rare, as it turns out."

That was all I needed to hear, given my already heightened state of anxiety. I had thought birds were one of the few remaining bastions of everlasting love. "What about birds of paradise?" I asked, trying not to sound desperate. "Aren't they monogamous?"

"Not in the least," he replied. "The male's goal is to fertilize as many females as he can. The females of the species are all pretty dreary looking, though, and like the male bowerbirds, there's every indication that they would even mate with a mechanical bird."

I felt my heart begin to race, and was unable to engage in any form of self-censorship. "Nigel, do you think it's just a little bit weird that you hand me an engagement ring and in the next breath you tell me that there's basically no such thing as monogamy?"

He let go of my hand and took a step back, as though I had just confessed to having a contagious skin disease. "Jesus, Ella, I never realized how paranoid you are," he said, scowling. "You should really get a grip on things. I'm not talking about us. I'm talking about the fucking birds."

He looked at me like I was mad, then walked over to an alcove in the gallery, where he sat down on an antique bench opposite a six-foot oil painting of a Eurasian blackbird. Within minutes, one of the artist types—an attractive young specimen, no less—sat, or rather, flocked, beside him on the bench.

"Your introduction was brilliant," I heard her say. Nigel smiled humbly and pulled out a notebook and began to write something down as he studied the painting.

I passed by him like a bitch marking her territory, and muttered something about meeting him in the gift shop in a while. I forced myself to fight back tears, thinking maybe he was right.

Maybe something was wrong with me.

Having failed to fix things on the personal front, I aimed to throw myself into the job wholeheartedly. I was determined to prove that I could do it all; that I could *focus*. Focusing was an easy, straightforward task that involved ordering more merchandise, designing a catalogue, and building a web page. There were a couple of languages I needed to master, as well.

My burst of enthusiasm was quickly sapped, however, upon checking into the institute. The front door was open when I arrived, and there were no less than ten men in the front hallway, hacking at things and stripping things and playing the radio loudly. I made my way through the din of noise and the fog of plaster dust and headed down the stairs unnoticed.

The office was even darker than usual, though it was not until I attempted to flip on the light switch that I made the connection: the workmen had switched off the electricity. In the darkness I tripped over a box, and then another box, and then felt my way behind the desk, where the few feet that had once separated my chair from the paint-chipped, asbestos-lined walls were gone, filled instead by a floor-to-ceiling wall of boxes. I managed to locate the scissors with the dim bit of light that came in through the basement window well and pulled out a T-shirt adorned with a smiling, bearded Karl Marx. Perhaps I had not been specific enough in my instructions. I had always thought of Karl Marx as more of a scowler than a smiler.

I then attempted to flip on the computer, planning to add the notes I had made at home to my small but growing wad of dissertation, before I recalled that the power was out. Instead I reached for the telephone, thinking I would call the Colonel's friend with cancer to talk about the web page, but the phone was dead, too.

I wandered back upstairs to inquire about the possibility of a return to civilized conditions anytime soon, but had difficulty getting anybody's attention given the general level of chaos. Then I saw Carmen sweeping the kitchen floor with an old-fashioned broom, the vacuum inert in the corner. She was sneezing and sniffling and her eyes were full of tears.

"Ah, Miss Ella! The Colonel, he is looking for you," she said, blowing her nose into a paper towel. "But now he is gone. He will see you tomorrow. He had some information about his friend who could help you with the website, he said . . . I believe the message was that you should not call him. Now he is dead."

"Oh," I said, looking at the floor, trying to seem appropriately mournful for the loss of someone whom I had never met. "I'm so sorry," I mumbled. "What's wrong, Carmen, are you crying . . . did you know the friend well?"

"Oh Miss Ella, it is my husband. Last night we have a big fight, you see."

"What about?" I asked, one foot already out the kitchen door, fearful of getting drawn into a prolonged conversation about Carmen's marital woes.

"What else? Money, of course. It is my mother-in-law, his mother back in Peru. She thinks we are very rich here in America. She calls us collect every week to ask for money."

"Collect," I said sympathetically. "That must be expensive."

"At least fifty dollars every call."

"Ouch," I said. "That's a lot. Can't you get her to stop calling collect? Maybe you could call her, instead."

"The calling is the least of the problem. She wants us to send her money and gifts, for the whole family. She no understand. She thinks because my husband has a job at the construction company that now we are very rich. But I want my son to go to college, you see. I want to save the money I make cleaning this house for my son. But my mother-in-law, she thinks everyone in America is very rich . . .

"Meanwhile, in Peru she lives very nicely. She has servants, even. But she says she needs better clothes."

"What does your husband say?"

"My husband, he is too nice to his mother. Yesterday she called and said she needed a new dress. He went to Bloomingdale's and he bought her two dresses. Three hundred dollars each. Six hundred dollars he spent on two dresses. Look at me, I dress in rags."

"Can't you get him to be more sensible?" I asked. I knew my question was naive but I didn't know what else to say. I wanted to add that he should at least shop at Filene's Basement, or Value Giant, even.

She simply shook her head and blew her nose loudly.

"Can you put some money away, in a secret account or something, for your son's education?"

"Yes, I have done that. But I am afraid he will find the money, and there is no one I can trust."

"What about the Colonel? Maybe he can help you."

"No. I need nobody's help," she said defiantly. "And I am giving you a headache with all my talking. You must go back to work now."

I looked at my watch and agreed, feeling guilty about the tacit lie; I had no intention of getting back to work. Maybe I should offer to help her, somehow, though she was undoubtedly more flush with cash than I was.

"Actually, I can't really get anything done downstairs what with the noise and the lack of electricity," I explained. "I think I'm going to head over to the Library of Congress to do some research. . . . I'll see you later. . . . We can talk some more."

I headed toward the door, apologizing to the workmen as I stumbled over a toolbox and sent a carton of nails cascading noisily across the hardwood floor.

It was a crisp spring day, and when I was unable to hail a cab, I figured I would simply walk the thirty-odd blocks to the library. Besides, I was in no particular hurry to either arrive or return. In transit seemed the best place to be.

By the time I reached the Library of Congress I had worked up both a sweat and an appetite, but I decided to press on. I wanted to see whether I could unearth anything new on Eleanor Marx beyond what I had found at the university's library in New York. I needed to discover something, I reminded myself. I needed to be thinking of my dissertation as a sort of science project. Although I had learned a few new buzzwords from my perusal of the *Deconstruction for Idiots* book that I had inadvertently shoplifted from Java Books the night of my meeting there with the Colonel (four books had been tucked under my arm, and I'd walked out, so flustered by the martini invitation that I'd forgotten to pay), I was still not sure I really knew what I was doing. I was hoping to come across something at the library—though I couldn't say what, exactly—that would put me on track.

The main reading room at the library had a motivating air of solemn scholarship; the rows of antique desks were outfitted with elegant green banker's lights and there were endless walls of important-looking books.

My inspiration was quickly sapped, however, by the library bureaucracy that began with the interminably long line that formed in front of the reference desk. After eventually being granted an audience with a librarian, I was directed toward the card catalogue room in the back of the stacks, next to a bank of noisy Xerox machines.

The librarian in the card catalogue room, however, told me that access was restricted; I needed special permission to view the index cards, which were off-limits to the general public. I asked how one received special permission and he explained that I would need a letter from my university or my employer. I then asked what the general public was supposed to do, and he suggested I take the elevator to the third floor and follow the signs to the computer research wing, located between the periodicals reading room and the men's room.

After a few wrong turns, I found the computer room, sat down at a terminal, and attempted to follow the instructions on how to conduct a simple search.

I typed in the keywords "Eleanor Marx," hit enter, chose from a selection of about sixty-seven different databases, and came up blank. I tried typing in "Marx, Eleanor," also to no avail. I wrestled with the computer for nearly an hour until I noticed that there was a librarian seated at a raised desk in the middle of the room, surrounded by a black wrought-iron rail, like a warden, or a king.

I approached from the side and tried politely to catch his attention. He, in turn, did little to hide his irritation when I was finally reduced to coughing while saying "excuse me, sir" in a tone loud enough to also catch the attention of everyone else in the room.

"I'm on my break," he said, turning a page of the sports section of the newspaper. The public was always disturbing him, his expression seemed to say, pestering him with question after question, too stupid to figure things out for itself.

"I'm so sorry," I tried politely. "I have a really quick question. Maybe you could just point me in the right direction. After your break, of course."

"What is it?" he asked irritably, setting his paper aside.

"Well, you see I've been conducting a search on Eleanor Marx, and I keep coming up blank. I know there must be something on her. I mean, I've read two whole biographies of her, and even those don't appear in your system."

"Did you try typing in the name 'Marx, Eleanor'?" he asked.

"Yes. I tried it both ways. Eleanor Marx, and Marx, Eleanor. I came up blank."

"Did you hit 'enter'?"

"Yes."

"Well, I'll have to check the card catalogue, then. The computer is pretty worthless, really."

"Is there any way that I could look myself?"

"At the card catalogue you mean?" he asked, stunned. "Absolutely not. We have to restrict access, you see."

"Why? I'm just curious."

"Too many readers these days. We have to restrict access to ephemera. As readers multiply, the individual needs of readers become less significant than those of universal readers. We now have to channel access to our storage and retrieval system more efficiently . . ."

"How can it be efficient if it doesn't work?" I asked, wondering what role the Colonel might have played in the design of such a system. "Unless it's more efficient in that more people simply give up," I offered.

The librarian simply shrugged his shoulders. "Ultimately it reduces the workload for everyone," he said, noncommittally.

"I see," I replied, nodding foolishly. The librarian said it would take him a while, that he would be back from his pilgrimage to the card catalogue in about an hour, if I was lucky.

This suited me just fine, as I figured I could use the time to write a short sketch of Eleanor as a child. I had spoken to Ira the previous evening and promised that I would absolutely positively send him what I had done by the end of the week. It had taken him a pretty long time to come to the phone when I'd called. His wife had answered, and I heard her yell irritably, "Ira! It's that Ella Kennedy woman."

I gave him a quick progress report, trying to disguise the main problem, which was that there was no progress to report, and his response could best be summarized as indifferent.

That's when I vowed to mail a package to him the next day, before he stopped bothering to take my calls altogether.

> **Abraham Lincoln.** By the age of nine, Eleanor had already begun to write regularly to Abraham Lincoln, giving him suggestions on how to conduct the Civil War. She told her father that the president badly needed her advice, and gave him the letters to post. Instead, he tucked them away in his desk drawer, proud but bemused.
>
> Eleanor . . .

My concentration waned when I noticed a bank of computers advertising free Internet access. I had heard a lot about the Internet, but was one of those three Americans who had never really tried to log-on before. I typed in the words "Karl Marx," and was stunned by the eventual response: there were no less than 30,286 relevant documents.

The first few hits, however, were misleading. I wound up on the home page for a chain of Karl Marx delicatessens, headquartered somewhere outside of Dallas. I found a couple of Karl Marx family home pages, one of which introduced me to a nice suburban family in Toronto—four kids, mom and dad, and a dog, all posing in front of their brand-new Dodge minivan. After a few more misses, I finally found the real thing.

It was hard to know where to begin amid an array of choices including CyberLeninism, Viva La Revolucion Cubana, Things for the Curious Communist, the Tito Page, the Mao Tse-tung Page, and the Essential Fidel Castro Home Page. There was even a specially featured Marxist website of the month, the distinction going this time to the Communist Party of Canada. I decided to take a peek at Living Marxism.

It took ages to log-on, and I wondered if that meant this was an especially popular sight. I tried to imagine a bunch of Marxists—

living ones, no less—sitting in their carpeted suburban homes around the world, all trying to meet up in cyberspace. Karl would be proud.

At last, a graphic of the bearded one himself began to slowly emerge, along with a few excerpts. "The point is to change the world," seemed to be the motto of the Living Marxism website.

The most striking thing was the relative sanity of the place. There was no calls to arms, no talk of revolution; no discussion, even, of labor unions or minimum wages or discriminatory labor practices. There were, instead, discussions about pornography on the Internet, the preponderance of bad drivers on American highways, and reviews of recently released feature films.

I logged on to another site simply entitled Marx Today, which appeared to be a cheat room stocked with term papers on a host of frequently asked academic questions. One of the more intriguing papers was entitled *Where To Art Thou, Karl Marx?*

Marx was still a dirty word, but the reality, at least online, was that it was slowly blurring into the mainstream—particularly if 30,286 hits served as any indication of the mainstream. It was really the right-wing extremists one needed to worry about, the armed militiamen, the radical pro-lifers, the Ku Klux Klan, the sorts of people who made good on their threats. The Marxists were just a bunch of washed-up idealists, clearly earning enough these days to buy the latest in computer software.

The cheat room website provided a direct link to a Marxist chat room, which I entered reluctantly, feeling slightly derelict. But again, the conversation was lacking spark. Should the EPA be more closely monitoring toxic waste sites in Montana, for instance? Should the nurses at the local hospital in Duluth, Minnesota, organize, or not?

I didn't really want to chat. And yet it all seemed so bizarre—being able to ask stupid questions without giving away one's true identity—that I hung out silently for a few minutes, and then braved a question of my own.

"Can anyone help me with some research on Eleanor Marx?" I typed self-consciously.

"Hi!" came the startlingly instant reply from someone who identified himself as Eddie Jr.

"Hi" I typed meekly in response.

"I can help! I know more than any history books will ever tell you! Remember, there are two sides to every story!" came the reply from Eddie Jr.

"What do you mean?" I asked.

"Things are not always as they seem!" he wrote.

At which point the keyboard literally froze, paralyzed, perhaps, by excessive punctuation. I tried everything I could think of short of smashing in the screen with the heel of my shoe, to no avail. But I couldn't walk away. What if I never found this Eddie Jr. character again? I wanted to know what he was talking about.

In the midst of my agonizing, the librarian reappeared, looking smug.

"According to our system," he said, "there is no such person as Eleanor Marx."

I tried again to convince him otherwise, lobbying for the chance to take a brief, discreet look at the card catalogue. He told me to come back with the proper credentials, and he'd see what he could do.

Chapter 5

I didn't want to badger Ira, but by my calculations, forty-nine hours and fifty-two minutes had elapsed since he should have received my work-in-progress. In that time I had begun to succumb to wide-ranging delvsional fantasies including the thought that he might have suffered a stroke laughing at my preliminary attempt at a so-called dissertation.

A general sense of unease was compounded by the fact that Nigel had gone missing. He'd been away for almost half the time that Ira would have been in possession of the dissertation, leaving a smeared and soggy note on the kitchen table explaining that something had come up, and he'd be back soon. Eeyore had sat beside the note as I read, licking cream spilled from the pitcher Nigel must have used for his tea at breakfast.

In an effort to distract myself after a mostly sleepless night, I stopped by the institute just long enough to determine that while outgoing phone service had been restored, incoming service had not. The electricity continued to be out as well, making working conditions as hopeless as usual. The only thing I could think to do to keep myself from flipping out over Nigel's unexplained absence was to work on my dissertation. But I couldn't go any further until I heard from Ira. A vicious cycle indeed. By the end of the day I had pretty much lost all self-restraint. I was either going to call the police and send them in search of my boyfriend, or I was going to call Ira. The latter seemed the less irrational of the two admittedly neurotic choices.

"It's Ella Kennedy again," his wife called to him, not even bothering to feign cheer this time. I wondered what she did all day apart from screen his phone calls.

"Hi, Ella," Ira said impatiently. "Listen, I really don't have time to talk right now and I've barely had a chance to skim your dissertation but I guess my advice would be to rethink things. This is way too predictable. You seem to be merely stringing together a bunch of biographical material. Did I mention that you need to at least posit a thesis? Something about how Eleanor's life affected her father's work, perhaps, or the future of Marxism, or the socialist view on the status of women? Or maybe you could do some research, find something new. You need to be thinking of your thesis as a sort of science project—"

"I was thinking of something along the lines of showing how the personal influences the political," I offered meekly. *Was I really a total idiot, or was there the remote possibility that Ira just didn't get it?*

"Hang on a minute," he said, muffling the receiver with his hand. I could hear him talking to his wife. "Listen, Ella, I'm really sorry. I've got to run. The dog needs to go for his walk and I've got to stop in at the laundry room and put our stuff in the dryer, but just keep on going, don't despair. You're smart and I'm sure you will figure this out."

I was not so sure I'd ever figure anything out; it seemed I'd been stuck between gears for years, using up gas while I idled. Still, there was no reason to fall apart; I had simply gotten off to a bad start. I just needed to rethink things. To write something that would jar him and demand his attention. To begin again, perhaps. Maybe this time from a less predictable place.

The main thing was to get out of the apartment, which made it difficult to concentrate on anything other than Nigel's absence. A nice strong cup of coffee might jump-start the brain—since Bob the bird had broken the carafe I'd been drinking only tea at home—and so I walked to the corner Starbucks, ordered two grande black coffees, and managed to produce at the unimpressive but steady rate of a paragraph per cup before I needed to use the bathroom, which was out of order.

Bitter Almonds. By the time Gerturde Gentry opened Eleanor's door to collect her washing, it was too late. She was dressed in white; her face was a pale blue.

The room smelled peculiar, not unlike bitter almonds, she would later tell the coroner.

There was a voice mail from Nigel waiting for me when I arrived home.

I tried to reach you at the office several times, darling, but the phone lines seemed to be crossed. I kept getting the Department of Transportation, instead. They've never heard of you over there. Anyway, I'm awfully sorry to disappear like this. Something came up suddenly, you see. An interview. A job interview. It's all out of the blue and quite unexpected and I really wanted you to come. In fact, if you get this message in time, you can still come, though I won't be here long. I plan to catch the first flight back from Miami as soon as I've finished. I love you, darling. Cheers.

I replayed the message several times and closed my eyes, savoring the sound of each word, but blocking out the meaning. Was it possible to be in love with a voice, I wondered? And if so, was it possible to sever the voice from its problematic owner?

We had been together for only six weeks, yet it felt like ages since I had been alone. I could not concentrate on anything more taxing than straightening up the apartment, which was no small feat. I then made some scrambled eggs and shared them with Bob. I tried to read, and I tried to write, and I tried to sleep, all to no avail. My mind kept drifting back to Miami, and I couldn't help but wonder where in the world this wife of his lived.

The sole conclusion I could reach was that I was mentally more sound just a few short weeks ago, before we ever met.

"I seem to be having a convergence of crises," I said to Lisa the next morning, straining to be heard above the din of the vacuum cleaner.

She didn't bother to look up from under her couch, where she was sucking up enormous dust balls and mumbling something about needing to have the air ducts cleaned.

"I mean, on the one hand I'm really blowing it with Ira. I just have a bunch of notes so far, a couple of half-formed chapters, and I can't seem to get any traction as far as an actual thesis is concerned. And this thing with Nigel is so distracting . . . I just can't figure him out. I think that something really tragic must have happened to him in New Guinea. Something that has left him sort of emotionally shattered."

"Like what?" she asked, pausing for a moment to switch attachments from the small, fuzzy brush to the plastic nozzle. She was wearing overalls and had a yellow bandanna wrapped around her head.

"I don't know. Maybe his wife died or something. Don't they

have a lot of volcanoes and earthquakes and poisonous snakes over there?" I shouted as she turned the vacuum back on.

"I wouldn't know," she shouted in reply. "Never been there."

"Well, anyway, I just get the feeling that something bad happened that has left him so needy. It's like he met me and he just . . . well, I hate to use the word, but he just sort of *flocked* to me. Sometimes he almost seems like one of these stupid birds he keeps talking about. He always brings me weird little gifts. Like these bracelets, and this ring," I said, producing my left arm to demonstrate. "And last week he brought me a snow umbrella from a garage sale. And before that, a cigarette case with someone else's initials."

Lisa didn't seem to be listening. She was busy trying to dislodge a wad of hair that was stuck in the vacuum hose. I followed her to the entrance hall, where she switched outlets and began to vacuum again.

"Lisa?" I asked. "Do you hear me?"

"I hear you," she said with some unexpected hostility. "I hear you trying to talk yourself into some romantic melodrama, some Greek tragedy or something, when I wonder if you've ever stopped to consider the other version."

"What other version?"

"That maybe the guy's just a schmuck. He's obviously married, right? I mean, maybe he's just a philandering jerk who attracts women like you who fall for the sad and eccentric type."

That was of course the very version I was trying hard to not consider. Why oh why was I such a idiot? Why was Lisa always right about absolutely everything? Nigel was two-timing me; or perhaps more accurately, he was two-timing his wife, because as his MERE *MISTRESS* I had no status by which to be two-timed. Or did I? But that didn't make a whole lot of sense. After all, we'd spent every night together until this week. And he was so sweet, so quietly solicitous. He said he wanted to marry me, and no one had ever said such a thing to me before. I thought of the warmth of his body pressed against me in bed, the taste of salt on his skin, his tender kisses bearing the distinct aroma of Camel cigarettes . . .

"Ella!"

"Sorry. I was just daydreaming. Listen, let's not talk about Nigel. Did you take any classes in deconstruction?"

"Deconstruction is dead. You need to be thinking postmodern." Lisa had won departmental distinction for her postmodern quasi-Marxist cultural critique of the *ex-Files,* which was later published by the university press.

"I have to confess that I really don't know what that means. I took all of these classes in classical Marxism. I never paid much attention to anything that happened after the nineteenth century."

"It's not that hard. Just think about context. Think about how you can't separate Marx's work from the conditions in which he wrote."

"Yeah, I know, but it's not about Marx, per se, it's about Eleanor."

"But that's even better. Look at how the women in Marx's life were marginalized. They were like footnotes to history, when if you look at it from another perspective, they were central. You know, like those pictures where you see both a candle and two silhouettes. One figure becomes dominant depending on how you look at it."

Yes, I knew exactly what she meant. I thought of the picture that my sister had drawn in kindergarten that had been hanging in the kitchen, eroding my self-esteem, for some twenty-five years. It depicted my family seated around the table. My sister, taking prerogative as the artist, had given herself straight blond princess hair that cascaded to the floor. She had red lips and wore a ruffled fairy dress. My parents and our oldest sister were all represented as small nondescript blobs with hands and legs. An infant at the time, I was a speck roughly half the size of a thumbprint but with big hair, clearly stuck in as an afterthought—a footnote—probably at the insistence of the teacher.

"Yeah, I know what you're saying," I replied. "I'm just having trouble articulating all this."

"Just keep it simple," she advised, switching outlets once again, "and use a lot of buzzwords."

I asked her for some sample buzzwords but she didn't seem to hear me.

"Anyway, Lisa, the other thing is that I think you should come back to work," I yelled over the whir of the vacuum. "I think this should be *your* catalogue. Honestly, I don't know what I'm doing . . . I'm getting nowhere and the Colonel seems to have no real interest in the project and his house is a disaster area and besides, my heart just isn't in it. What I really want is to concentrate on my dissertation full time. And it's not like I'm really doing anything useful, I'm just putting together a mail-order catalogue . . .

"We could organize a coup and oust the Colonel," I continued in jest, hoping to get her attention. "I know there would be plenty of support. I could start circulating a petition tomorrow. I'm sure Carmen would sign it. Maybe we could rally the decorators, too. And, hey, if that doesn't work we could just take the man out ourselves. Hang his corpse from the chandelier in the living room, kind of like they did to that guy in Afghanistan, or to Mussolini."

"The Colonel is beside the point," she said, barely audible.

"The point being?"

"The point being that *I don't want to work anymore.*"

"You'd rather vacuum?" I asked, instantly regretting my words. I had meant to sound provocative, but I realized I simply sounded obnoxious.

"Can't you get a cleaning lady or something?" I asked, trying to redeem myself. Lisa dragged the canister into the kitchen, suctioning up bits of shriveled Cheerios and mashed baby biscuits from under the high chair.

"I enjoy taking care of my house," she said. "I've never done this before." She turned off the vacuum and continued with her soliloquy. "You know, I have a friend with cancer, and I was listening to her say that it turned her life around. She suddenly realized that there was more to life than all of this competitive bullshit. That the real satisfaction was not in clearing off a stack of papers from your desk but in *nurturing:* growing flowers and reading to children and baking fairy cakes . . ."

I was trying hard to follow her; Lisa was my mentor, and if she was suggesting that we should stay at home and bake and garden, I felt I should at least listen. In my mind's eye, however, I pictured not a bed of flowers, but a mass of prickly weeds.

"What are fairy cakes?" I asked, trying to sound like I cared.

"Oh they're these lovely little cupcakes, very light and fluffy and decorated on top with bits of candy and sprinkles. Would you like the recipe?"

"Maybe some other time," I said. This was all very confusing. I couldn't tell from looking at her whether she'd undergone some kind of profound spiritual conversion or had been kidnapped in the night and replaced by a Stepford version of her former self. In either case, I was still not quite ready to let go. Everything I believed about my own future as a woman with the potential to reproduce was crumbling in her decision to quit: I had always figured, in the back of my mind, that first I would make myself indispensable at my wonderfully interesting job; then I would get married and have a baby, taking only my allotted maternity leave; next I would hire Mary Poppins and go back to work, where I would achieve brilliant things.

"Are you really happy at home?" I asked earnestly.

"You really don't get it, Ella, do you?" she shouted from under the table.

Not only did I not get it, but I was hurt. I had thought that close friends would consult each other when contemplating drastic alterations to their life plans. To me her decision seemed the equivalent of suddenly tithing all one's money to the Church of Scientology, or deciding to become a nun. I would have liked the opportunity to have joined her for a beer to explore this maternally inspired change in sentiment.

"I guess you can't really get it until you've had kids," she said, adding further insult.

"Get what?" I knew what having kids was about; I was an aunt, after all. I had even spent the weekend with my sister's three kids while she and her husband went to a wedding in New Hampshire, once.

"Get that there are different phases of life. Different times for different things. Right now, I really couldn't give a shit about the Institute of Thought. Maybe I'll feel differently in a few years."

"Geez, Lisa," I said bitterly. "You gave enough of a shit to drag me down here. The least you could do is help me figure out a few things," I tried.

Hayden suddenly bounded into the room crying, stammering something through his tears about his chocolate milk having spilled, and Lisa pulled him close and held him, uninhibited by the chocolate smeared all over his face.

I felt I had lost her attention but proceeded nonetheless. "Who is Eddie Jr.?" I asked, hoping the question was sufficiently interesting to compete with Hayden's dramatic entrance.

Lisa looked up at me with an amused smile.

"Not Eddie Jr. again," she said, wetting a paper towel and cleaning Hayden's face before turning her attention to the puddle which, with increasing speed, was heading toward the dining room carpet she had just vacuumed.

"Why? What do you mean?" I asked, squatting down with a cloth to help her.

"Eddie Jr. is just a netmyth," she yelled from the kitchen, where she had gone to get some more paper towels.

"What's a netmyth?" I asked, feeling, not for the first time, one step behind the curve of contemporary culture.

"A netmyth is a story or a rumor that starts circulating on the Internet and then, before you know it, people confuse fiction with fact. Like the one about John Glenn."

"I managed to miss the one about John Glenn," I quipped.

"Apparently someone put a story out on the internet about John Glenn's next-door neighbor . . . his neighbor from back when he was a kid. According to the story, the neighbor's wife once said to her husband, 'I'll give you a blow job when the little boy next door walks on the moon.'"

"I don't get it."

"How can you not get it? John Glenn actually did walk on the moon. See? It's a joke."

"So he got the blow job, then?"

"Ella," she said, exasperated, "that's not the point. The point is that this story, which probably had no basis in reality, circulated around the world. It took on a life of its own. Like Eddie Jr."

"Well, what about Eddie Jr.?"

"Eddie Jr. is some crank who claims to be the great-grandson of Eleanor Marx."

"But Eleanor never had any children. Not that I'm aware of, anyway."

"That's right. But Eddie Jr. has been floating around on the Internet claiming to be Eleanor's great-grandson for a couple of years now, and people are starting to get their facts confused."

"What people?" I asked. "I mean, how many people could there be who have ever even heard of Eleanor Marx?"

"True. And that's a fair question," said Lisa, "but enough people have become interested in all this that Eddie Jr. has made a small name for himself. . . . Besides, Ella, I think the more obvious lesson is that you should be paying attention to what's going on in the world today . . .

"Never mind that you know nothing about deconstruction or postmodernism, but remember how I urged you to take that class on political theory and the new media? You laughed at me at the time, but personally, I found it really useful."

I was beginning to think it was really too much of an emotional drain to be friends with someone who was always right. ·

Lisa picked Hayden up and headed toward his room. I followed behind her and collected a few stray toys along the way, wondering why she, in turn, seemed so irritated with me. I began to play with a noisy pop-up bunny as I watched Lisa strip off Hayden's soggy clothes and wrestle him down on the changing table.

"I tried to sign up for that class," I lied after a few minutes of forcing the bunny to squeal, "but it was full. I'm teaching myself HTML, though, and in fact I wanted to pick your brain a bit about the website. I wanted to interview various American Marxists, maybe create a link to their sites. Since you know so much about modernism, maybe you could point me toward some modern Marxists . . ."

"What modern Marxists? You're the only one I know," she said mischievously as she removed Hayden's stinky diaper.

"I'm not a Marxist," I practically screamed. "And I don't understand how you can be so cynical. You of all people."

"Ella," she said, looking at me like I was crazy, "it seems to be the consensus that Marxism failed. I mean, if you look hard enough, you'll find a few diehards left. But basically, the party's over."

"Yes, well, since you got me invited to this particular party, why don't you just help by giving me some names?"

"Let's see . . . there's Professor Neiman at Berkeley. He argues that we should keep Marx alive as a tribute to all of those who have died in his name. You might give him a call."

"Right," I said. I had heard of him. He was rumored to be something of a lunatic. I looked around Hayden's room for something to write on, and picked a scrap of cardboard from the trash bin. It appeared to be the remnant from the packaging of some toddler-sized undershirts. "Can I write on this?" I asked, pulling a pen from my pocket.

"Sure. Have you talked to Hannah Bloomstein?" Lisa asked as she held both of Hayden's feet in the air like he was a trussed turkey and slipped a fresh diaper beneath him. "She's at Michigan. . . . At least I think she's still there. The gist of her thesis is that the declaration that communism is dead comes too soon. Capitalism has survived many a crisis, and so will communism. You know, Marx declared the death of capitalism, and he was wrong. And now capitalists have declared the death of communism. They might be just as wrong."

"Is there anyone else?"

"Well there are the revisionists," she said as she applied cream to Hayden's chapped bottom while he thrashed around unhappily. "They'll claim that Marxism was never meant to be a science written in stone. It's just a theory, a way of looking at the world. The world changes, economic conditions change, hence the theory changes. As in capitalism, right? I mean who would have been writing about junk bonds a hundred years ago?"

"Or bulk discounting," I added enthusiastically.

"Exactly." She attempted to slip a new pair of overalls on Hayden while he tried to dive headfirst off the changing table and I wondered if I should offer to help pin him down, or possibly even tie him up.

At last she declared him properly dressed and we headed back downstairs to the kitchen, where she began to mix a new cup of chocolate milk.

I silently placed odds on how long it would take for this new milk to spill.

"Why don't you buy one of those tumblers with a lid?" I asked, having observed my own nieces and nephews toddling around without incident gripping plastic spill-proof cups emblazoned with the smiling faces of various Disney characters.

"I don't believe in those," said Lisa. "Children shouldn't be babied."

Her conviction gave me pause: I suddenly saw myself as spineless, lacking strong opinions on anything, from the relevance of Marxism in the twenty-first century to the political correctness of spill-proof cups for kids.

"Then, of course, there's the chief argument," she said, as I followed her down another flight of stairs to the basement.

"Which is?"

"Which is that we have not seen a single example, in China or in the Soviet Union and Eastern Europe or in Cuba or Latin America, of anything that can be called Marxism. That Marx wrote about liberation, not oppression."

"Of course," I said. "That's my very point. That's what I was trying to tell the Colonel. I mean, my feeling is that Marx's predictions came too early on. Maybe he was right. Maybe capitalism will self-implode, but it may have hundreds of years yet to go."

"Well, you can certainly make that thesis, but what is to say that the logical outcome is communism? It's more likely to be something like total global destruction. You know, the melting of the polar ice caps or nuclear war or colonization of outer space.

"I mean, it's interesting to posit that history adheres to any scientific laws," said Lisa, pulling out the ironing board and a pile of her husband's shirts. "But I think it's safe to say that, as far as communism being the next logical phase, well, capitalism is clearly proving itself the winner."

I was losing my train of thought. I was more interested in watching her fill the iron with water and plug it into the wall. No one had ever taught me how to wield an iron. My mother always said that if it needed to be ironed, it went to the dry cleaner, and I considered that one of the few useful things she had taught me in life.

"Can you hand me the spray starch?"

Now I felt even more stupid. What was spray starch? Did it come in a can?

"Where?" I asked.

"Right in front of you," she said, pointing to a shelf full of cleaning fluids.

I began to read each of the names aloud: "'Mr. Clean, Ajax, Lysol bathroom cleaner, Mop & Glo . . .'"

Lisa put down the iron and with obvious irritation grabbed the spray starch off the shelf herself.

"I don't think you need to fret so much, Ella," she said, unbuttoning the collar of a blue-striped cotton shirt and flattening it on the ironing board. "People will continue to study Marx regardless of his relevance. What does it really matter? I mean, unless you were planning to go out and start a revolution or something. Just order your umbrellas and write your thesis and get on with it . . ."

As she finished her sentence, Hayden tripped down the basement stairs, sending what remained of his chocolate milk into a trickle down the steps. I stared at it for a few minutes until it occurred to me to offer to help, and I went running up to the kitchen to get the paper towels.

By the time I returned Lisa had armed herself with a bottle of Woolite carpet cleaner, and we mopped up spill number two before tromping upstairs, en masse, to the kitchen to refill Hayden's glass.

Lisa then looked at her watch and announced she had to leave for a doctor's appointment. I offered to baby-sit Hayden—anything seemed preferable than going into work, or back to my empty apartment, wondering why Nigel was interviewing for a job in Miami. But Lisa declined my offer, and I couldn't decide if the awkward undercurrent I detected was simply a function of my own anger, or if she was mad at me, too.

I offered again, lying about how much I would enjoy spending time with Hayden, but she made some excuse about having to go to the grocery store directly from the doctor, and how it would take too long.

"Is something wrong, Lisa?" I asked. "It seems like you're kind of mad at me, which I don't really understand."

"I'm not mad at you, Ella. It's just that I thought you were more sensible."

"More sensible than what?"

"More sensible than to be having an affair with a married man," she said.

"Oh, is that it?" I asked, almost relieved. "It's not an affair . . . we're just sort of living together," I said nonsensically. "And besides, like I said before, it's more complicated than that."

"Complicated how?"

"Well, I'm not really sure, but it's complicated."

Lisa screwed up her face, making it clear she had no sympathy for my reply. She attempted to stuff Hayden into a snowsuit and he started to cry, protesting quite reasonably that it was not cold outside, and Lisa began to make sweet cooing noises and suddenly I couldn't stand to be in her presence anymore, my own life being such an undernurtured mess.

I went back to the library the next chance I had, armed with an official-looking letter written on the Institute of Thought stationery. I signed my own name at the bottom, granting myself permission to riffle through the precious card catalogue.

As it turned out, I could have saved the paper; the guard posted at the entrance to the card catalogue room was slumped in his chair, snoring. I flashed my letter at him as a formality, and then proceeded to solve the mystery of Eleanor's existence in five minutes flat. The index card for Eleanor Marx did, indeed, have a giant X through her name, suggesting that she had perhaps been the product of some sort of cosmic mistake. What the first librarian had failed to realize, however, was that a small arrow had been drawn at the bottom of the card, indicating that it was meant to be flipped over. On the back read the simple notation "Eleanor Aveling."

I had forgotten. No sooner had the ink dried on their Great Russell Street lease than Eleanor changed her name to Aveling, thereby losing herself in the great card catalogues of history.

Madame Bovary. Eleanor Marx was the first person to translate *Madame Bovary* from the French into English. She trudged each day with her books and reams of paper to the British Museum Reading Room, where she sat with her sharpened pencils, agonizing over the choice of every word and the placement of each comma. She had always loved this little book, and was partial to the suicide scene: "Now her chest began to heave rapidly. Her tongue was sticking right out of her mouth; her eyes, rolling about, were turning pale, just like the globe of a lamp as it expires, as if she were already dead . . ."

"You see I'm not clever enough to live a purely *intellectual* life," she wrote to her sister, "nor am I dull enough to be content to sit down and do nothing." She considered literary work the middle ground.

She looked up from the page and noticed that a man was staring at her.

He approached and spoke to her casually, as though they were old friends. We meet again, Madame, he said.

Eleanor was at first confused. She looked quizzically at the man. Perhaps she had seen him before. There was something memorable about his odd looks. The long forehead, the pale, almost sickly skin, the crooked, stained teeth. Was he lovely or hideous? He was both at once, she decided.

At the Orphan Working School, he explained. In Hampstead.

She felt her cheeks flush with embarrassment. He looked vaguely familiar, and yet she had no idea what he was talking about.

The man did not seem insulted but rather amused. He seemed confident that, at some point, she would catch on.

Insects and butterflies, he said, offering another cryptic clue.

And then she did remember something at least; she saw a pale man with an improbably long face wield his pointy stick from behind the lectern, like a baton. That man had had more hair than this fellow, hair lighter in color, even, but that memory was from a long, long time ago. The speaker had been oddly engaging, his voice impassioned as he droned on about the life cycle of insects. But now she couldn't decide how much of this was real and to what extent she was forcing herself to conjure up a memory.

Anyway, said the man, he remembered, even if his lecture hadn't left much of a lasting impression on her. It was the only time he had met her father, he explained. After the lecture you came to the podium . . . you and your mother and your father. Your father shook my hand. You hid behind your mother's skirts.

How is your father? he inquired.

Her father's health was not so good just now, she heard herself explain. Her mother had died recently, and Marx, who was sixty-three, seemed to be having trouble with his own health.

The stranger offered his regrets. He said he had read about her mother's death in the newspapers.

Eleanor was beginning to remember something. It was ages ago, she said. Father had wanted to go to a lecture because it had something to do with Darwin. Was this correct?

It was, he said with his crooked smile. I am a great admirer of the man, he explained. In fact I have arranged a meeting with him in a few weeks time . . .

Eleanor was no longer listening. She was dredging her brain for more pieces of the memory. She found herself strangely intrigued by this stranger. She had a feeling about him: perhaps this odd man was compensation for her having, finally, let Lissagary drift back to Paris.

I was only a child at the time, Eleanor finally said, by way of apology.

You were never only a child, Eleanor, he said knowingly. And then he excused himself. He was late for a class, he explained. But he hoped that they might meet again.

It wasn't until he left that she realized she didn't even know his name. But it didn't take more than a few inquiries. Everyone knew who Edward Aveling was. And everyone had something to say about him.

Chapter 6

My lack of progress on the NUTS project was not for lack of trying: I was toiling under impossible conditions. The electricity had been shut off for almost a week, the Colonel had all but disappeared, and the construction foreman warned me not to even think about entering the basement, as the ceiling was quite literally caving in.

Then there was the small matter of lacking incentive: I still had not received a paycheck, and remained in a familiar state of debt to my parents. The Colonel kept promising he would pay me soon, invoking a variety of excuses ranging from misplaced checkbooks to inexplicable banking errors. In the meantime he had given me a temporary membership card for his health club with instructions on how and when to get my photo taken, and had also deposited a wad of health insurance forms on my desk. I had simply shoved all of the documents under a pile of papers: it seemed ridiculous to bother, as I would be leaving soon. In fact, any sensible person would have packed her bags and fled already. But I was not thinking in sensible terms. I was thinking only that I needed to stay in Washington for a while, to figure out Nigel.

After a few more wasted days, I decided to chose a course of unprecedented action. I bullied my way past the construction crew, negotiated for a couple of hours worth of electricity, brushed the bits of crumbled plaster from the top of the computer, called and screamed until someone showed up to install the modem, arranged for an online connection, and set out to design a web page.

The first bit of bad news, however, was that the HTML book—the one that was supposed to enable me to create a web page in five easy steps—fell about forty-three steps short of enlightening me.

I had this idea that the NUTS website would, of course, contain a picture of Karl Marx. By clicking onto different parts of Marx's image, one would link to different parts of the page.

But it had not occurred to me that making Karl Marx's body user-friendly would involve math, which had never been my strong suit.

```
<IMG SRC="USEMAP=#name>
<MAP NAME="name">
<AREA SHAPE="RECT" COORDS="n,n,n" HREF="">
<AREA SHAPE="CIRCLE" COORDS="n,n,n" HREF="">
<AREA SHAPE=POLYGON" COORDS-,n,n, . . ."
  HREF="">
```

The more I read, the worse it got. There were things like FRAMESET COLS that involved percentages. There were hexadecimal number representations to determine elements as simple as color. There were profound questions that I found difficult to answer, like the relative value of JPEG vs. GIF.

Adding to my general level of frustration was the discovery that although I had succeeded in getting the electricity turned on, the water was now turned off. This was a discovery made only after depositing a tampon in the toilet—the same toilet that was used by the construction crew, no less—which I was then unable to flush.

After a full day at the office, I had failed to produce any fancy graphics, but I had managed to name our website and write an explanatory statement about NUTS's aim to "put a human face on Karl Marx." I also succeeded in establishing an address through a free browser offer: www.karlmarxstuff.com. (Just about every other name I could think of relating to Karl Marx was already taken.) These were no small feats, particularly given the steady rain of plaster on my head, the frequent power surges, and the deafening noise from the workmen, plus the fact that I had to walk several blocks to a restaurant every time I needed to use a bathroom.

By the time Nigel called to say he was back in town and had won a couple of free tickets to the theater inside a bag of cheese-flavored nacho chips, I was ready to call it a day.

"How's your play going?" I asked Nigel, shifting my weight in the creaky folding chair. We were seated in the first row of the aptly named Hole Theater, which had the same ambience, not to mention the same damp smell, of an unfinished basement, or of my office, come to think of it.

The theater had recently become popular in the same campy way that it becomes fashionable, from time to time, to frequent unsavory parts of town in search of alternative eating establishments. In New York, for example, the meat-packing district enjoyed a brief stint as the hip place to go for breakfast: a group of us would travel by subway, groggy before our first cups of coffee, and then step over puddles of blood on the way to the latest trendy café.

While there were no freshly slaughtered animals on the premises of the Hole Theater, there was a heating problem and a parking problem and the likelihood of encountering a stray bullet along the way.

Nigel's tan contrasted oddly with his winter coat, which he persisted in wearing despite the balmy weather in D.C. He had handed me a string of amber beads when we met outside the theater. He said he'd found them at the airport, and I hung them around my neck hesitantly, wondering where, precisely, he had found them—in a gift shop, in a sticky puddle on the floor, around the neck of his wife?

Again I asked Nigel how his play was going, but my question hung midair. He was absorbed in the Playbill, such as it was—a bunch of poorly Xeroxed pages fastened together with a paper clip. His eye stopped for an unconscionably long time on the photo of the lead actress. I read over his shoulder: graduate of University of Maryland; an extra on *L.A. Law;* disc jockey for an alternative rock radio station in Boston.

"Nigel," I repeated, shaking his arm gently. "How's *your* play going?"

"What?" he answered without looking up.

"How's your play? The Value Giant play? The one you described to my parents? You know—birds and shopping or whatever . . ."

"Yeah, I know the one. It would be coming along fine if I only had the time to write. When I do manage to sit down with it, I find it flows rather nicely, though."

Nigel went back to studying the program, unabashed. What he said was absurd: he had nothing *but* time.

"What's this play about, anyway?" I asked, deciding to do the mature thing and simply change the subject. I reached for his program. We had been allotted one per couple.

"It's supposed to be a nineties interpretation of *A Doll's House,* he replied.

"Really!" I said excitedly. "I didn't get that from the name . . . what's the name again?"

"Nora and Nellie," he said.

"Who's Nellie?" I asked.

"I think Nellie is supposed to be Nora's lover," he whispered. "It's a lesbian interpretation you see. It's an all-woman cast."

"Good Lord! I wonder what Ibsen would have to say. Did you know Eleanor was a big fan of Ibsen?"

"Eleanor? Eleanor who?"

"Eleanor Marx. Or Eleanor Aveling, rather." I had been telling him the saga of Eleanor bit by bit, and wanted to believe that he was paying attention to the details of my life. It was part of the whole self-delusion package that was the basis of our relationship. And so, in order to preserve the status quo, I decided to give him the benefit of the doubt: he'd been away for almost two days and had important things on his mind, so it was understandable that he might have forgotten about Eleanor.

"She translated a number of Ibsen's plays," I continued. "She helped bring him to the attention of English audiences. Eleanor aspired to be an actress, you know. She took acting lessons, and appeared onstage several times. The reviews were mixed, though, and she was very easily discouraged. She and Edward Aveling and George Bernard Shaw held a reading in her apartment, once. Shaw played Krogstad. In fact, Eleanor once wrote a satire of *A Doll's House*."

"Hmmm . . ." he said.

"She cowrote it with a man named Israel Zangwill. It was meant as a sarcastic response to English audiences who thought that the ending of *A Doll's House* was too radical. You know, their Victorian sensibilities were totally offended by the idea that Nora could walk out on her husband and leave her kids. Ibsen even wrote a completely different ending for German audiences, though he felt sick about it."

"Hmmm," he said.

"I wonder what he would make of tonight's performance." I thought about that for a moment. "If Ibsen was the same kind of radical guy now that he was a hundred-plus years ago, he would *have* to condone Nora walking out on her husband and kids to live with Nellie. Right? But, well really, no. The new Nora would *take* the kids! Screw Torvald! 'See you in court!' she would say."

"Uh-huh," he said. He took my hand and squeezed it tight.

What was my problem, really?

It seemed, for the moment at least, like there was nothing more one could ask for from life than a night at the theater and a warm hand to hold.

I leaned my head on his shoulder, urging myself to be content. Still, even in my self-deluded state I knew it was dangerous to base a relationship on a series of small good moments.

I had regained my senses by the time we arrived at the restaurant—an insufferably cheerful café with a vaguely Southwestern theme—where we sat awkwardly at the table for several minutes before I broke the silence.

"Tell me about your interview in Miami," I said at last. "What sort of job is it?"

"A totally degrading job," he replied simply, pulling his coat tight as if to shield himself from the thought. "One I may be reduced to taking, if offered."

"Well, what sort of totally degrading job is it?" I asked, fondling a cactus-shaped salt shaker.

"Have you heard of Parrot Jungle?"

"I have! I went there as a kid. It's like a zoo with mostly birds, right?"

"Exactly. And they have animal shows. You know, the kind where some idiot gets up there and makes the bird fly through a ring or say something clever."

"Yeah! I love those shows. Actually they have a pretty good one at the aquarium in Baltimore—with dolphins, of course, not birds. . . . I took my niece there last summer."

"Well, they want me to be the idiot, so to speak. They have a show where the birds ride bicycles and land on people's heads and say amusing things into a microphone. They said I was overqualified but would consider me in light of my having a British accent. . . . They said it might appeal to tourists."

"When will you hear?" I asked, pouring bits of salt on the table and tracing a pattern through the grains with my finger.

"Not sure. It was a bit vague, but probably in a week or two."

A waitress with impossibly long legs extending from a yellow miniskirt showed up before I could reply.

Nigel ordered a bottle of wine with a confidence I found enviable, particularly given his inability to pay for it, and then with equal self-assurance, able to put aside the fact that we were in the middle of a potentially explosive personal situation, he asked for the pressed duck Santa Fe.

"Would you like a salad with that, darling?" the waitress asked in a seductive southern drawl.

"Yes, darling, the house salad sounds lovely."

She stared at me, as I stared at the menu. I was distracted by this "darling" business.

"And I would like the catfish," I replied at last. "Without the peppers and broiled, not fried."

"I'm sorry," she said with no audible trace of pity. "We're out of catfish. But the trout is excellent."

"Is it filleted?"

"No, none of our fish is filleted."

"But the catfish came filleted." I pointed to the menu as proof.

"Yes," she replied, putting down her little pad and crossing her arms. "But like I said, *we don't have any catfish.*"

"Why don't you try the duck?" said Nigel, helpfully.

"I don't like duck. If I had wanted duck I would have ordered duck. . . . And besides, have you ever heard of a duck in Santa Fe? Isn't Santa Fe in the desert? Is this a desert duck?" I asked the waitress, who was now looking at me distrustfully.

I felt the tears begin to trickle down my cheeks.

Nigel and the waitress continued to stare at me.

"I'll come back in a few minutes, darling," she said, touching Nigel on the shoulder, as if they were intimate friends with a mutual problem.

"What's going on with you, Ella?" he asked, appearing genuinely baffled.

"What's going on?" I practically shouted. "Did you apply for this job in Miami, or did they just find you, like through some psychic job hot line or something? Could we have maybe talked about it, first? You ask me to marry you. You won't talk about your wife. Now you may move to Miami. I'd say we have a bit of a communication problem!"

I was aware the fact that my complaints were perfectly rational seemed negated by my tears.

"Well, you'll come with me, of course, I mean, I just assumed . . . if we're going to be married. But don't worry. I'm not even sure that I'll get the job. And if I do, maybe I won't even take it. I mean, never mind that the job is degrading to me. It's humiliating for the birds. . . .

"Did you know that birds' brains are something like ten times larger than those of reptiles? I mean, birds are smart. They deserve to be treated with dignity. . . . I had a parrot once that could count—and I don't mean mimic—but he could actually count to five. Every morning my wife would give him five pieces of fruit, and they'd count together—"

"Your wife?" I asked, hoping for more information.

"Yeah," he said flatly, and then returned to a monologue about the intricate level of care birds give to their young before embarking on a recitation of the whole miraculous migration thing. Flying without radar and all that.

I was beginning to feel that I could write a book on avian trivia. He was practically unstoppable once he got going on his fieldwork, reminiscing about the family of bowerbirds with whom he had become intimately acquainted during his months in the rain forest. He described each member of the flock in such detail (this despite the fact that they looked exactly alike) one might suppose that the bowerbirds were a family who had hosted him on his school year abroad. Which, in a manner of speaking, I suppose they had been.

I had nothing against birds, and had even grown fond of Bob the small green parrot in an odd and probably perverse way (Bob sounded exactly like Nigel). But I was not a bird person, per se. I was a cat person. And cats and birds were not the best of friends, though I tried not to read too much into that fact.

"I tried to get them interested in the idea of including bower-birds in their show," he continued. "Although I must say I have mixed feelings about it. On the one hand it would be amazing to get the birds to sort of steal things from the audience—a spotted bowerbird once stole one of my wife's bracelets, he hung it from a twig to decorate his little bower—but on the other hand I think the best thing to do is of course leave the birds where they belong."

I stared at the now shiny bangles on my wrist, pained. Nigel had unwittingly disclosed the most intimate details yet about his wife: she had been with him in New Guinea and she wore bracelets. Now I had a picture to plug into my mind. A woman in a rain forest. A woman with bracelets, possibly like mine. It wasn't much but it was something.

Things had been different, once, he explained, not for the first time. There was a time when he would never have considered working in a theme park. He had once had that job at the London Zoo, for example, as well as a subsequent position lecturing part time at Cambridge, both of which he recalled with an almost pathetic air, not unlike a soldier who cannot stop talking about the war.

He was an up-and-coming ornithologist, he explained again. But he had fallen from grace in some unspeakable fashion that may or may not have had something to do with his unspeakable wife, and I tried to fight the observation that his descent had landed him here, with me.

"Why don't you just marry me now," Nigel said suddenly, though it seemed to me he was not staring intently into my eyes so much as studying the waitress's legs as she took an order at the next table. "We'll go find a justice of the peace, or a sheriff or a ship's captain or whomever you are supposed to find in this country. Then we can approach these choices together, you know, as a team."

I felt tears begin to well up in my eyes again and I began to babble. "You know, the more research I do on Eleanor Marx," I said, wishing I could stop myself from saying something disastrous, "the more I feel like I have something in common with her. It's almost spooky."

Nigel sighed and gave in. "Like what?" he asked. "What do you mean?"

"I'm not sure. I mean, I think we probably look alike, a bit. And then there's this whole latent Judaism thing, you know. Karl Marx was Jewish, but his family became Lutherans. And fathers who are writers . . . well sort of, in my case. And then there's her relationship with Aveling, which is obviously going to be a disaster from the start."

"Ah," said Nigel. "So that's the point of all this. If you're Eleanor, I must be this Aveling character who is a disaster from the start."

"I didn't mean that," I countered. I looked up at him cautiously, fearing the consequences of what I had just said.

"That's great, Ella. I'm asking you to marry me, and you're comparing me to some chap who's a disaster from the start."

I began to fear I was falling into some sort of diagnosable psychotic paranoid state; I kept catching glimpses of the waitress and her voluptuous breasts in my peripheral line of vision. She seemed to be hovering around our table more than necessary.

"You're overreacting . . ." I insisted, knowing he was not. "Look, Nigel," I said, tears now actively streaming down my face. "She's more your type. I'm all wrong for you."

"Who's more my type?" he said, baffled.

"The waitress."

"*The waitress?*" He threw up his arms in despair. "I don't even know the waitress. What's wrong with you anyway?"

"I don't know."

"What don't you know?"

"I don't know, Nigel. It's just that your vagueness is driving me mad."

He looked genuinely confused. "What vagueness? There's nothing vague about my intentions. I want to marry you. That's about as concrete as it gets, wouldn't you say?"

"But you seem to have so many secrets. Your whole relationship with your wife is a secret. And your play. And now this Miami thing has really thrown me for a loop."

Again that sad look, which made me feel like a shrew for inflicting pain.

He took my hand and squeezed it. "I love you, Ella," he said simply. "It's been a long time since I've felt like I could go on again. It wasn't until I met you."

The waitress returned with her little pad and I looked at her, helpless.

"I'll have the pressed duck Santa Fe, darling," I said in as cheerful a tone as I could muster.

I wiped my tears and tried to smile. Nigel smiled back.

Perhaps this was the key to a successful relationship: glossing over the troubling details and the gaping black holes. Just faking it.

Aware that I was doing nothing to fix the central problem of my thesis, that I was, in fact, failing in pretty much every aspect of my life, I found myself standing in front of a mirror, thinking about Eleanor's physical appearance.

Eleanor, Observed. "She was the gayest creature in the world—when she was not the most miserable," observed one friend of Eleanor's. "Her appearance was striking. She was not really beautiful, but she somehow gave the impression of beauty by reason of her sparkling eyes, her bright colouring, her dark locky mass of hair . . ."

"A lively young girl of slender build with beautiful black hair and fine dark eyes . . ." noted Eduard Bernstein.

H. M. Hyndman wrote of her resemblance to her father: "A broad, low forehead, dark bright eyes, with glowing cheeks, and a brisk, humorous smile, she inherited in her nose and mouth the Jewish type from Marx himself, while she possessed a physical energy and determination fully equal to his own, and an intelligence which never achieved the literary or political success . . . of which she was capable. Possibly she felt herself somewhat overshadowed by her father's genius, whose defects she was unable to see."

The *New York Herald* was more succinct: "A German-looking lady with eyeglasses," its correspondent observed.

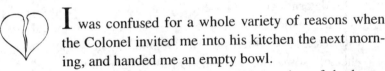 I was confused for a whole variety of reasons when the Colonel invited me into his kitchen the next morning, and handed me an empty bowl.

His kitchen was by then the only visible portion of the house that did not resemble a war zone. The living and dining room areas had been cordoned off with floor-to-ceiling sheets of plastic; inside the rooms stood men wearing Hannibal Lecter–type face masks, wielding noisy power tools. The front hallway had been stripped bare, illuminated only by a single, dangling, wire-caged bulb.

I deduced from the shipment of distressed wooden cabinetry that had just arrived from Ireland and was sitting in crates outside the front door that the kitchen was likely the next area slated for demolition.

I stood leaning against the microwave on the granite counter that would soon be reduced to rubble, holding the empty bowl, wondering why I had been summoned.

"Tell me, do you prefer cornflakes or Froot Loops?" the Colonel asked, holding a box in each hand.

"Um . . . generally I prefer cornflakes, but I'll pass right now. I've just eaten. . . . I picked up a cranberry muffin at the 7-Eleven on my way in to work," I explained. "You know, the one on the corner of Q and Wisconsin," I added, to bolster my claim.

The microwave suddenly lit up and the disk inside began to spin and I realized I had accidentally hit a button. I jumped away, startled, and the Colonel tried to shut it off by punching a series of numbered panels, to no avail.

"Carmen!" he yelled. "Damn! I think she had to go to the doctor or dentist or somewhere this morning. I never learned how to work this thing."

I opened the microwave door and the disk stopped spinning. Inside was an imploded banana and a goo-covered phone bill.

"There it is!" he exclaimed, retrieving the mangled bill. "They were threatening to disconnect us. You've saved the day again." He motioned for me to join him at the table.

"I'm leaving for London in the morning," he said, pulling two British Airways tickets from his jacket pocket while he spoke, "and I'd like for you to join me."

"That's very kind of you," I replied cautiously. "But the thing is, I'd really rather not go to London right now. . . . I have some personal business to attend to. The timing's all wrong. . . . And besides," I ventured boldly, "Lisa never said anything about travel in this job."

In truth I felt mildly panicked about leaving Nigel; I felt very much in a state of emotional limbo, and wanted to sort things out.

"What about your house?" I asked, trying to scheme up a plausible way out of the trip. "Don't you think you should be here right now, just to make sure things are going smoothly? You never know what might come up," I offered, as though speaking from vast firsthand experience of mansion remodeling.

I counted silently as the Colonel heaped five teaspoons of sugar on the fluorescent loops of his cereal, and then doused the bowl with low-fat milk. As I spoke, a chorus of hammering began, and plaster fell from the ceiling, landing in his bowl.

"Actually the timing is perfect," he said, scooping out chunks of plaster with his spoon, unfazed. "I was going to suggest you take some time off anyway, as it's getting difficult to work in here.

But then this London thing came up—the woman from NUTS called and said she'd be in London and, well, frankly, it seemed perfect. Besides, I thought it might be good if you took a look at the souvenir selection at the Marx Memorial Library."

I thought for a moment and countered that I could see no professional reason for me to accompany him. "I've been there, to the library, several times, and there is no souvenir selection. They have *postcards*."

"Postcards! What a good idea! I hadn't thought of that."

"I'm, um, actually just starting to make good progress on the website," I tried. "I've managed to get us an address and when I logged on this morning, it appears that we've even had two visitors already."

"But this place is a wreck. . . . I never envisioned having visitors here right now," he said, a bit of milk dribbling down his chin headed toward his tie.

"No, no . . . I mean visitors to the website. They don't actually come in person. . . ."

The Colonel looked confused. "You're quite a feisty one, Miss Kennedy. Lisa neglected to mention that you were quite so argumentative. Or so whiny, for that matter. Pack your bags, if you will, and meet me at Dulles in the morning."

He handed me a ticket and told me to take the rest of the day off. And I should have, but first I felt compelled to make a few more notes.

I was beginning to feel like an outlaw, like Thelma or maybe like Louise, energized by my own delinquent behavior in pursuing this abhorrent thesis. Seeing this thing through to the bitter end was my own version of driving off a cliff, and in many ways, the metaphor seemed apt.

Enigma. Edward liked to play with details. He toyed with his age and with his résumé; even his name was subject to change. He penned many plays under the name Alec Nelson. He claimed to be either French or Irish, or sometimes a little bit Scottish, depending on the circumstances. But he was invariably generous, often to a fault, ordering up a round of drinks for everyone in the pub, even if he had no intention of paying the bill. He was friendly as a puppy: anyone might have fallen for him, and plenty did.

As usual, the fight with Nigel had been mostly my fault and was sparked by the letter—the one that had arrived that same day from Cambridge.

Arriving home early, I collected the mail from the lobby and paused to chat with my neighbor about the dreary weather and the new parking regulations and the condition of Mr. Hermann across the hall whom I didn't even know, but who was apparently recovering from double bypass surgery. While feigning interest in our conversation, I noticed that a letter had arrived from Ira. More to the point, however, a letter had arrived for Nigel, which was unprecedented.

I continued to make small talk with my neighbor about plumbing problems in the building, but my mind was elsewhere: I was studying the postmark, which was from Cambridge, England.

The British did not, as a rule, use return addresses, which placed quite a burden on a person like myself; I had no way of knowing whom the letter was from. If the letter was *not* from his wife, I would be glad to pass it on to him, unmolested. But what if it was? I needed to know. I had a *right* to know. After all, the man had proposed to me and yet he refused to discuss his marital status. There were laws prohibiting that sort of thing, somewhere, possibly.

I opened the door to the apartment and called Nigel's name. He didn't seem to be there, though his loafers were sitting on the floor and the kitchen smelled like fresh cigarette smoke, which I had come to decide had a slightly less offensive smell than stale cigarette smoke, though the two odors were admittedly related.

I studied the letter again and then concluded that I had little choice: if there was any chance the letter was from his wife, I had a duty to myself to steam it open. That much seemed clear.

I had never steamed open a letter before—I had only read about it in books. I didn't even know whether steaming was actually a physical part of the technique, or whether steaming was just a romantic metaphor from the past for something now far more advanced, like dissolving the envelope glue with a tiny handheld laser. I fantasized about bluffing my way into a radiologist's office, where maybe I could sneak a look with his X-ray equipment while he was busy with another patient.

Old-fashioned steam would simply have to do. I put a kettle on to boil, and while I was waiting, I pulled back the curtain and pressed the envelope to the window. Miraculously, I was able to read the bold print of the letterhead. Regina Lark, The Little Green Cottage. Cambridge. His wife, I presumed, living in a little green cottage!

Then I noticed something else, too. On the other side of the window was Nigel, sitting on the tiny terrace adjacent to the kitchen. The curtains were usually drawn to provide a bit of privacy, and so I had barely registered the fact that the terrace even existed.

The once drab cement area now had dozens of potted ferns hanging from hooks in the ceiling, as well as several bird feeders. Nigel didn't notice me right away; he seemed to be hunched over in the corner, studying something. I dragged open the creaky sliding door and stepped out into his makeshift bird sanctuary.

"Nigel?" I inquired gently. I felt like I had just caught him in the act of something illicit, though he didn't seem particularly startled by my own, unexpected, presence.

"Shhh . . ." he said, motioning for me to come toward him. He pointed to the ground, where a haphazard nest had been hastily assembled from a variety of items pulled from a trash bin, including shredded newspaper and Q-tips and paper towels. Inside lay four tiny eggs.

I didn't care about the nest. I was more interested in the letter, which I handed to him. He glanced at it and said thanks and nonchalantly stuffed it in the breast pocket of his shirt. Then he pulled me toward him and brushed the hair from my face and kissed me. He eased me back against the sliding glass door and pressed his body hard against mine.

I was troubled by the letter, as well as wary of having a sexual encounter on the balcony facing onto Connecticut Avenue. I could see a group of school-aged children leaving the zoo, holding balloons, staring up at us and giggling. More important though, I was distracted by another thought: I had left the kettle on the stove.

"Do you want a cup of tea?" I managed to mumble in between kisses.

"Sure," he said, sweetly nonplussed by the abrupt change in plans. We went back in the kitchen and I made him a cup of tea with the boiling water, which he mistook for a nice gesture until I hit critical mass. I felt I was having some sort of apocalyptic meltdown: I threatened to leave him unless there were immediate and meaningful disclosures regarding his marital status. I told him I couldn't take his mysterious ways anymore.

Was I missing something? I asked, in perhaps the wrong tone of voice. Was he having some sort of breakdown? Suffering some form of post traumatic stress disorder? And if so, what was the trauma? Precisely how much time each day did he spend sitting on the balcony, facing onto Connecticut Avenue, pretending he was back in the goddamned rain forest or whatever it was he was doing out there?

The louder I spoke, the louder Bob began to shriek "hullo, hullo." Eeyore padded into the room and began to hiss at the birdcage and

I momentarily turned my wrath on the cat. Nigel put an arm over his head in a mock gesture to protect himself from our screaming missives but really he seemed remarkably unperturbed; his other hand held tight to the handle of his mug as he sipped his tea.

I didn't leave it at that. Since I was already hysterical and had no more dignity to lose, I began to taunt him about his refusal to let me read any of the Value Giant play. Although I didn't actually say it, I kind of let it be known that I doubted the existence of any manuscript in progress. He had replied that I never gave him the benefit of the doubt about anything, including his love for me. Which was true.

Our fight did not conclude with passionate makeup sex, but rather with painful silence. Later on that night, when I couldn't lie beside him anymore, I left the bedroom—I left my own bedroom (well, my father's bedroom, technically speaking) while Nigel slept in my bed—and curled into an uncomfortable ball on the sofa. I left for the airport before he woke, feeling tired and anxious and confused.

The Honeymoon. The Derbyshire countryside had been, on the face of things, the romantic ideal. They took long walks together, pausing to pick wildflowers and berries. They read poetry to each other. But though she tried to gloss the memory, those romantic nights were quickly over and seldom consummated, as Edward repeatedly drank himself into a stupor, leaving her wide awake and wondering.

He spent most of the morning asleep, as well, which left her plenty of time to sit on the veranda with paper and pen, trying to explain to her friends why she had chosen to declare herself married to a man who already had a legal wife.

He and Isabel Campbell Frank had separated years earlier, she explained, not untruthfully. Edward claimed

Belle would not grant him a divorce on religious grounds; other versions of the story had it that Edward refused Belle the divorce, hoping he might stand to inherit something, someday. In any event, there were no children, and neither party seemed to have suffered from the split.

She wrote to her friends that Dr. Aveling was "morally as free as if the bond that tied him years ago . . . had never existed," not realizing the irony of her own words. Aveling was, if anything, a bit too morally free. Bourgeois conventionalities didn't stop him, even when it came to things like paying his bills.

Eleanor learned that she had been an unwitting accomplice to the act of stiffing the proprictress of the Nelson Arms Inn, where they had honeymooned. Edward retorted that she had not deserved to be paid. The old cow had always been so terribly rude, he said, waving her greasy spatula about and chiding them for being late for meals.

Eleanor launched a small protest. The woman was a widow, she argued. She was barely eking out a living as it was. This was the sort of person any self-respecting socialist would want to help out.

Edward disagreed. The old woman was capitalism at its worst. She had offered room and board but no real sense of hospitality, thereby reducing their otherwise lovely holiday to a brutal business transaction.

They argued for a while, until the larger issue became lost in a muddle of philosophical debate. Derbyshire was far away by that point, and Eleanor had no money to spare anyway.

A dim bulb went off in my brain as I sat on the airplane, wedged uncomfortably in a middle seat in a middle row between the Colonel on my right, and a man who looked like my pale reclusive dentist in New York on my left. A severely overweight woman with some sort of tiny pet stuffed in a small crate occupied the aisle seat beside the dentist-like man. I had my reading material balanced on my lap—the completely incomprehensible *Deconstruction for Idiots* on one thigh, the new issue of *Glamour* magazine on the other. It was the magazine that set the bulb alight.

DOES YOUR MAN HAVE INTIMACY PROBLEMS? screamed the headline, as though it were speaking directly to me. "Rate your man in the following quiz to see whether he is really an intimaphobe," the subhead suggested.

While there were no questions that addressed my specific concerns: e.g., "Does your man refuse to talk about his marital status?" or "Does your man seem more comfortable in the company of birds than women?" there were still plenty of other questions that were not irrelevant. "Does reply in monosyllables when you ask him personal questions?" for example. Or "Does he seem preoccupied and self-absorbed most of the time?"

Needless to say, I passed the test with flying colors: I was living with an intimaphobe of the highest order.

The stewardess walked by and tapped me on the shoulder to point out that I had failed to buckle my seat belt. I looked up and noticed that the man who looked like my reclusive dentist was reading over my shoulder, seemingly quite engrossed with my answers, and the Colonel was falling asleep.

I strapped myself into the seat and the Colonel began to snore. The animal in the crale began to yap. The dentistlike man pushed a few strands of greasy hair over a budding bald spot and introduced himself as John Updike—no relation to the writer, he apologized—and said that he had once had a wife with an intimacy problem. I smiled politely, but all I really wanted was to be left in silence so I could read the accompanying article about how to get your man to open up. I plugged in the complimentary airline earphones in a subtle attempt at telling John Updike that I was not available for further conversation.

I also had my nearly maxed-out credit card poised, awaiting the outcome of the raging battle between my brain and my heart over the question of whether or not to call Nigel from the GTE airphone and tell him about the quiz.

John Updike did not get the hint. He tried to strike up a number of different conversations, on topics ranging from the nasty traffic conditions he had encountered on his way to the airport to fun things to do in London.

I told him that I hated London, and began to catalogue the reasons why the place had outgrown itself about half a century ago: its quaint narrow streets, originally designed for horse-drawn carriages, were now clogged with off-road vehicles the size of tanks; an impulsive jaunt to Canterbury generally meant sitting on the M-something or other for hours at a time; and when I had lived there as a student, the grocery stores had been so small one could barely push a cart down the aisle without knocking the can off their shelves.

They had Safeway now, he countered. With big parking lots and men who bagged your groceries for you.

Well, there were still other problems, I continued, like everyone was very grouchy, and practically laughed in your face when you spoke with an American accent.

John Updike looked at me, disappointed. He said I was the first person he had ever met in his life who failed to appreciate London, and then he opened his book and began to read.

An hour into the flight all seemed well. Mr. Updike had clearly gotten my rude hint, the Colonel's head bobbed about as he slept, and no one had disturbed me except for the stewardess, who had returned to scold me for not having properly stored my carry-on baggage under the seat. Meanwhile, I had learned a thing or two: never ambush your partner with unexpected questions (like when he is trying to make love to you on the balcony, possibly). Try to bring up important issues when you are engaged in something mutually enjoyable (and physically excruciating, it seemed), e.g., rock-climbing or Rollerblading or white-water rafting. Or take a drive together, the author advised. According to her extensive research, men start talking—they are almost reckless with their words—when they get behind the wheel of a car.

I wanted very much to share these amusing, and possibly useful revelations with Nigel, but was fretful about the emphasis on adventure sports plus I did not want to cave in so easily after our fight. My credit card was still clutched tightly in my hand, bathed in the sweat of indecision.

Two hours into the flight I grew fidgety. I was unable to concentrate on the deconstruction book even in its watered-down form, and the accompanying *Glamour* articles on amusing birth control blunders and new foreplay techniques also proved too intellectually demanding. My brain was failing to absorb; it was mostly leaking thoughts of Nigel.

I finally gave in and decided to call my apartment. I felt the need to apologize to Nigel, even though I was not convinced I had been entirely at fault. Calling, however, would require leaning over John Updike's tray table in order to reach the airphone. I would then have to say excuse me, while taking care not to spill his Diet Pepsi. Once I managed to accomplish all that, I would then have to conduct a very private conversation while John Updike, and possibly the Colonel, depending on the depth of his slumber, listened. It was this last thought that gave me pause.

I spent another full hour hoping that John Updike might decide to get up and stretch or walk to the bathroom to no avail.

At last I drummed up the courage. "Excuse me," I said, reaching for the phone. "I'm uh, I'm uh just trying to get to the phone." He looked up, startled, as the cola went cascading into his lap.

"Oh my God!" I exclaimed. "I'm such a klutz. I'm so sorry!" He was very very wet. His expensive-looking trousers were soaked through. "Can I get you another soda or something?" I offered stupidly.

He didn't reply. He tried to blot up the pool of Pepsi that was still swimming around on the tray table with his tiny cocktail napkin. The Diet Pepsi was now beginning to drip on to the leg of the woman next to him, and she, too, began to fuss with her pathetically unabsorbent napkin.

I didn't see what further use I could be so I reached for the airphone again, which I managed to do somewhat more gracefully this time around.

Still, there were many more obstacles to overcome. I ran the credit card through the slot in every conceivable direction—with magnetic strip up, sideways, and upside down—until John Updike reached over and, again without saying a word, grabbed it from my hand and inserted it in accordance with the little picture that I had failed to notice, the one that accompanied the instructions.

Then punching in the numbers presented a whole new set of problems having to do with international dialing codes, again requiring his silent intervention. After some ten minutes of fumbling, I finally managed to get through to what I assumed was my apartment. A female voice answered and said hello, and then the line went dead.

Stunned, I looked at Mr. Updike, but he was buried in his now soggy book.

Then the faucets in my brain quit leaking and turned on full blast. Had I simply dialed the wrong number? If it was the right number, there were probably many logical explanations, though I couldn't name a single one.

I decided to call again, but I only got the voice mail that time. After some struggle I got the phone to stick back in its receiver, and the stewardess came around with the lunch trays. I had a glass of wine with my free-range curried chicken, which loosened me up and made me feel quite chatty. I started to ask the Colonel about the details of our NUTS meeting, but he had not touched his lunch and looked like he was in a coma. So I turned to John Updike, intending to ask him what shows were worth seeing while in London.

As I began to speak, however, he put his earphones on and gestured to me that he was busily involved in watching the in-flight movie about a boy and a large swimming mammal.

This life was exhausting, this endless thrashing about in search of some awkward human connection, one that was free of wives and wounded egos.

Better to take a vow of silence, fortify oneself with food and books and music. At a cruising altitude of 35,000 feet, I felt I had finally achieved a state of alienation in its purest form to date.

If I could blame my work problems on the Colonel, I thought it not entirely unfair—almost reasonable, really—to blame my academic problems on Ira. He was so uninspiring, prone to drone on and on about stuff like Kantian imperatives. He spoke in a monotone, had no sense of humor, and demonstrated a flagrant disregard for the aesthetics of self-presentation with his wiry nostril hair and eyeglasses that had been broken for at least two years. I considered him a walking advertisement for the personal perils of academia.

I suffered no illusions that Ira liked me either. Although he never said so aloud, I knew he considered me an intellectual lightweight, an advisee who was dragging him down with her failure to produce a groundbreaking thesis that he could take credit for having fostered.

It should go without saying that Lisa had a most enviable advisor—a beautiful young Kenyan woman named Vanessa with beaded hair and a brilliant smile who had written her own dissertation on the Marxist influence on women's independence movements in sub-Saharan Africa. Vanessa had thought Lisa's *X-Files* idea was entirely worthwhile; she did not seem to view her objective in advising as inflicting self-doubt. They even liked each other: they hung out together watching *X-Files* videos and drinking wine; they frequently dined together; and the two of them had become such good friends that Vanessa served as a bridesmaid at Lisa's wedding.

This is all to explain why I did not rush to read Ira's letter, why I let it sit in my bag overnight, festering like the cancerous sore it was. When I finally forced myself to pry open the envelope, after checking into the hotel, I was not so much surprised by his essential message—cease and desist immediately—as much as pissed that he had not had the nerve to pick up the phone and speak his mind.

He had given my papers to his wife to read, he explained in his handwritten note that was scrawled on a small monogrammed card (the sort of card you might select when writing a letter of condolence), and she found the whole thing too treacly. She had also pointed out that I had not posited a thesis, per se. Yes it was true that his wife was not a political theorist, that she was, as it happened, a midwife, but she had a good eye for these things, he continued.

Had I considered any contemporary topics? What about a Marxist analysis of AOL's potential takeover of the media—might this be the sort of "control of the means of production" that Marx was getting at? What about a Marxist analysis of events at Columbine? Or what about attempting a new equation to define surplus labor versus necessary labor in the age of e-commerce? I didn't like the sound of any of these, plus the last one sounded likely to involve math.

I knew intellectually that I should have listened to Ira, but I was in too deep. I needed to finish what I had begun, even if the driving-off-a-cliff metaphor became more resonant with each word I wrote.

Divorce and Remarriage. Eleanor knew that the subject of divorce and remarriage was liable to make Edward explode, yet she couldn't help but bring it up from time to time. They had been living together for three years, and so far as she was aware, he had had no contact with his wife. Why not just end things, she would ask bluntly on those occasions when she could no longer contain the question. Then she'd cringe, fearful of his reaction.

Edward's answer was relatively consistent: divorce was beside the point, he'd say. They were revolutionaries! Their own love was so strong that they didn't need the specious documents of a capitalist society to cement their bond.

Then Edward would either take Eleanor in his arms and profess his unending love and eternal devotion, or he would walk out the door in a rage, shouting words to the effect that an official exchange of vows couldn't possibly make the relationship any more stifling.

Why didn't she just chain him to the door, he'd ask on his way out. And then he'd be gone.

"I am *very* lonely," she wrote to a friend. "I never felt lonelier than I do just now . . ."

Chapter 8

When I was small, maybe four or five years old, my mother suggested we have a picnic in our garden. This was years before my father had become the Karl Marx of retail—he was working as a buyer of ladies' sportswear for the now defunct Woodward & Lothrop—and we lived in a modest split-level house in Rockville.

A picnic! I was thrilled. What child does not love a picnic? What child is not inordinately thrilled by the prospect of schlepping otherwise mundane food outside and then sitting on the ground and eating it while batting away bees and stomping on ants?

My mother was not exactly the picnicking type; she was more inclined to dress me up and take me out to the country club where we could order tuna fish sandwiches held together by ribboned toothpicks that were aesthetically, if not gastronomically, far superior to our own white-bread-and-mayonnaise concoctions.

It had been a beautiful day, and my mother suggested that perhaps Nixon, our parakeet, could use a dose of fresh air, too. I readily agreed, and recall that we went inside and retrieved the cage and then brought it out and set it on the picnic blanket. Nixon chirped.

Then my mother had another idea. Why not see if Nixon wanted to fly? It was at that particular moment in time that I had my first, if not terribly insightful, vision of the tragic end: *If we open the door to the cage, Nixon will fly away, and he will never come back.* I may have only been four or five years old, but I recall lodging a small protest to that effect.

Never mind, my mother had said, and she opened the latch. She had always loved animals, and had been going on lately about how cruel it was to keep a bird in a cage. She loved animals so much, in fact, that my eldest sister regularly accused her of loving her pets more than her children.

Nixon flew to the top of a tree where he sat for a while. He chirped some more before he eventually worked up the courage to leave the airspace of our garden, never to return.

I felt a familiar twinge in the pit of my stomach as the Colonel and I sat on Hampstead Heath eating the tuna fish sandwiches we had bought from the small grocery in town. It was not just the sandwich that sparked the memory, but the sense that I was dining with a member of the human race unaccustomed to sitting on the ground.

We were stretched out in the tall grass on a hill near a pond. Children with dirty overalls were sailing miniature boats while others flew kites.

Our meeting with the NUTS woman was scheduled at the Marx Memorial Library the next morning, and in the meantime we were discussing catalogue logistics. He began rattling off a stream of manic ideas again: I should order mouse pads, pocket diaries, wristwatches. Had I looked into pillowcases, screen savers, tote bags?

I said I had only ordered T-shirts and reminded him that he had specifically prohibited me from acting without his consent, which was hard to get given that he was never around. Speaking of which, I said a bit irritably, as long as I had his attention, he should be aware of the fact that I was still having trouble with PageMaker . . . some hundreds of text blocks and multilayered rectangles had now disappeared into cyberspace and was there any way we might be able to outsource the catalogue? I also mentioned in as subtle a way as possible that a paycheck would not be unwelcome.

The Colonel nodded and answered my questions in reverse order. Yes, of course, he was glad I had reminded him. The NUTS people would be giving him an installment of the grant money tomorrow—that was part of the point of the meeting, he explained—and he would pay me as soon as he had deposited the check. And no, outsourcing was not an option. The project was too important to be entrusted to foreign hands, he said.

I watched him chew his sandwich. I had devoured mine already and was still hungry. First he ripped the crusts from the bread, then he then tore what remained of the sandwich into tiny pieces, dropping healthy clumps of tuna onto the tinfoil. Occasionally he would place a small, select piece of food in his mouth. Had he been family, I would have volunteered to eat his discards.

The Colonel swallowed and then asked me to remind him to stop at John Lewis on Oxford Street later in the day. He needed to replace the dress shoes he had picked up there last year. I considered asking him whether he could afford to purchase shoes before the NUTS check was deposited, but decided not to be too cheeky.

As he pulled a monogrammed flask from his breast pocket and took a sip, I tried to calculate how much alcohol he had consumed since we left Washington—there had been at least three gin martinis on the flight before he had fallen asleep, and that was only what I had actually seen him order.

"Ah, isn't this sun just heavenly?" he asked.

I agreed that the sun was heavenly and said that I hoped it would do something to dry out the mud that was caked on my shoes. (I realized I had forgotten to tell John Updike that mud was among the things I disliked about London.) I looked at the

Colonel to see if he was equally muddy, but as always he looked meticulously tidy.

Meticulous, even in the mud. We had checked in at the hotel before our Heath excursion, and while I had deliberately dressed down, changing into blue jeans, the Colonel had dressed *up*. He had put on a suit, swapped his bow tie for one that appeared to be sporting tiny crowns, grabbed a slim umbrella, and donned a bowler hat. It looked like I was picnicking with a bespectacled Prince Charles.

He crossed one creaseless trouser leg over the other and spoke in what sounded to me like a subtle attempt at a British accent. "I hear it may rain later in the day," he said, which made me think not so much about the weather, but about Nigel.

I nodded my head and we sat in silence for a moment.

"Do we have a specific agenda for our meeting tomorrow?" I asked, mostly to make conversation. As I was speaking, I felt something on my leg. I was about to swat at my knee, thinking there was a bee on it, when I looked down and saw, more alarmingly, that it was the Colonel's hand.

"No, there's no specific agenda. Just a get-together, a chance to actually meet in person, in this impersonal cyber age," he said, causing me to wonder what he could possibly know about the cyber age given that he didn't even know where the ON switch was on the computer.

"Not to mention the handing over of a very large check," he added, grinning. He began to trace circles on my knee with his finger as I stiffened. An amorous advance had never really occurred to me. Sure, there had been that conversation about a martini, but I had thought his suggestion was mostly meant to throw me off guard. Now I didn't know what to think or how to respond. Not only did his light touch tickle, but it was causing me to think tangled thoughts.

I asked myself a hypothetical question: if push came to shove and there was no Nigel in my life, could I fathom a relationship

with the Colonel? Would it help to picture him not as my enig-
matic boss, but rather as his namesake—Marlon Brando, playing
the role of Colonel Kurtz in *Apocalypse Now*? I pictured him
large and sweaty and delirious with power, ensconced in a
thatched hut, surrounded by skulls. It was all too confusing to
contemplate.

"Did I tell you about Eddie Jr.?" I blurted out of the blue, just
for the sake of having something to say.

"Who?"

"Well, it's pretty weird. There's this guy I found on the Internet
when I was over at the Library of Congress—he calls himself Eddie Jr.—and he suggests that he knows something secretive about
Eleanor."

"Which Eleanor? The Arthurdale Eleanor?"

"No, no. The Marx Eleanor . . . You know, the one I'm writing
my dissertation on."

"Right, of course. So?"

"Well, Lisa says that this Eddie Jr. guy claims to be the great-
grandson of Eleanor."

The Colonel said he didn't understand why that was weird and
asked me to elaborate. I told him that Eleanor had never had any
children so far as I knew, and then relayed all that Lisa had said
about Eddie Jr. being a netmyth, consciously avoiding the part
about the blow job for fear of sounding provocative given that his
hand was now on my inner thigh. I figured when it moved one
inch higher I would definitely need to act.

"That's absolutely fabulous," he said.

"What is?"

"This Eddie Jr. story. This could be our big breakthrough." He
pinched something between his fingers and then flicked it. I
looked at him, confused.

"An ant," he said. "There was an ant crawling up your leg."

"Oh. Thanks," I said, my face burning. "I don't follow your
drift about the Eddie Jr. thing. The guy sounds like a crank to me."

"It doesn't matter," he said, crossing his arms. "Eddie Jr., whomever he is, could put the institute on the map. Imagine the press we could get. Some descendant—some illegitimate descendant perhaps—of Karl Marx shows up in Washington. The press will go nuts! As soon as we get back to Washington, I want you to track down this Eddie person. Now that you bought a modem thing for the computer you can find him, right? And then find us some media contacts. Like at *People* magazine. And try some of those TV magazine type programs. You know, maybe *60 Minutes,* even."

"But we have no reason to believe Eddie Jr. is in Washington. He could be anywhere in the entire world," I protested, staring at his hand as it rested on his chest. I had never really noticed his hand before, which was long and thin and elegant, like a pianist's. Nor had I noticed quite how large he was. Larger than life, really, I mused, thinking about his immoderate résumé of past exploits.

"Spare no expense," he said. "Find your Eddie Jr. friend, wherever he is."

"As long as we're here, let's go take a look at Highgate Cemetery before it gets too late," I suggested.

"What's at Highgate Cemetery?"

I explained it was where the Marx family was buried.

The Colonel rose and brushed the crumbs off his suit and said that was an excellent idea. "Do they have souvenirs, do you suppose?"

I said that actually I supposed not, and we trekked silently through the Heath, eventually joining up with a small group of Japanese tourists who had also come to ogle at the tomb of the bearded one.

Eight hours. Together they moved crowds, like modernday rock stars. Eleanor was able to translate her father's scientific views of socialism into something tangible for the people. Marx had been misunderstood, she insisted: he never advocated taking anything *away* from the working man! He wasn't after their winter coats or their firstborn sons! He was talking only about reclaiming for the workers what was rightfully theirs: the means of production. And at the very least—in the meantime, anyway—they needed to make the working day tolerable by launching a campaign for an eight-hour day.

And Edward, with his voice like a euphonium, would get the crowds on their feet, roaring with assent. Together they penned several essays, including "The Factory Hell" and "The Woman Question."

Although they worked together seamlessly, even appearing together onstage in the plays that Edward wrote, other sorts of cracks continued to appear.

If the tap in my brain had been running on the plane, then by the middle of the night I was in a state of full-scale psychic flood alert. I felt like my eight-year-old niece after a sleep-over party: shattered. Physically and emotionally drained from both lack of sleep and overstimulation.

My entire body ached for sleep, to no avail. I couldn't so much as relax despite the fact that I had dropped $12.95 at the airport on a book about combating jet lag and had followed all of the advice. I had taken care to avoid caffeine, and I had eaten plenty of crunchy green things without even asking why. I also wore the prescribed eyeshades, alternating them with the dark glasses, which were apparently designed to play some sort of cosmic trick on my circadian clock. But all of this merely worked as an amulet to ward off sleep.

So I lay in bed, my heart racing, thinking about the Colonel. I had to confess to having experienced a certain tingling sensation that was not altogether unpleasant as his hand had moved along my leg.

I kept thinking about the fact that the Colonel was alone, across the hall, wondering what might happen should I pay him a visit, but this thought was so emotionally complex that I wished I were Catholic so I could go to confession and purge myself of such notions. I began to dredge my brain for other things to think about and met with instant success: images of umbrellas and refrigerator magnets began to haunt me, as did visions of missing text blocks. Then I thought about Nigel, quickly moving on to thinking about wives who looked like supermodels and had important jobs and could conceivably be lying in my bed. I so thoroughly alarmed myself that I had no choice but to pick up the phone.

This time it took only four attempts to figure out how to use my international calling card. Nigel answered on the first ring.

"Nigel?"

"Darling!" he said, sounding unexpectedly pleased to hear from me. "Where are you? I was really freaking out. I woke up this morning and I couldn't find you."

"Did I wake you?"

"No, darling . . . "It's only ten o'clock" I'm just lying here watching the Weather Channel. They say it might rain tomorrow. . . . But I was mostly worried about you." Again I found myself drowning in his sensuous voice and was instantly reminded of the pathos of this relationship.

"I'm so sorry about last night," he continued. "I really do hate to fight with you. I thought you'd left me again. Well not again, but . . . please come back. We can talk. I promise."

It was staggering, really. That was all that I needed to hear. He was like a good fix. I felt I could get on with my life again. At least until the next misunderstanding.

"Oh, let's just forget about it," I said casually, as if we *could* forget about it, as if we had fought about something trivial, like what to eat for dinner. "What's new?" I asked awkwardly.

"Well, let's see. . . . It's been an excellent day, really. I got a lot of work done on the play, and I've been offered the job in Miami. Where are you, anyway?"

"In London, You've been offered the job in Miami?"

"In *London,*" he mimicked with surprise.

"Yeah, sorry. I never got a chance to tell you. It's for work . . . just for another day. I'll be back late tomorrow. No big deal. So, *Miami,* huh?"

"Yeah. And you know, I really think we shouldn't let geography get in the way. I mean, I'd like for you to come. But if you don't want to, we can sort this out, somehow. Actually, I was over at your mum and dad's this afternoon. They agreed that the job in Miami isn't the end of the world. And they thought you should go, too. Your father said you had nothing holding you back. And they were incredibly helpful with the play. You are so lucky to have such wonderful parents . . . your dad took me over to Value Giant. He got me some golf balls."

"But you don't play golf," I said. Besides, *What was he doing shopping with my father when he should have been busy worrying about me* "I can't believe my parents really said that I had nothing holding me back," I whined.

"The golf balls were on special. Sixty balls for only $17.95. Can you believe it?"

"Is that a good deal?"

"I don't really know. Honestly, I don't know a golf ball from a cauliflower, but your dad gave them to me as a gift. He said he'd take me over to his club and teach me to play sometime."

The idea of Nigel hanging out with my parents, never mind wearing a polo shirt and swinging a golf club, made me wary all over again. What could possibly be motivating this man? Did Nigel want something from my father? Was this about his money? Or citizenship, perhaps? Did he want to marry me for my American passport? On the other hand, there was always the smallish possibility that he loved me and was simply trying to establish a relationship with his future father-in-law.

He was so charming and chatty on the phone. Yet at home he never seemed to have anything to say. But maybe he did. Maybe I was just too demanding, asking for a round-the-clock summation of his every thought.

All of which contributed to the return of paranoia. There might be some conspiracy afoot, one designed by my father to get me to stop asking for tuition money, perhaps. The fix was suddenly bad. Some weird foreign stuff or something.

"Nigel . . ." I hesitated, wondering whether I would be tedious enough to ask him another wife-related question.

"Do you miss me?" he interrupted.

"Of course I miss you. But that's not the point—"

"Do you love me?"

"Yes. I love you *and* I miss you. But we still have some problems to sort out, as far as I'm concerned."

"Shall we marry, then?" he asked sweetly. "We can just do it when you get back. We don't need to plan a big event or anything. I'm lonely here without you."

"Nigel, really, I think we have a number of issues to clear up first."

"Like what?" he asked in earnest.

"Wait, there's someone at the door." I quickly donned the terry-cloth robe that was hanging in the bathroom and opened the door. There was no one there, but an envelope was lying on the floor, addressed to the Colonel.

"Sorry," I said, returning to the phone. I began again with renewed energy: "Before we can get married, I need to know about your wife. This is absolutely idiotic. I'm starting to feel as stupid as Eleanor Marx—"

"Oh please," he interrupted. "Not that again."

"I mean, she was so smart. Much more talented than I am,

certainly. She acted, translated, wrote, spoke publicly. She was an avid reader, a do-gooder. And yet her love life was so obviously doomed. The guy was married!" I was thinking out loud mostly, reflecting on my own question about smart women and bad men.

"Look, Ella, you're looking for problems. You want to make our relationship into some fucking tragic self-fulfilling prophecy. But we're not Romeo and Juliet, you know. We're not even Eleanor and what's-his-name. We're just two people who are trying to establish a future together. Granted, there are a few practical problems, but this isn't Shakespeare. This is about whether or not I should take a job at Parrot Jungle!"

This was sadly true. Then again, there were obvious extenuating factors, genuine problems interfering with the prospect of a happy marriage. But perhaps I should have had a more open mind. Surely there must be some call for political theorists in Miami: they have a university. It was right near Parrot Jungle, as I vaguely recalled. Besides, what was wrong with lying on the beach for a few years? I could get a bikini wax (though I would probably be best off avoiding the bikini itself) and work on a tan.

"I called you from the airphone today," I said in an overly accusatory voice, "and I could swear a woman answered the phone."

"You must have dialed the wrong number. . . . Hey, they're calling for rain in London, too. . . . You should see the storm front moving across the Atlantic . . . most of Europe will be hit, actually. You'd better be careful."

"The rain is not the point, Nigel. The point is that I doubt I dialed the wrong number."

"No, Ella. The point is that you seem to doubt everything. Why not try and believe for once? What would be the harm in seeing the glass half full, just for fun, for a change of pace, even? I mean you have no faith . . ."

I put a hand over the receiver so he wouldn't hear me crying.

"Ella, listen to me. My first marriage was a failure, and it's too painful for me to hash it out right now. Can't you just let it go for now? Everything is under control."

The disclosure was oddly touching. It seemed a reasonable enough suggestion that I let it go. I thought I could let it go. But apparently I could not.

"What do you mean, under control?" I asked sarcastically. "Will I be under control someday, too, do you think?"

"Look, Ella," he interrupted gruffly. "You're being very neurotic. Maybe you'd better find someone with no past whatsoever. Someone like God might suit you."

"Nigel, I've just remembered something!" I tried, recalling the *Glamour* quiz. "We should go for a drive when I get back. Let's go off to the country . . ." I was beginning to brighten but he had already hung up. He hung up *my* phone in *my* apartment in *my* ear. (Well, technically, of course, it was my father's phone.) The line went dead before I could finish. And he had called me neurotic, to boot.

I sat on the bed and cried for a while and then I walked across the hall and knocked on the Colonel's door.

I handed him the envelope and he invited me in without asking any questions, or impolitely noting the time, which was nearly three-thirty A.M.

The Swimming Pond. Eleanor took a deep breath and threw herself into the icy swimming pond. Her plan, insomuch as she had one, was to either find some sense of clarity, or to freeze and sink. She didn't really care which way things went, as long as the frigid waters would stop her mind from churning.

She had come to the Heath alone, wandering through the same paths she used to trek with her father and her sisters. She sat on a bench on Parliament Hill for a while, and watched a group of schoolchildren fly kites.

She was ready, at last, to change things. George Bernard Shaw had just told her of the latest rumor: Edward had been seen around town on more than one occasion with a young blond actress. She had pretended not to care at the time—she'd heard such things before, of course—but it tore her up inside.

The chief question was whether to leave Edward, or to simply kill herself and end the misery for all concerned. In the meantime, she had ceased to eat again.

When she arrived back at the flat in the early evening, she was shivering. Her lips were blue and her hair was straggly, and Edward grew so alarmed that he whisked her into bed and insisted on fetching the doctor.

Eleanor protested that she had never felt better.

You need to leave here, Edward, she announced almost joyfully. I can see things so very clearly now. I had an epiphany while I was swimming, she said, launching into an irrelevant anecdote about a picnic and a goose and a passage from Shakespeare, furthering Edward's belief that she was, indeed, breaking down.

Edward told her she was mad, that she should sleep. That he would send the maid, Gertrude, to fetch the doctor.

I'm not at all mad. In fact I've never felt more sane. You must go, Edward. You deserve better than me. I'll give you the money to live. I'll borrow more from Engels. I'd do anything to end this. I simply can't go on like this.

She had meant to sound more rational. She had planned to have the conversation over dinner, to make her points slowly and deliberately.

It was a good offer, she thought. Surely it was what Edward must want, and she fully expected him to stick his hat on his head and walk out the door.

Come to New York with me, he said instead, and pulled her close.

New York?

I've been invited by the Socialist Labor Party of North America, he said. They want me to speak. They'll pay for my passage, and for food and lodging. We'll have to pay your way, but we can manage.

I don't know, Edward, she said skeptically. I need to know things will change. I can't live like this anymore. I think that if we were only married, legally married, maybe we could have a child. I think my body simply won't conceive out of wedlock.

You're awfully religious for a communist, Edward laughed, taking her in his arms. You're so damn ethical. You *must* come to New York. I can't do it without you, you know that.

He had a valid point, she thought.

I crossed my arms tight against my chest to prevent the hotel-issue bathrobe from flapping open as I perched awkwardly on the edge of the queen-size bed.

"Would you like a drink?" asked the Colonel, rummaging through the minibar. He had positioned himself on the opposite side of the room but was still within spitting distance of the bed; our supposedly deluxe hotel suites were each barely larger than a Buick. I noted with envy as I watched him squat ineloquently that his movements were not restricted by his nightcloths; he was clad in pinstriped pajamas that were nearly as formal as his daytime attire and exposed nothing unseemly even as he bent forward and stuck his head inside the small refrigerator. After some clanking of bottles he finally produced a miniature whiskey.

"No, I'm fine, really," I said, sniffling. "I shouldn't have come over. I honestly don't know what possessed me."

"Not at all," he said, in a tone so stiff it betrayed his words. "Is there something you would like to talk about? Some matter that needs discussing?"

"Definitely not," I answered. "It's too stupid and my personal life is a mess and don't get me started. Are there any pretzels in there?"

The Colonel looked around for a minute and tossed me a tiny packet of honey-roasted almonds instead.

"What about you?" I asked boldly, contemplating the package of nuts. I didn't like almonds, but the honey-roasted part sounded tasty. I could lick the seasoning off, I figured.

"What do you mean, what about me?" he asked, leaning against the credenza.

"Well, I don't know much about you. I know what I've read, but there's got to be more to you. I mean, on the one hand you're this tragic Pnin-like man, on the other hand you're like a comic book character, or a stick figure."

"A stick figure? I'd rather like to be a stick figure," he quipped, putting his hands on his belly to emphasize that he was, of course, the very antithesis of a stick figure. "What kind of stick figure did you have in mind?"

"You know, like a kid draws," I said, not sure where I was trying to go with this idea. "Stick figures are kind of one-dimensional. And what I'm trying to say is that I know you're not. Not one-dimensional. That's why I'm asking," I said, well aware I was babbling. I shoved half the packet of almonds in my mouth to shut myself up.

"Who's Pnin? Does he have something to do with Arthurdale?"

"No." I laughed. "He's a Nabokov character. Funny but sad."

"Yes, well, I suppose that's what my wife would say about me, too."

"You have a wife?" I practically shouted as a nut slipped down my throat.

"Yes, well, we've been separated for years. Ten years, to be precise. She keeps threatening to file for divorce. Until then, though, I still have a family membership at the health club. That's why I was able to give you the card. Are you all right?"

I wasn't, really. The nut was lodged in my throat, and I ran to the minibar to find something to help wash it down. The Colonel gave me a hard pat on the back, which seemed only to secure the nut in place.

"What happened?" I asked through my gasps. "With your wife, I mean."

"Oh, it was pretty straightforward. She said she had had enough of me. She said I drank too much. She said I needed help, etcetera, etcetera. It was when we were living in Nepal. When I was with the World Bank. She ran off with Ted. He's a yak farmer."

"A *yak farmer*? For real?" I asked, sipping a sickly-sweet Ribena from a small box.

"Yes, and what a lucky yak farmer Ted turned out to be. Esther set him up in his own business when they returned. They live in Vermont, where he imports yak products—you know, cheese and milk and herbal sorts of things made from its hoofs and ears—and he sells them to health-food stores. He does quite well apparently."

As he spoke he began to raid the minibar again, cursing what was left of the selection. There were five tiny, empty whiskey bottles lined up on top of the television, and I could sort of see Esther's point.

"I need to lie down," he announced suddenly, and he more or less hurled himself at the mattress, landing next to where I was sitting.

"Can I tell you something personal?" he asked, as if he had not done so already.

"Sure," I said nervously.

"I think I've made a really huge mistake," he said, propping himself up on an elbow. "There's this one decorator in particular, you know, the plump blonde debutante one, the one who wears all those cute little tennis outfits . . ."

I nodded though I wasn't sure she had ever come down to the subterranean portion of the mansion.

"Well, she's talked me into going sleek, ultramodern. I have no idea how that could have happened. I'm a French Provincial kind of guy, at heart."

"What have you done so far? Have you actually ordered anything?"

"I'm afraid so," he said, his words beginning to slur. "Sofas and lamps and coffee tables and lord knows what else. I can't really remember. . . . She seemed so convincing at the time."

"When was this? When did you actually agree to work with her?"

"Just before we left," he said.

"It might not be too late to cancel," I ignorantly assured him. "Though she wouldn't be in the office this late. Why don't you call her in the morning?" I said, glancing at my watch. "In fact I really should be going myself."

"Wait!" he demanded. "Have I told you what a really great comfort you are, Ella? You seem to know how to solve every problem. You're so smart and so very *sensible*." As he said this he reached for my hand and squeezed it. "And you're very lovely, too."

At the time that seemed, like one of the nicest things anyone had ever said to me. Not to mention this was arguably the most intimate conversation I had had with a man since Raj had read me the bio of his bride-to-be. I lay down on the bed, close to him. Eventually we both fell asleep, his hand still clasping mine.

I woke at dawn, terrified by the possible implications of having just slept with my boss, and tiptoed back to my room.

Later that morning—so much later, it seemed, that I was already in need of a nap—I found the Colonel leaning against a street sign outside the Marx Memorial Library at our previously appointed meeting time. He was huddled behind a newspaper, waiting for the building to open.

I approached and stood beside him hesitantly. I wasn't sure what to say. I felt awkward and embarrassed and unsettled by my confusing feelings for him. We had slept together, holding hands. It wasn't much but it was certainly something beyond the scope of ordinary employee/boss relations.

"Arsenal lost," he said.

"How interesting," I replied without enthusiasm. I vaguely recalled from my London School of Economics days that he was talking about British football.

That was it for the conversation. I sat and watched the cars creep by; it was the tail end of rush hour—assuming the traffic ever did thin in Central London. I wished that we could talk about what had happened between us, or perhaps about what had not happened. A small part of me wanted to try the experiment again, just to see what might develop.

He folded his newspaper and tucked it under his arm. "How was your morning? Productive?"

We had to shout to be heard above the drone of traffic. Clerken-well Green—the scene of many a labor rally—had not been left exactly untouched by the march of history. A mere hundred years ago, Eleanor had walked this same ground. I tried to picture her standing at an open window of the library, which was then a socialist meeting hall, waving to admirers below. Maybe she had broken into song, like Madonna playing Eva Perón, while the crowds fell to their knees in frenzied adoration. Or maybe not.

Now the most striking thing going on below, apart from the appalling traffic, was a noisy construction project to renovate the town house to the right of the library. An excellent earring shop had opened a few years earlier in the building to the library's left, and I had wasted a fair amount of money there as a student.

"It was productive," I replied, grateful to have settled on a nice, mundane subject. "I worked a bit on my dissertation, though I'm still just taking notes mostly. My advisor suggested that I deconstruct the material, and I don't even really know what that means, and in any event, I'm struggling. I mean, I haven't actually figured out my actual thesis."

"I thought deconstruction was dead. I had a deconstructionist designer once. That's what her card said anyway. She thought I should just sort of blend all the styles together. She urged me to do a Greek fresco on the living room wall and get rid of the kitchen table and instead put down giant pillows so we could eat on the floor . . . I think it was supposed to be Ethiopian style. I almost listened to her, too. But thank god now I realize I'm a French Provincial kind of guy . . ."

"What's with this library?" I asked, glancing at my watch. "It should have opened half an hour ago. And where are these NUTS people anyway?"

Was it too much of a generalization to say that Marxists were never particularly good at precision timing, I wondered, reflecting on many a graduate school seminar that seemed to start basically whenever people managed to ingest enough coffee to show up.

"Relax. We're in no rush," he said, reaching, I feared, for my hand.

"Actually, I am in a rush," I said suddenly, completely freaked out by this hand-holding business, this dancing around our nonexistent relationship. "I have to go." The Colonel looked at me, surprised. "I forgot, I have something to do before our flight. I'll meet you at the airport."

"But you can't go," he said reasonably. "We have our meeting now. That's the whole reason we came here . . . to meet with the NUTS people . . . they sent me a fax last night to confirm . . . you need to see about the souvenirs . . ."

I heard his voice grow distant as I fled. In my rush to get away from him I crashed head-on into a stunning Slavic woman in a trench coat. I apologized and helped her pick up her papers. I then forgot to look in the proper direction and was nearly struck by a taxi as I stepped into the oncoming traffic.

"You could put our project in jeopardy, Ms. Kennedy," he yelled.

"I understand that. And I'm really really sorry," I shouted back. But I couldn't tell if he heard me what with the honking of horns and the general chaos I had just caused.

"I'm sort of possibly engaged, you see," I yelled, certain now that my words were lost in the sea of traffic. "And it's all very confusing."

Chapter 9

It might be most telling to describe what I did not do with my one free afternoon in London: I did not, for example, go wandering through Eleanor's old neighborhood to soak up local flavor or learn more about her. I did not go to the British Museum to wonder about which space in the reading room Eleanor had once occupied. And I did not visit the National Portrait Gallery, or attend a West End show, or, more remarkably, go anywhere near Harrods.

I bought a round-trip train ticket to Cambridge instead, in search of Nigel's wife.

I didn't have much to go on in my role as sleuth. My only clue was from the letter Nigel had received before I left, from a Regina Lark, The Little Green Cottage, Cambridge.

I wandered down the High Street in Cambridge, irritably. What kind of an address was "The Little Green Cottage?" Could it be located on an A-to-Zed map? And what kind of name was Regina, anyway? I couldn't help but observe that Regina rhymed with vagina. And thinking of Nigel having a wife with a reproductive system made me so anxious and jealous that I wanted to just go home and lock myself in a closet until such inappropriate thoughts ceased to flow through my brain.

Maybe this wasn't such a good idea, afer all. I mean, what would I say to the woman if and when I found the Little Green Cottage? Perhaps, instead, I should just wander down the High Street, which looked suspiciously like every other High Street in this United Kingdom, with its quaint cobbled roads and a preponderance of pretentious cafés. I could buy overpriced items from the Body Shop, the Disney Shop, the Gap, and that omnipresent shop filled with hundreds of oddly shaped wax candles that seemed destined to slam its doors shut and go out of business at any minute. Then I would go back to London on the train laden with shopping bags like a good tourist. As opposed to a scheming, paranoid one.

And yet I just wanted to see her. A mere glimpse of her would give me some sort of insight, I thought. I could sum her up, categorize her disparagingly, and move on. And since I was feeling so very masochistic, why not give in to my intense urge for a cigarette, which I wanted very badly, even though I had quit five years earlier with no small degree of difficulty. I bought Nigel's brand, ducked into Ye Olde Café, and decided to sit in a chair and jointly smoke and caffeinate myself to death until some better option decided to present itself.

I was on the verge of fulfilling my death wish when I noticed the bank of tourist brochures at the café entrance. Which is when I went over and picked up the one on the Little Green Cottage, which advertised itself as an antiques shop, Regina Lark, proprietess. Which is when I began to cough profusely, stubbing out my cigarette, which did not really help.

At last I caught my breath, took another sip of coffee, and stumbled out the door, apologizing to no one in particular.

Once I stepped out into the street I realized that I had to use the bathroom. That my need, after four cups of coffee, was urgent, bordering on emergency. But I soldiered on in search of the Little

Green Cottage, which sounded like the sort of place in which one might expect to find not one Regina Lark, but rather a Mr. McGregor and a Benjamin Bunny.

I asked several people for directions to the Little Green Cottage, pulling out my little green brochure hoping to demonstrate that the place really did exist, but to no avail. So I wandered on in search of a bathroom, half figuring that I would bump into the Little Green Cottage if it was meant to be. *Inshalah,* as they say when you board an airplane in an Islamic country: this aircraft will have a safe journey, if, and only if, God wills it, and with absolutely no bearing on the pilot's ability to fly.

And moments later, I bumped into a McDonald's on an otherwise staid corner in downtown Cambridge. God was on my side this once. I found a rest room, and as I emerged, I noticed the Little Green Cottage directly across the street.

I paused and took a deep breath before opening the door to what was, in fact, a cute little green brick cottage, with green and yellow awnings. The shop looked a little too cute, like the Hollywood set for a Jane Austen novel.

There was nothing to it. I was just another tourist, out to exercise the flailing dollar. I needn't identify myself, which would be preposterous anyway.

Chimes on the door prevented me from making an inconspicuous entrance. The woman at the counter put down her newspaper, took off her reading glasses and greeted me.

She was quite attractive, if a tad frightening in that well-dressed, more English-than-thou sort of way.

"Ella?" she asked. "How very remarkable. The resemblance . . ."

I felt faint.

"Nigel told me just this morning that you were in London, but he never mentioned you were coming to Cambridge. . . . Dear, it's so lovely to meet you at last," she said rising from her chair. She kissed me once on each cheek, the smell of her flowery perfume serving as an astringent to keep me from passing out.

She was everything I had feared, except about thirty years older. I couldn't think of anything to say, so I just stood there feeling as frumpy as I no doubt looked, and suddenly acutely aware that I stank of cigarette smoke.

"Nigel has told me so much about you," she said excitedly.

"He has? How did you know it was me?"

"Um, I suppose he must have sent a photo, of course," she said nervously. "And Nigel has told me all about your work and your dissertation. I think that's so interesting. You know a friend of mine is writing a biography of Shelley, and he knows quite a lot about Eleanor Marx. I ought to introduce you."

"That would be nice," I said, hearing my words from a distance. I was lost in shock, several mental miles away. "What a lovely shop you have," I added, trying to ground the conversation in something present and concrete.

"Let's go out for a walk," she said, grabbing her coat. "Better yet, do you have time for lunch?"

I nodded dumbly.

"Gretta," she yelled to someone who was in the back room. "I need you to tend to the shop for an hour. I'm going to lunch with my future daughter-in-law."

His mother, I said to myself with a sigh of disappointed relief. Regina Vagina was merely his mother!

Over a plate of greasy fried things at a dark pub called the Woolly Sheep Inn, I tried to absorb the fact that Nigel had a mother. A mother who owned an antiques shop. A mother with whom he communicated.

In fact, it seemed, Nigel was a most dutiful son, who corresponded with his mother on a regular basis. She was proud of Nigel, and carried a fading graduation picture of him around in her wallet. She also had a picture of Bob the small green parrot, to whom she had become quite attached, apparently, while Nigel had been in New Guinea.

Nigel had spared her few details of our relationship. She knew that he had moved into my apartment. She knew about his marriage proposal and was aware of my slowness in responding: "-That's all right, dear, take your time. It's the most important decision of your life." She knew about my family, and said she would like to visit a Value Giant when she came in for the wedding. Or possibly for the premiere of the play, she added, depending on which came first.

"But what about his wife?" I asked hesitantly after we had covered most of the other ground. She seemed open enough: I figured I would try to milk her for all the information I could.

Regina looked at me worriedly.

"Lily?"

"*Lily?*" I replied, perhaps with too much bitterness, given that I had never met the woman. "He still wears a wedding ring, you know."

"Oh good Lord," she said, burying her face in her hands. "I would have thought that meeting you would have pulled him out of denial. I mean . . . I had thought it was such a good sign. . . . He hasn't really been the same since it happened."

"Since *what* happened?" I nearly shouted.

"Really, dear. I think this is something the two of you need to discuss. You can't possibly dream of marrying the man when he won't even talk about Lily. . . ."

"Yes, well, that's sort of my point. . . ."

. "I'll talk to him, dear. I'll urge him to open up. I mean, he's clearly moved on, but it won't do him any good to continue to suppress the whole thing."

"I really don't get it. It's all such a big secret, like he murdered her or something," I blurted out in my usual socially inept fashion.

"My goodness, dear," she said, visibly distressed. "Do you

have reason to believe such a thing? I mean he was quite angry, he had every reason to be, of course, but I only talked to her last week. Funny the coincidence."

"What coincidence? Do you mean our names?"

"Your names? Oh, yes . . . no . . . what?"

"Lots of L's," I offered, reading something into nothing, as usual.

"No, I mean that you both live in Washington."

"So Lily is alive and she lives in Washington," I announced, like Sherlock Holmes accumulating scraps of evidence. "Can you tell me anything about the dalmatian?"

"Who, Spotty?" she said, surprised.

"Yeah, probably. Unless there's some other relevant dalmatian in his life."

"Spotty died long ago, bless his heart. He was the sweetest dog. You should have seen him as a puppy. He was this little tiny pup, covered with spots—"

"So Spotty wasn't in New Guinea?" I interrupted.

"Certainly not. Spotty died when Nigel was eleven. Hit by a car. It was quite shocking. We thought about replacing him, but I just couldn't bear to go through that puppy phase again. It was as bad as having babies, I tell you. In some ways worse because, well, they don't wear nappies."

"So Spotty has no bearing on the present," I said, just to clarify things.

"Certainly not."

"All right. Tell me another thing. Did it have anything to do with the rain? I mean, he seems to get really flipped out by any form of precipitation. It's kind of an odd phobia. . . ."

"Well, of course one knows it is bound to rain in a rain forest," she said ominously. "I think it was just a matter of bad timing, you know, when Lily chose to raise the subject . . . she didn't know they were about to have a horrid storm. But yes, dear, you're quite right. This rain thing is a bit problematic. I've urged him to talk to a therapist about it . . . I mean, *it does rain*. Rain is a fact of life.

At least here in England. You must have noticed that, my dear. Does it rain a lot in Washington?"

I thought for a moment and then replied that it rained a reasonable amount in Washington. Sometimes it snowed, too. Then we sat in silence for a while.

"What about Mr. Lark?" I asked innocently, after a while. Maybe I could learn something by coming at this from a different angle.

"His father?" she nearly shrieked.

"Yeah."

"He didn't tell you that either?"

"What should he have told me?"

"Well, his father is doing well, considering." She began to rummage through her pocketbook, and I wondered if she planned to produce another photograph.

"Considering what?" I was by then beginning to feel aggressive. If she wasn't going to fill me in on her son's wife, she could at least discuss her own husband.

"Well, there was a little scandal a couple of years back. You may remember . . ." She produced a tube of brownish lipstick and a small mirror from her bag and began to paint her lips. She then checked to make sure she had no food stuck in her teeth.

I tried to remember. There were so many scandals in England it was hard to keep them separate. "I remember about a zillion royal family scandals," I said, "and there were a few more recent ones about a bishop, and of course there was the quintuplets thing, though I suppose that's not technically a scandal. When I was a student at LSE there was this terrific scandal about some member of Parliament and women's clothing and fruit . . . an orange, or a tangerine or something . . ."

"Yes. That's the one," said Regina Lark, distractedly, pushing her food around with a fork.

"No," I said. "He was the one who . . ." I suddenly realized that she was not kidding. My mind raced back to the grainy black-and-

white photos that had been splashed across the tabloids, images too torrid to contemplate over lunch.

"But . . . But I thought that guy died."

"He almost did. He suffered minor brain damage from oxygen deprivation. But he's all right now. I mean, he'll never be able to work again, but he's at home. He likes to putter around in the garden, which is quite helpful as I'm so busy with the shop."

I was speechless. I knew that each life was full of its little secrets, its skeletons in the closet and all, but this was particularly hard to comprehend.

Regina could tell I was horrified.

"Listen, dear," she said. "All men have their little weakness. It is up to us to forgive them. . . . Look, I need to get back to the shop now."

Regina threw a few bills on the table and I offered feebly to contribute.

She waved off my offer, and I felt vaguely unwell as we parted with a kiss and a hug.

Whatever had happened between Nigel and his wife was unspeakable. Yet suffering brain damage as the result of some bizarre masturbation episode was apparently considered appropriate lunch conversation.

I may have been stupid and blinded by love, but I still had the feeling that this was not a good sign.

Regardless of any personal implications, however, the thought of the Mr. Lark scandal inspired me to find a nice park bench and begin to pull together my notes on Eleanor and Edward's own little transatlantic scandal.

A Not Unlovely Oval Face. So it was that Eleanor found herself leaning on the deck of the *City of Chicago*, clad in a plain blue traveling suit, her tangled mass of hair blowing in the wind.

The week at sea had begun to blur into a series of fiery settings of the sun, the long days punctuated only by the occasional flying porpoise and, on one solemn morning, the burial at sea of a fellow passenger who had died of natural causes.

While many of Eleanor's fellow passengers kept to their rooms, racked with nausea, Eleanor strolled the upper decks, euphoric. She had never been to America before, and Edward had been so kind the past few weeks—and charming, but for the occasions now and then when he would pass out at dinner.

America was in a caustic mood in 1886. This was the year that Albert Parsons along with August Spies and six other labor activists were sentenced to die in the Chicago Anarchist trial—the trial of the century back in the days before every other trial earned that label. They were accused, essentially, of having inspired the throwing of a bomb that killed eight policemen during the Haymarket riot.

The *Chicago Tribune* had a suggestion about what to do with men with ideas like Parsons's: you decorate every lamppost in the city with their carcasses.

It bears mention that to most American eyes, communists and socialists and anarchists and foreigners in general were all part of the same problem. Which didn't make Edward and Eleanor very popular visitors.

As the vast ocean liner pulled into New York Harbor, Eleanor saw a sight so remarkable she tugged on Edward's sleeve. A half-erected Statue of Liberty stood on a small chunk of island. Workmen hung from ropes and scaffolding around it like spiders on a web.

A gift of friendship from France, said Edward. Eleanor slipped her arm through his and leaned her head on his shoulder, skewing her hat.

As they docked, a reporter from the *New Yorker Volkszeitung,* the German-language organ of the Socialist Party, came on board to greet Edward and his wife, and to record his own little piece of history: The man wore a grey travelling costume and a broad, black felt-hat. Hastily observed, he made the impression of a Quaker. Briskly flashed his dark eyes. The young lady, who leaned on his arm, had rich, glossy, black hair, dark-brown eyes and a not unlovely, oval face. Her complexion was heavily browned by the sun during the voyage. The cotton garment which the young lady wore, was gathered together at the waist by a black girdle, above which a kind of blouse with delicate creases fell and from there a steel watch-chain stretched towards the girdle. The intelligent face of the lady was covered by a large, white straw hat with a white bow.

Chapter 10

My anxieties about spending eight hours sitting next to the Colonel pretending to gloss over my erratic behavior and our questionable intimacy had ebbed when I learned he had had his seat reassigned. He was in first class, where those very same airline stewardesses who routinely tormented me about every minor tray table infraction were probably busy refilling his champagne glass and massaging his feet. I presumed he had requested a change in his seat assignment in order to get away from me, and I couldn't really blame him, although I found it incredibly irritating that he had probably succeeded in getting himself bumped up to first class simply by smiling sweetly at the airline clerk. Whenever I tried to smile sweetly at airline clerks I got bumped *down*. If I grinned any wider they would probably stick me in the baggage compartment.

With that thought in mind, I settled uncomfortably into yet another cramped middle seat—the place where the gods of seat assignments seem to have permanently banished me. This time I was in a row of three: On one side of me was a sari-clad woman with a baby in her arms. A young student with an abnormal psychology text sat by the window.

I studied the card stuffed in the seat pocket with instructions for what to do should the plane accidentally fall into the Atlantic. Not fully satisfied that taking off my shoes and sticking my head between my legs would enhance my chances of survival on a plummeting aircraft I decided to think more productive thoughts and went straight to work making notes:

—In Ohio, they encountered their first socialist cowboy, who waxed eloquently about the exploitative practices of ranch owners.

—In Chicago, Aveling commiserated with one of the accused anarchists, Samuel Fielden, a fellow Englishman. Fielden was one of the lucky ones: the day before his scheduled execution the governor of Illinois commuted his sentence to life imprisonment. Another of the group committed suicide, and the rest eventually hanged

—In New York, Eleanor was harassed by a policeman who stopped her on the street, looked her up and down, and quipped what the hell is that? *Edward later said that the man was an idiot. What could he possibly know about British fashion?*

The pilot announced that we were delayed for take off on account of bad weather in Toledo, the logic of which I did not quite grasp. The baby beside me began shrieking directly in my ear, giving me the excuse I needed to slam my notebook shut and reflect on my own lack of fashion sense. I wondered what Eleanor had been wearing. Surely not wrinkled khaki pants, chunky loafers, and a black V-necked sweater: it was pitiful but it was me, almost thirty years old with scraggly hair and no sense of sophistication—this despite my invariably large credit card bills and my weakness for designer labels. I stared at the family sitting across the aisle. Attractive, intellectual-looking man my age reading some thick history of the world type book, a cherubic toddler next to him engrossed in *Go Dog Go,* and a woman nestled against the window seat, reading a literary novel. She wore what could properly be called a grown-up outfit, including a silk scarf tied cleverly around her neck, and she had an expensive-looking haircut. Disturbed by my own irrational feelings of hostility, I cast smug looks of detachment in the direction of the happy-looking family.

I then put on my eyeshades and reflected on how I had no desire to speak to anyone ever again. It was not simply that I was feeling hostile toward all members of the human race—which of course I was after my disturbing meeting with Nigel's mother—but I genuinely wanted to get some sleep after forty-eight hours of mental overload.

So I wondered if I was already dreaming when I heard the Colonel's voice.

"We have a problem," he said simply. "We need to talk."

I glanced up and saw him standing in the aisle. I stared at his multicolored moose tie, slowly working my way to his bloodshot eyes. He looked stricken, his expression was grave.

"What's wrong?" I asked. "Did everything go all right at the library? Did the NUTS people show up? I'm really sorry about running off like that . . . I know it was very immature of me. I'm just a little confused, about last night and all . . . Are those reindeer or moose? Or mooses . . . or *moosi?* What's the plural of . . ." Both the abnormal psychology student and the Indian woman were staring at me, listening intently.

"Listen, it's not about that. It's about the project . . . "

The Indian woman began to scold us for waking her baby.

"But the baby was already awake. It was screaming. Just a minute ago I watched it spit up milk on your shoulder," I said self-righteously, pointing at the spot on her dupatta.

"Babies routinely spit up," she explained, as if talking to a moron. "They spit up even when they are asleep. Do you suppose you might do me the favor of conducting your conversation elsewhere?"

I felt like clobbering her with my dissertation notes, which were sitting on my lap in a heavy three-ring binder, but the Colonel had a more tempered suggestion. "Would you be so kind as to switch seats with Miss Kennedy here for just a moment?" he asked as he stood awkwardly in the aisle. "That way we can speak without disturbing you."

"I'm sorry, sir, but my husband spoke personally with the minister of transportation to ensure that I would have an aisle seat. I will not be moving."

"Just for a moment?" asked the Colonel. "Just so that we can talk? It's an emergency."

The woman was not interested in any emergency. "I will not be moving," she repeated. "It will disturb the baby."

The Colonel gave up and we continued to hold our conversation over the high pitched shrieks of the infant.

"I called Carmen from the airport just to check in," he explained, "and she said that we're being picketed."

"Picketed?"

"Apparently. Yes. You know, people are out there, outside my house, holding banners and shouting things. Nuke the Commies; Save the . . . baby Numbats . . . That sort of thing. Can you imagine?"

"What's a baby Numbat?"

"Excuse me, Henri . . . I think you should come back to your seat. The ice is melting in your martini." A tall, slim, dark-haired woman who looked like Natasha in the *Bullwinkle* cartoon came up behind him and put a manicured hand on his shoulder. She looked vaguely familiar.

"Oh, Veronica," he said, putting an arm around her waist, "I want you to meet Ella. Ella works for me, at the institute . . ." I tried to smile but some other evil emotion was already getting the better of me, and it felt suspiciously like jealousy.

An airline stewardess interrupted. She had been trying to get the Colonel's attention for a few minutes before she finally tapped him on the shoulder.

"You must return to your seat, sir. We're going to be leaving in just a few moments."

"That's what I've been trying to tell him," said the Bullwinkle woman.

"But, my friend," he said to the stewardess, "are we really going to take off in a few minutes? We've been sitting here for quite some time, actively not taking off. The fact is, we are still sitting at the gate, as you can plainly see." Though his tone was meant to be playful, I sensed borderline belligerence.

"That's an excellent observation," said the stewardess, "but according to regulations, we cannot take off until you have returned to your seat." She had her hands on her hips, and looked toward Veronica, her eyes pleading.

Veronica shrugged her shoulders.

"It's a cat and mouse type situation," the Colonel said, smiling. "Or no, I think it would be more accurate to say a chicken and an egg situation, am I right, Miss Kennedy? . . . Miss Kennedy is our resident intellectual," he explained to the stewardess.

"A chicken and an egg," I replied nervously.

"Look, Kimberly," he said to the stewardess, reading her name off the tag on her navy blue lapel. "You must see my point, as well."

"Actually, sir, I'm not sure that I do see your point."

"My point is that since we are not even *prepared* to take off, I see no reason why I should return to my seat. I have business to conduct with my colleague here. And furthermore, I have no guarantee that even if I do comply with your request and return to my seat, the plane will take off. Am I right?"

Kimberly told him that while she was enjoying their little chat immeasurably he really did need to take his seat or she would have to call the pilot.

"If I take my seat, Kimberly," he asked, "will you bring me a fresh martini?" Either I was beginning to imagine things, or he winked at Ms. Bullwinkle as he spoke. I think he winked at her. He had never winked at me in all of our time together.

Kimberly said that she would happily bring him a martini and the Colonel said that he would sit down in just a minute then, that he just needed to tell me something first.

This time Kimberly looked at me, pleadingly. I shrugged my shoulders and tried to relay without words that I was not responsible for this man's behavior.

Kimberly and Veronica left and the Colonel began to tell me about the unfolding disaster at his house. The protesters apparently went by the name of the Republican Cyber Police. They had seen my neophyte web page, and had called a cyber rally to protest what they viewed as the dangerous proposal to reconsider anything Karl Marx had to say.

"But if it's a *cyber* rally, why are they actually out there . . . I mean, physically out there," I asked. "Shouldn't they be rallying in cyberspace somehow?"

"Hell if I know. You know Carmen, her English isn't so good, and she gets a little hysterical sometimes. It's hard to tell what's really going on."

"Well, there's obviously nothing we can do right now anyway. We'll have to deal with it when we get back. So what's the story with the Bullwinkle woman?"

"Who?"

"You know, your femme fatale," I said, gesturing toward the front of the plane.

"Oh, Veronica you mean. Her name is Veronica, not Bullwinkle," he said, confused. "She's our contact. You just missed her at the library yesterday."

I realized then that I had not missed her at all. She was the woman I had bumped into as I was accidentally flinging myself into oncoming traffic.

"Hmm . . . I see you became fast friends," I said, feeling ridiculous.

"What's wrong with you, Ella? Don't you see that we work for her now? She's our deep pocket."

"So that must mean you got the check."

"Well, not exactly. . . . There's just the matter of the conversion of foreign currency, but when we get to Washington—"

He was interrupted when Kimberly returned with the pilot, and the two of them urged the Colonel to return to his seat. The woman next to me chimed in with renewed complaints that we were waking her baby, which was by then fast asleep on her lap and snoring loudly.

The Colonel began his chicken and egg monologue again and Kimberly interrupted. "Sir," she said calmly, "I do not care to engage in a Socratic debate with you—"

"A Socratic stewardess!" said the Colonel gleefully, at which point it occurred to me that he must have ingested a drink or two prior to boarding.

"Sir," said the pilot quite soberly, his uniform boasting a host of very shiny medals. "We want nothing more from you than to see you comply with our regulations."

"And I want a guarantee that this plane will take off sometime before the next century. We're already"—he paused, checking his watch—"we're already fifty-two minutes late for takeoff. And I have a meeting in Washington at ten P.M. Don't I, Ella?"

I couldn't recall any meeting, but I nodded nonetheless. I could always tell the grand jury that we had our own little meeting, I supposed.

"I'm liable to sue you for damages if you don't get me to my meeting on time."

"I must warn you, sir, that if you do not comply right now with our simple request, I will call airport security and have you removed from the aircraft."

"Call in your troops, my friend. Bring on the army. Bring on the revolution! Have you ever noticed how many songs have been written about revolution," he began again. "Tracy Chapman and Chrissie Hynde, not to mention the Beatles. 'Re-vo-lu-u-tion . . . '" he began to sing, horribly out of key.

"I mean, with all this talk about revolution you have to admit that the NUTS people are on to something. The time is ripe to at least take a closer look at a man like Karl Marx. He may have something to offer us, as a purely intellectual matter. That's what our friend Ella here would say."

In retrospect I think it was the Karl Marx reference that truly alarmed the pilot. It was one thing to have a slightly drunk self-important passenger on board—that sort of thing probably happened every day. But it was quite another thing to have a passenger espousing revolution. I began to recognize the potential gravity of the situation.

"Sir," I said, "I think you should sit down for now, and after the plane has taken off we can talk some more."

"Quite a reasonable idea, Miss Kennedy," he replied, and then, addressing Kimberly: "Do you realize that this woman and I spent last night together, and she still calls me sir?"

"I'm sure you command respect," Kimberly said with some hint of sarcasm, and she and the pilot turned and headed back toward the cockpit.

"Sir," I urged again, "I really think you should sit down. Maybe drink some coffee. We can talk when we get to Washington."

He seemed unmoved by the sight of Kimberly and the pilot and what appeared to be a security person standing together outside the cockpit. I couldn't hear their conversation, but Kimberly pointed several times in our direction.

After a few minutes they approached, and the security man grabbed the Colonel by the wrist.

"Oh *bloody hell*," he exclaimed. "What do you people want from me?"

"I'm afraid we're going to have to escort you off the plane, sir," said the small but beefy security man in a delightful cockney accent.

"Siddown and put your goddamned seat belt on," boomed a voice from behind me. The happy family looked up from their books to see what all the commotion was about.

"I'd like to see you try," the Colonel replied dangerously. He looked like he might explode, and then I began to remember those stories about his temper. He grew all fidgety, looking around as if he'd dropped something. Then he grabbed the binder off my lap.

"Oh, please, don't!" I shrieked, grabbing at his arm. I knew that my interest in Eleanor Marx was not necessarily coming from a healthy place, but it had never occurred to me that my work might serve to inflict actual bodily harm on others. But I was too late. He threw it overhand, like a tennis serve, knocking the pilot hard on the head. My notes were not terribly thick, but the plastic binder did the trick. Pages drifted out of the side pocket, floating slowly to the ground.

The pilot yelled in surprise, and a small trickle of blood began to stream down the side of his face where the edge of the binder had nicked him. The security man grabbed the Colonel under each armpit and practically lifted him off his feet.

"You're going to have an international incident on your hands, gentlemen," the colonel yelled as he was pushed toward the exit. "Do you know who I am?"

"No idea," said the pilot, which did not improve the Colonel's spirits in the least. The pilot pulled a handkerchief from his pocket and dabbed the blood from his face.

Veronica appeared, carrying her briefcase and pocketbook, and she followed the Colonel as he was led off the plane.

I waited until I could no longer see them, and then I unstrapped my seat belt, crawled over the woman next to me, and knelt in the aisle to salvage the fragments of Eleanor's life.

Unpaid Bills. Edward bought her exquisitely perfumed corsages, ordered bottles of the finest wines, and produced so many theater tickets that Eleanor begged him to stop. The trip to America was like a second honeymoon—one better than the first. But she couldn't help but wonder who would ultimately foot the bill.

They spoke in auditoriums filled to capacity. Eleanor made an impression that would last, in certain circles anyway, for years. A branch of the Scandinavian Workers League would later name its club in Chicago after her: The Eleanor Marx Kvinno-klubb.

The trip was not to conclude on this high note, but with political disaster, the catalyst for which was a farewell speech by Edward, who managed to say, decidedly and not for the first time, the wrong thing.

He inadvertently insulted the people who had paid for his trip. The Socialist Labor Party of North America was too intellectual, he said, in so many words. It was not the party of his choice.

Even if he spoke the truth, Edward erred in the callous delivery of his remarks, the result of which he was unaware until he reached the shores of England again. The story hit the papers when they were just a few days from home, and would remain headline news for much of January.

AVELING'S UNPAID LABOR, trumpeted the *New York Herald* in a banner headline. "The Socialists are Disgusted and Say So about his Exorbitant Bill. Cigarettes and Corsage Bouquets. Some of the Items which he calls 'Legitimate Expenses.' The socialists will nevermore import a professional agitator from the effete monarchies of Europe."

The article was rather lengthy and detailed, with subheads such as "A Deadhead at the Hotels," and "Crisp Bills Flung in His Face," the thrust of which was that Aveling had racked up charges totaling $1300 for thirteen weeks of work. The party paid these, however reluctantly, only to be presented with an additional bill of $600, which included receipts for corsage bouquets for Eleanor, cigars and cigarettes for them both, and theater tickets, even though Edward had boasted of being admitted to the theater for free by virtue of his journalistic credentials. There was also a bill of $42, for wine at a four-star hotel in Baltimore.

The *Herald* had taken the liberty of wiring this story to the *Telegraph* in London. By the time the couple climbed the steps off the boat they were already notorious.

A reporter blocked Edward as he made his way along the dock. Sir, he said, I understand that the chairman of the party threw a hundred-dollar bill at you and pronounced "here is enough to pay your passage back to England. We are glad to get rid of you." Do you deny this to be true?

Edward pushed the man aside in anger, nearly sending him cascading into the harbor.

Another reporter read aloud from the London *Evening Standard,* " 'Altogether, delivering lectures on socialism seems a lucrative business.'" Sir?

And another reporter to Eleanor, with the typical, eternal question: What would your father make of this?

Chapter 11

Okay, Ira, I said to myself, preparing my silent defense, my preliminary motion for summary judgment in the case against me and my right to continue depleting the natural resource of paper on this endangered planet. Yes. I understand that I am fucking this up. That my so-called dissertation more closely resembles the script of a soap opera than an academic treatise purporting to deconstruct or otherwise shed light on the past, present, or future state of Marxism. But I need to keep going with this—I feel some morbid connection to this material and if it will not illuminate the political state of the modern world, perhaps I can gain at least some small insight into my own tortured little love life.

And then—you have my word—I will do something productive. I will settle on a conventional topic. Either that or I will throw myself wholeheartedly into waitressing. Or possibly peddling Marx-related merchandise online, which is suddenly looking like a pretty good little gig.

The first thing I noticed was the smell, which seemed to be emanating from the general direction of the bedroom. Sort of fishy, I decided after a few whiffs. Not quite intolerable, but potentially so. I dropped my suitcase in the hall and called Nigel's name as I walked through the apartment, cursing the extraordinary mess he had left in his wake.

Golf balls and toilet paper and several large bags of bird seed were piled knee-deep in the hallway. The cat was sitting on the counter amid piles of dirty dishes, staring menacingly at Bob, who was perched high in his cage, his green feathers ruffled. Papers were strewn about the table and floor. I bent down and picked up a few stray sheets and began to read.

I absorbed only a few key words and phrases, but enough to realize that the papers were a part of Nigel's play, the gist of which seemed to be as advertised: it was about birds. I caught something about the Vogelkop Peninsula and about the rain. More to the point, I caught something about a bracelet hanging from a twig at the entrance to a cave. And then I heard his voice.

"Ella, darling, is that you?" he asked sweetly. I didn't reply at first; I was trying to commit to memory another sentence or two, dredging for clues to the Lily story. Nigel walked through the apartment and into the bedroom, still calling my name.

"Nigel! I didn't know you were here," I replied guiltily, dropping the fragments of his manuscript and making my way through what appeared to be more sale items from Value Giant: a bunch of exercise videos; a three-year supply of cat litter; and as I headed toward the source of the smell, I found about a zillion pounds of once-frozen shrimp, now defrosted and picked through by the cat and lying in an oozing puddle on the hardwood floor. It occurred to me that I might be able to find that new form of mold Ira had referred to, after all.

The bed was not made and Nigel's dirty clothing had been tossed in the general vicinity of the laundry basket, which was not a big surprise. But there were things . . . weird things like children's tennis shoes and a pogo stick and wood-chip mulch and a full set of outdated encyclopedias lying on the bed.

And there was Nigel in the midst of it all, his hair sticking up funny and a few green feathers stuck to his wrinkled shirt and a thick tome on penguins tucked under his arm, and even before he could speak another word, I forgot about Lily and about our tiff on the phone and I threw myself at him and pulled him down on the bed atop the piles of junk, scattering things further.

We poured our collective doubts about each other into a singularly passionate physical event and then fell asleep, my body tucked perfectly against his, holding tight.

Why couldn't we just stay like this forever? Or at least until the next mealtime? I was thinking about apologizing for everything. I was contemplating telling him that I was ready to bear his children, possibly even in Miami, and that I didn't even need to know what really happened in the Vogelkop Peninsula.

Then the phone rang.

Nigel sat up and lit a cigarette as he spoke into the receiver. "Yes. . . . She is here, but she's asleep . . ." I rolled over to indicate that I was conscious, but he was already winding down the conversation. "Yes, I'll tell her," he said, and put the phone down.

"Who was that?" I asked, burrowing my head in his chest, looking for a comfortable spot in which to watch his smoke rings rise to the ceiling.

"It was that Colonel guy," said Nigel without emotion. "He said to tell you that he'll be back home tomorrow, and he found one of your earrings in his bed when he was packing."

I instinctively reached for my left earlobe, which was, in fact, earring free. "Damn! . . . It must have fallen out while I was sleeping. I can't believe I've been walking around all day with only one earring. How embarrassing!"

Nigel continued to blow smoke rings expertly, first a large ring, then a series of smaller rings that shot right through the first.

"It's not at all what you think, Nigel," I said, suddenly realizing the likely interpretation of the Colonel's message. "It's really not. I can explain."

"Yeah, sure. It never is what you think, is it? I forgot to tell you, some guy named Eddie Jr. called about seventeen times while you were away. He says to tell you 'Things are not as they seem.' He said you'd know what he meant."

He relayed this message without much emotion. I rolled over and looked at Nigel cautiously, wondering what he was thinking, but his expression was inscrutable, as it so often was.

"That's weird. How did he know who I am? I didn't even give him my real name. . . . I'm telling you, Nigel, don't get the wrong idea. I don't even know who Eddie Jr. is. He's just some guy I met on the Internet. And nothing happened with the Colonel, either. After I talked to you on the phone last night . . . I was just so upset and confused and a fax arrived for him and . . . I don't know. It's very complicated. One thing led to another . . ." I stood up and began to pace around the room.

I headed toward his pack of cigarettes, which was resting on the night table on the other side of the bed. But midway round the room I slipped inelegantly in the puddle on the floor and landed with a painful thud.

"Ouch. Jesus, Nigel, why didn't you put the shrimp in the freezer?" I shrieked. "They've melted all over the floor and . . . jeez, I think I've twisted my ankle or something. And it stinks!"

The tone of my voice was incorrect. It was not what I had intended.

He extended a hand and helped me into a chair, where I sat trying to will away the pain while he dressed in silence.

"I'm sorry, Nigel," I offered.

"I'm sorry, too, but truthfully I'm just starting to think this has no real future, Ella. We're not at all in sync. If it's not one thing, it's another. I go out of my way to bring you all these gifts from Value Giant, and you just get angry. I accidentally dropped the shrimp on the floor. I was going to clean it up, but you don't even give me a chance. . . . Never mind the fact that you've got some sort of twisted relationship with that lunatic Colonel chap. Plus you're having some kind of cyber relationship or something with some guy named Eddie. I mean," he said, his voice suddenly growing loud and angry—a tone I had not previously known him capable of—"I mean, I'm not even going to get started on what that's all about."

"Nigel, forget all that . . . I have an idea," I said suddenly, jumping up from the chair and wincing with pain. "We have to take a ride," I announced, hopping around the room maniacally, looking for my car keys.

"A ride?" He looked at me like I was crazy. "What do you mean, a ride?"

"In my car. We'll go to the country!" I enthused, suddenly envisioning a romantic getaway. "In fact, we'll go to the country and we'll stay overnight. Maybe two nights. Whatever. Why don't you pack a few things?"

"I don't know, Ella," he said, looking apologetic. "I'm not sure I really want to go for a ride. I've got a lot of work to do on the play. Did I tell you the premiere is Friday? Your dad has organized this for me at his Rockville Value Giant. He's been extraordinarily kind. He even called some of his media contacts."

"You're kidding." It seemed I'd simply been cut out of the loop—the loop involving my boyfriend and my parents, no less. Nor could I recall the last time my father had invested any enthusiasm in *my* ambitions, such as they were. He paid my tuition, admittedly, but not without complaint. Still, I was convinced (though, as always, conscious of the self-delusion involved) that this ride concept was the key to salvaging our relationship.

"We'll just stay one night, then," I said, tossing a change of clothes in a plastic shopping bag and donning a clean pair of khakis and another V-neck. Nigel stood quietly, staring at me, as I threw a pair of his underwear in the bag and collected our toothbrushes.

"I'm going to get the car from the lot. Meet me in the lobby in ten minutes," I instructed.

In retrospect, I suppose I have to admit that Nigel did insist, repeatedly and rather vociferously, that he didn't want to go for a ride, never mind be designated as the driver.

"I'm a lousy driver. I hate driving . . . I even hate riding. I get carsick. I failed my driver's test three times," he pleaded. "And I never learned to parallel park," he added, for good measure.

Given these disclaimers, it might have occurred to me to inquire as to whether he had ever driven on the right side of the road. But I was too busy trying to get him to talk. I had planned to be subtle in my attempts to encourage him to open up, so I figured I wouldn't start right in on the wife situation.

"I met your mom," I offered cheerfully as he put his directional signal on and began to pull into traffic on Connecticut Avenue. I hadn't realized that it was already rush hour. Traffic was barely moving, and given my poor sense of direction, I wasn't entirely sure where we should be headed anyway.

"You met my mom!" he replied in a voice that could well have contained anger though it was hard to tell whether the edge in his tone was a response to my disclosure or to the impact of the crash as the front of my car slammed hard into a Pepsi truck that spanned the length of a city block. The collision threw me back into the seat and inexplicably shattered the side window. Horns honked, people shouted, a messenger who had been knocked off his bicycle gave Nigel the finger, and the truck driver shook his head with pity as he alighted from his cab and came to offer assistance.

I limped out of the car, shaken but largely unscathed except for my already wounded foot, and began to apologize to all concerned. I exchanged registration and insurance information with the truck driver, and some of my fellow motorists helped organize a break in the traffic so that we could push my car to the side of the road. The driver of the Pepsi truck then offered to call a tow truck from his cell phone as steam had begun to pour out from under my hood. At some point in the midst of all this chaos Nigel tapped me on the shoulder.

"Listen, darling," he began in that accent that very nearly transported me from an anarchic rush-hour scene in Washington, D.C., to some romantic sheep pasture in Cornwall. "I'm really sorry about this."

"Oh Nigel, never mind," I said, putting my arms around his neck, nuzzling my face in his pilly sweater. "My car was a piece of crap anyway."

"No, darling," he said, politely wriggling free of my embrace. "I'm sorry about *us*. It's very difficult for me to explain, but I just don't sense this moving in the right direction. I'm a very loyal man, you see. Loyal to a fault."

"Loyal? What do you mean, *loyal?*" I genuinely didn't understand, plus I had to shout to be heard above the roar of traffic. "Are you saying you're loyal to your wife? Or are you saying that you are loyal to me, and I'm not loyal back? Because I am. Loyal."

"Both?" he said, but I could barely hear him and it sounded more like a question.

"What do you mean, both?" I shouted as he began to cross the street, dodging traffic. This was no way to end a relationship. There were supposed to be violins playing in the background, or at least some rock song with melodramatic breakup lyrics that I could later listen to and weep. Something other than the sound of cars honking their horns amid the smell of diesel fumes.

He didn't answer, though I wasn't sure if he had heard me. In any event a police car arrived just then and I was forced to turn my attention to the more urgent of the two disasters.

When I returned to the apartment it appeared that Nigel had already come and gone, taking with him some of his things, including the fragments of his manuscript.

I stood in the kitchen staring at Bob, holding the plastic bag containing Nigel's toothbrush, and it dawned on me that he had walked off before I was able to deliver my last means of defense to explain my otherwise inexplicable night with the Colonel.

I would have called it the Bowerbird Defense had he been willing to listen. A female bowerbird visits an average of 3.6 bowers in a local area before choosing a mate. I had planned to tell Nigel I was just visiting bowers, hoping he would be so impressed by my knowledge that he would overlook the fallacy. The fallacy being that I was not a bird, strictly speaking.

GBS. Legend has it that once, when George Bernard Shaw was standing in a packed crowd listening to the Avelings lecture on the eight-hour workday, he grew bored and scribbled a note that was passed through the throngs of people up to the podium and then on to Eleanor. The note instructed her to stop talking and to stand on her head so that he could get a clearer view of her legs.

It was her ankles, in particular, of which he was rumored to be fond.

Shaw insisted that the story was false: he would never have been so crude and besides, he added, Eleanor Marx was incapable of giving a boring speech.

Still, this apocryphal tale holds the suggestion of what might have been had Eleanor not been sick in love with Edward.

Sick in love, indeed, I thought, putting my pen down. Lovesick. An excellent word. So excellent that I looked it up in the dictionary: **lovesick** adj. 1. so much in love as to be unable to act in a normal way.

I took mild comfort in the fact that this was a condition worthy of definition. There was an adjective available to explain my compilation of lists analyzing deep feelings of loss and regret over Nigel's absence after only two months. I had to confess that other than noting his good looks and his charming accent in the column labeled "pro Nigel," most of the entries were in the form of negative positives. Or were those, technically speaking, positive negatives? In any event, he was not a sexual pervert, so far as I knew, nor was he a racist, or an ax murder, or an abuser of children and puppies.

Sure, certain things were missing in our relationship, e.g., communication, meaningful conversation, and intimacy, but who really needed that from a man? Wasn't that what girlfriends were for? And yes, granted, he might be married, but there were worse things a man could be, as demonstrated in my list. So why be so hard on the guy?

If the last thing I wanted to do was attack the mess in my apartment, the next to last thing I wanted to do was go to work and face the protesters, who had, apparently, mustered sufficient attention with their cyber rally to have earned mention in the morning newspaper—it was not every mansion in Georgetown, after all, that had people parading about outside chanting things like "Long live capitalism."

So, for lack of any better ideas, and in need of some female companionship, I limped my way through the metro station and over to Lisa's pansy-shrouded doorstep.

She was back in black, and looked like her old perfect self again, albeit more visibly pregnant. We exchanged niceties while she prepared a pot of herbal tea.

"He's not a bad man," I said of Nigel, musing out loud. "He's just confused."

"Possibly," she replied, producing a bottle of black nail polish and an emery board. "He also seems pretty dull."

"I've never seen you wear nail polish before," I observed. "Dull?" The idea of dull was stunning to me. He was the very opposite of dull. He was the most splendid man I'd ever seen.

"It's sort of a thing I do when I'm pregnant," she said, referring the vampish nail polish. "I like my fingers and toes to look nice. I figure they are the only parts of me I can salvage right now." That said, she attempted to reach her toenails with the brush, but had difficulty bending over the mound of her stomach.

"I'll do your toenails," I offered, "if you'll help me figure out my life. Why do you say he's dull?"

Lisa shrugged her shoulders noncommittally, as if I were somehow getting the better end of the deal.

"The whole bird thing is sort of a drag. And besides, British men are passé. Eastern Europe is in."

"Jeez, Lisa. I'm not trying to make a fashion statement out of my love life."

"That's a good thing 'cause he's not much of a fashion statement, is he?"

"What's with you?" I asked while performing my first pedicure. "You've been snippy ever since I got to Washington." It occurred to me that she might be experiencing wild hormonal mood swings: the last time I saw her she was dressed like mother earth. Now she wore black nail polish and was dressed in what looked like the latest in Euro maternity wear.

"Look, I'm sorry," she said, softening her tone. "I'm just being silly. I just don't get good vibes from the guy, that's all."

"But you don't even know him. You saw him, what, once? On the street? And you're passing judgment?"

"No, you're absolutely right. Tell me what's going on. I'm just kind of edgy today."

Relieved to have her attention, I launched into my pathetic saga: Nigel had just walked out on me; I had learned a few more confusing pieces about his life from his mother; the Colonel had been escorted off the airplane in a drunken rage; my bank account was in serious arrears; never mind the fact that the Colonel was now hanging out with some beautiful Natasha-like woman, which in theory should not really matter to me but bugged me nonetheless. Oh, right, and my car had been wrecked!

I noticed at some point while speaking that Lisa wasn't really listening.

It wasn't as though she was distracted by Hayden, or preoccupied with her mission to maintain the tidiest house in America. She just seemed kind of lost in thought as she sat on the overstuffed sofa, staring idly out the window while sipping her tea, taking care not to smudge her nails. Her nods and uh-huhs came at peculiar intervals, like five minutes after I had ceased to speak.

I continued to pour my heart out to her, though I couldn't say why. Possibly because even in her own apparent confusion, she had a whole lot more than I did; she had everything I thought I wanted. So on I went, posing a series of unanswerable questions. How could this man have turned my life inside out so quickly? What did that mean? Did it mean this was true love? Was there such a thing as true love? Or was I so lonely and pathetic and fundamentally insecure that I was able to self-destruct over any schmuck who told me he needed me?

And what did she think about these Eleanor Marx parallels? Was God trying to hit me over the head with the obvious, and was

I too stupid to see the light? Or alternatively, did I have an overactive mind in need of therapy and medication?

And how was it that I had turned out to be the bad guy in this drama, I asked in a tone of near hysteria, when the only thing I wanted to know was why he still wore a wedding ring? I mean, that seemed to me a reasonable enough question, didn't she agree?

Lisa nodded her head and shrugged her shoulders simultaneously. "All relationships are confusing," she said. "The important thing is self-respect."

What was that about? She sounded like the blurb inside a fortune cookie and I decided right then that I hated her. I hated my best friend. She really had nothing useful to say to me in this moment of crisis, plus, was she implying that I had lost my self-respect, or was she suggesting, rather, that I never had any self-respect to begin with?

She prevented me from verbalizing the rash response I was busily formulating by asking if I wouldn't mind applying a second coat of polish for her since I had done such a nice job with the first.

Perhaps it was unfair to ask Lisa to untangle my love life for me. But as a married woman I thought she would have some advice, some secret womanly truths to share, something to say to make this sorry scene at least worthy of a chick flick, complete with nail polish and true confessions.

Besides, I had no one else to turn to: my parents were not exactly the sort of people I leaned on in times of emotional trauma. My mother had once told me my problems would be solved if I would simply lighten my hair color and get a proper manicure myself, while my father recommended the management training program at Value Giant as a means to realizing self-worth.

If she wasn't going to be of any use in sorting out my love life, the least she could do was help me out with the work situation.

"You should be proud of me," I urged, summoning all the self-respect I could muster. "I spent a couple weeks reading this

HTML book and I've actually started up a website. I'm not real far, though . . . I'm finding it pretty complicated, especially the color stuff . . . but, hey, I'm getting there."

"HTML? I think you're supposed to be learning something else now. Like XML or something. Besides, you don't really need to learn all that. Just go to WebChimp."

"*WebChimp?*" There was really no way to one-up this woman.

"It's a website that will walk you through setting up a website. It makes it really simple. Hayden could practically do it."

Hayden. Where was our little friend anyway? I was hesitant to ask because I was enjoying his absence. I had more to tell her, certain that somewhere along the way I would spark her interest, or possibly earn her compassion. I told her about the protesters outside the office. I told her that Eddie Jr. had been calling my apartment. When that failed to get her attention I told her I had spent the night with the Colonel, holding hands.

Still no reaction.

I then stood up and waved my hand in front of her face and said, *"Hullo? Anyone home?*

"What's going on, Lisa?" I asked. She was still staring out the window intently.

"Sorry, what did you say?"

"Are you still mad at me for having a relationship with Nigel? Even now that it's fallen apart? Or else what is it? What am I missing? I mean, you're not even listening."

Lisa sighed. "Look, Ella, it's all right. About Nigel, I mean. I understand. These things happen every day. In fact you've helped me more than you know. Would you like more tea?"

"No thanks. Don't you have anything with caffeine around here? And that's not true. They don't happen every day. Not to me anyway."

But she seemed disinterested again. She was completely gone. I began to wonder if she was on sedatives perhaps. Or had gone in for an outpatient lobotomy, because she used to be my friend. She used to care about me! But she did not seem unwell; if anything she exuded good health from every pore. I was the one who, in my post-travel daze, looked like I was slightly under the influence of something or other.

"Lisa, where's Hayden?" I asked, wondering if perhaps I should be worried.

"He's with Francesca," she said, checking her watch. "She took him somewhere. I don't know, maybe to the playground."

"Who's Francesca?"

"The nanny. From Sweden or Switzerland. One of those countries. She's from Scandinavia. Somewhere in Scandinavia, I think. Maybe Norway."

"When did you get a nanny? I thought you didn't want to have nannies anymore. I thought that was part of why you quit your job. I suppose you have a cleaning lady now, too?"

"Well, I did, but she's thirty minutes late and if she's not here in five minutes, mark my words, Ella, she's history."

"What's going on, Lisa? . . . You've changed . . . I don't get it. . . . It's like you've gone through three different phases in the last month. Is everything all right with you and Roger?"

"Look, Ella. You're not the only one with problems in life, okay?" she said with obvious irritation. She began pacing around the living room.

"You know, this will sound really stupid, but back in college, in this Feminism 101 course I took freshman year, they talked about the different phases of women's emancipation. I can't really remember all the steps, but you basically went from like, bonded chattel to the total eradication of men."

"So what's your point? That I'm evolving backward?"

"Of course not. But I really don't get this, Lisa. You invite me down here . . . no, 'invite' is the wrong word. You insist I come to Washington and then you totally betray me . . . which is fine, okay? . . . I'm not dwelling on that, even though you might want to note, I haven't gotten a single penny out of this job yet . . . but fine . . . that's not the point, either. . . . The point is that you've gone from this brilliant intellectual woman to supermom and now . . . well . . . now I no longer know what you're up to."

"And is there something wrong with supermom?"

"No. Supermom is great. It's just that it seemed so sudden. And so intense . . ."

I pressed on, suddenly caring less about preserving our friendship than about proving my point. "Within days of giving up your job you completely lost interest in all the knowledge you'd spent a lifetime accumulating."

"You know what they say, Ella. 'With your episiotomy they give you a lobotomy.' This cleaning lady is history. I need to call the agency—"

"Wait!" I said, putting my hand down over the phone. I was determined to see this through, for whatever reason. "Listen to me a minute. You can't use the old episiotomy story because you are one of the smartest people I've ever met in my life and besides, Hayden was born almost three years ago and you were functioning just fine until a few weeks ago."

She began to pace around the room again, pretending not to hear me, and I felt like an idiot all of a sudden. Why was I pursuing this? The point didn't really need belaboring: Lisa was clearly having some kind of breakdown, and here I was, her friend, trying to push her over the edge just to prove my point, whatever it was.

I felt sorry for myself as well. What do you do when your heroes fall? Lisa had it *all*. I mean, I had even planned to be her someday—a slightly less physically attractive version of course, living in a less pricey neighborhood.

But it was Lisa who had allowed me to entertain romantic visions of the future, of a husband with whom I would lie in bed on weekends, reading the newspaper while our children brought us toast and coffee. The baby would lie between us on our white down duvet, happily sucking her thumb and gurgling. On weekdays I would go to work and the children would grow up incredibly well adjusted because we would have figured out the right answer to the whole child care thing. On the weekends, after we read by the fire, we would visit museums and cafés and the children would behave well in restaurants. People would come over from other tables, even, to compliment us on our lovely family.

By quitting work, Lisa had suggested that this career and family thing just wasn't working out. It was the equivalent of telling me that the baby would spit up sour milk on the white down duvet, and that the children would all wind up delinquents because I was working too many hours, but I had no choice since my husband had left claiming I had become an intolerable shrew on account of years of sleep deprivation but I would know the real reason was because I had gained forty pounds and had hideous stretch marks.

And now that she had more time on her hands, not only did she not want her children around, but she didn't seem to have any interest in me either.

I stood up and pulled my hair back and took a deep breath. My mind was cycling out of control.

"Lisa," I tried more sympathetically this time. "What's going on? You seem . . . you seem kind of anxious."

"Do I?" she asked defensively, looking at her watch. The doorbell rang, and she ran to it as if fleeing from my accusation. I couldn't see, but I heard the cleaning lady begging for her job in pidgin English.

"Please, Señora . . . the car it is broken and the baby . . . the baby she is sick. And now I am here, Señora. Now I will clean."

"You've brought the baby!" Lisa shrieked. "And just how do you plan to clean with this baby hanging around?"

"Oh, Señora, this is not a problem. The baby she will sit in her basket. She is a good baby. She will not cry."

The baby began to cry on cue.

"Look, Maria, you are forty-five minutes late. Time is money, you know."

"Consuela," she said.

"Excuse me?"

"My name is Consuela. The baby. She is Maria. Señora."

"Yes. I see. Consuela. Thank you. Goodbye."

I heard the door slam, and Lisa came back into the living room with a look of contempt. She gazed out the window and then her face lightened as she waved to a sporty-looking man wearing an Orioles cap behind the wheel of a green Jeep.

"Look, Ella," she said, grabbing her sweater and keys, "I hate to do this to you, but I have a meeting. Can you lock the door behind you?" She gave me a kiss on the cheek.

"A meeting? Who's that?" I asked, stunned.

"That's Paul," she said. "Our kids are in the same playgroup," she added, as if that explained things.

"Oh," I said. "And where's Roger?"

"Detroit. On business."

"Lisa," I said stupidly, "are you having an affair? Were you having an affair when you quit work? Does Roger know? What about Hayden?"

"Look, Ella, I had a revelation, and it's all thanks to you." Paul honked the horn of the Jeep impatiently, and Lisa said we'd talk soon, as she ran off toward the vehicle. I watched her from the window for a moment. She hopped into the Jeep and gave the man named Paul a long kiss.

I watched, feeling sad and angry and sick in equal parts. The Lisa I knew in school would have never talked to Consuela that way. And was there really no such thing as a happy marriage? If Lisa couldn't pull it off, who could? I was also furious, really, on a thousand different levels, not the least of which was the realization that she was a married woman who had given me a lot of grief for having a relationship with a married man.

But what did I know, in my unmarried naïveté? Perhaps this was just an inevitable phase of marriage—the brief fling phase. I wondered worriedly what might come after this phase. Revolution? Total destruction of the existing marital system? Radical lesbianism, perhaps.

I stood up and hopped to the door, thinking maybe I should see a doctor about my foot.

Freddy Demuth. The wine flowed freely at Engels's Primrose Hill house, and the company was typically as rich as the food. Eleanor found herself a bit flushed and giddy after one such Sunday night meal. "The usual round of dinner, drink, cards, supper, and more drink," she wrote. But on that particular occasion, the drinks had got the better of her.

Two glasses of wine was all it took to get her going, and she had to watch her tongue. Though she loved Engels as a father, there was something unspoken between them.

She didn't mean to be offensive, but as Engels refilled her crystal glass and the cook offered her a second helping of pheasant, she brought up the volatile subject of Freddy. She had seen him at the back gate that morning, Eleanor said. Visiting with Helene. Engels glared at Eleanor, and she ran from the room, ashamed of her indiscretion.

Eleanor had reason to believe that Freddy was the result of a secret liaison between Helene and Friedrich Engels.

Freddy had maintained no contact with Helene as he was growing up, but as an adult he began to visit his mother on the weekends. By then he had found work as a skilled engineer. Freddy's wife had left him, draining the bank account and leaving their son, Harry, behind.

Freddy Demuth weighed heavily on Eleanor's mind. After wrestling with her conscience for years, Eleanor did what seemed to her only obvious; she figured out where Freddy lived and began to visit him regularly, bringing small gifts for his son.

While no one else in the family seemed to acknowledge his existence, Eleanor couldn't help but think that Freddy was the skeleton in the closet that negated all of Engels's good intentions.

Chapter 12

Although I had been given advance warning, the sight of the cyber-rally people with their KILL THE COMMIES and DEATH TO MARX signs was still astonishing. Who were these scruffy, angry people, and didn't they realize that Karl Marx was, indeed, quite dead already? I couldn't help but think to myself that these were the very sort of people who might actually benefit from a full-scale societal revolution of precisely the sort that Marx had envisioned.

I got the overall impression that the protesters were planning a long-term siege of the Institute of Thought. They had brought with them enough equipment to scale Mount Everest, including tents and coolers and large backpacks, and seemed to have designated the north side of the lawn as a sort of child-care area, with playpens and portable cribs set up in a shady spot under a tree. On the other side of the house a man was busy assembling a badminton net, driving a stake into the ground with a large mallet.

The spectacle of protesters outside the institute only added to the general sense of chaos on this otherwise quiet corner: construction debris littered the front lawn, the builders' trucks were double-parked and clogging traffic, and the entire right side of the house was shrouded in plastic and scaffolding. It looked like the property had been condemned, and squatters had taken over.

A policeman had been stationed at the front door, and he tried to block my entrance up the steps. I insisted that I was an employee of the institute, but was unable to produce any physical evidence to bolster my claim. We were midargument, and I was about to panic, recalling that a good chunk of my dissertation notes was lodged in the Colonel's computer, when Carmen opened the door to vouch for me. Still, before letting me through he insisted on searching my handbag for god knows what—bombs or guns or biological weapons, perhaps—and probably due to my generally disheveled appearance, he chose to frisk me, as well. I told him that this was bound to be the highlight of my day and anyway, if I did have a gun I probably would have pulled it on someone already, it having been that kind of morning.

The policeman did not seem to find my observation in any way amusing, but he waved me through the door nonetheless.

I looked around, shocked. I had only been gone a couple of days, but in that time the walls had been literally torn down: exposed electrical wires hung from the ceiling; the staircase railing had been disassembled so that the act of descending to the basement office now involved the risk of falling about eighteen feet. The workmen had moved on to another wing of the house, and I could hear them in the distance, demolishing things.

"Where is he?" I asked Carmen, listening to my voice echo in the dark, empty hallway.

She tilted her head, and we both looked up, as if we could see him through what was left of the ceiling.

"He is in the bed, upstairs," she said. "He says he has a big pain inside his head."

"Is he alone?" I asked reluctantly.

"You mean is he with *that woman?*" asked Carmen with obvious disdain. "She was here. Now she is gone. . . . She made quite a mess in the kitchen this morning. How difficult is it to make coffee without spilling it all over the counter, I ask you? She left it for me to clean up."

I shrugged my shoulders noncommittally, reminded, naturally, of the mess in my own kitchen.

"Well, back to work," I said in as cheerful a tone as I could muster.

"Yes. Be very careful down there," she advised.

I studied the staircase for a moment and decided that sitting on the ground and sliding down was the safest way to travel. Without any railings, it seemed certain that I would fall to sudden death if I tried to negotiate the narrow passage vertically, particularly given the pain in my foot, which made it hard to balance even on flat terrain.

So much had changed and yet nothing was different: there was not a single message on our voice mail, not one new piece of mail on my desk. The sole indication that a couple of days had passed was that more T-shirts had arrived, and in order to get to the desk I had to climb over the boxes and step down into the chair.

At home and at work, my life was being taken over by superfluous consumer goods. I would soon be squeezed out altogether.

What was I doing here, anyway? I was waiting to be paid, of course, but that seemed increasingly unlikely. The only logical thing to do was to print out my dissertation, gather my personal items, and flee. As soon as I flicked on the computer switch, however, I heard Carmen shout my name.

"Miss Ella! The television people, they are outside," she said, yelling from the top of the stairs.

"What television people?" I yelled back.

"I don't know. Channel 62, I see . . . and channel 103—Holy Mother of Mary, I didn't know there was such a big channel—and I think that one says CNN. Yes. CNN."

"*CNN?* What in god's name are they doing here?"

"They say they want to talk to someone. I started to answer

their questions but I'm not sure I'm the right person. They want to talk about Karl Marx, for some reason. I said to them, 'Isn't he dead?' "

"What about the Colonel?" I asked, hobbling over to the bottom of the stairs, growing increasingly alarmed.

"I tried to get him, but he's in a very heavy sleep. I couldn't wake him up."

"Holy Mother of Mary," I couldn't help but agree.

I didn't really have authority to represent the Institute of Thought on television, as I saw it. I was just the souvenir girl. We needed to establish a public relations department for these sorts of things. I dialed the Colonel's private line and listened to it ring, suspecting that he would simply designate me as the public relations department (you're smart, you'll figure it out, he would no doubt say), but he didn't answer. I started to dial Lisa's number, but then thought better of it, reflecting on her newfound total lack of interest in anything whatsoever.

So I made the usual halfhearted attempt to coax some order out of my unfortunate hair and wished that I had worn something more presentable. I crawled up the steps with no small amount of effort—my ankle had swollen to the size of a small tangerine, and shards of pain shot through my leg and up to my thigh when I put any pressure on it.

This was only one of many small moments of reckoning in life, I told myself. I took a deep breath and decided to move forth boldly.

My fifteen minutes of fame were over rather abruptly. They were more like a minute or two, at best. The bright lights from the cameras forced me to squint as I stood at the top of the institute's marbled steps, prepared to humiliate myself on national television.

I positioned myself beside a piece of discarded drywall, and thought of Eleanor. I scanned the crowd for the likes of Bernard Shaw—the literary man, as opposed to the CNN anchorman—thinking what a thrill it would be to receive a note complimenting me about my legs. Instead I saw a few landscapers and men with leaf blowers who had wandered over from the neighbors' yards, as well as a homeless man pushing his few belongings across the lawn in a Safeway shopping cart.

"There are rumors that the Institute of Thought is being funded by a dissident group of Russians intent on destabilizing the current government," shouted the reporter from Channel 103.

I stood frozen, staring at the bright lights. This was certainly a possibility. Quite a clever possibility, actually, and one that had never even remotely entered my mind. "That's completely untrue," I said unsteadily. "Our client is intent only on advocating freedom of thought and expression."

"There are reports that Henri Finkel, the founder of the Institute of Thought, has helped a leading member of the Russian Mafia gain entry to the United States," said the reporter from Channel 62.

"That's completely untrue," I reiterated, flashing on Natasha.

"There are reports that your institute is engaged in fund-raising through the sale of Karl Marx paraphernalia," said the CNN reporter.

"Is that illegal?" I heard myself shout in reply. "Since when is that a crime?"

I was startled by how big my otherwise little voice sounded as it echoed through the bank of microphones jammed up against my face.

There was silence from the crowd. They seemed to expect some follow-up to my pronouncement.

"Karl Marx was a misunderstood man," I repeated, "and at the very least, his life, and his work, deserve a second look."

I felt trembly and could not believe what I had just said, but was mildly encouraged by the sound of barely audible applause that seemed to be coming from a man with a NO MORE SPEED BUMPS banner.

"You might as well go ahead and burn every book in this country if you are unwilling to consider—to simply even *consider*—that Karl Marx may have had something worthwhile to say. That in order to understand Karl Marx's politics, you have to understand something of the conditions of nineteenth-century Victorian society. That Karl Marx had the germ of an idea for a better world. Yes, he might have said some pretty scary stuff, but he also called for things like the liberation of women, the abolition of child labor, free public education!" I felt an unprecedented swell of confidence. My voice would be heard around the world. My voice would be heard by my father. . . .

I studied the faces in the crowd to gauge their reaction. Had I provoked passion? Scorn? Surprise? If anything, the prevailing mood appeared to be one of boredom.

But I did not care. Instead I went on, in what was increasingly becoming an out-of-body experience, to give a speech about how much of Marx's analysis of capitalism was quite prescient; about how the Soviet Union was not a true expression of what Marx would have advocated; about Eleanor Roosevelt and Arthurdale and democracy and equality; and then I went on to explain that I was a registered Democrat with a weakness for designer labels but no real sense of style and at last I inspired three people to get on their feet and applaud while a few others threw rocks and I saw Nigel in the way back of the small crowd, waving to me, and I felt breathless and euphoric and like life had meaning.

I was so happy to see Nigel that I threw myself at him and buried my face in his scarf, hoping to obliterate the memory of what I had just said, though the event was no doubt now preserved for posterity on videotape.

"Sorry about your car," he offered.

"Yeah, so much for our romantic ride in the country." I laughed. "I'm afraid the repair estimate is more than the car is even worth. I think I may just take it back as is."

"Listen, let's take a walk," he said. "I didn't mean to be so abrupt the other day. I think we should talk, and I'm better on my feet than behind the wheel."

I didn't want to be a complainer, but my foot was killing me and taking a walk was not likely to improve my condition. "Come," I said, pointing to a red, white, and blue tourist trolley that had stopped in front of the institute so the out-of-towners could gawk at the television cameras, and I grabbed his hand and pulled him on to the back of the bus.

Our free ride ended at the zoo, which was, conveniently, just a block from my apartment. Nigel proposed we see the baby lions and wander around for a while, but first he coaxed me into the gift shop. He wanted to buy me a present, he said, despite my protestations. I was thrilled by this return of affection, but knew he was broke. I was not into souvenirs, I argued, aware of the irony given my job description. And besides, wasn't it more sensible to buy a souvenir on the way out, rather than on the way in, so that one wouldn't have to lug it around the zoo?

Nigel said no. He wanted to buy me a present. It would make things easier. I suspected only then that this was not going to be a romantic reconciliation sort of trip to the zoo.

I noticed gray clouds begining to gather overhead, and I took Nigel's arm with one hand, both for solace and for physical support, and held a giant stuffed toucan in the other.

As we studied the llamas I told him that I was pretty sure my job was over. I took a deep breath of smelly llama and told him that I hadn't been paid yet and that the whole institute was quite literally falling apart.

"So you spoke to my mum," he said in response.

"Yeah. I told you that already. She's really nice . . . and I'm sorry about that whole thing with the letter and meeting her on the sly and all. I didn't mean to be so deceptive. It's just that, well, I just really needed to know who you are. All this mystery was driving me kind of mad. It still is, I suppose."

We wandered over to the giraffes, where a baby was demolishing a small tree.

"How much did she tell you?"

"Not much at all."

"She didn't tell you about the logger?"

"The what?"

"Did she tell you how much you look like Lily?"

"No. But what's the big deal? People are attracted to certain types."

"The point is that I can see history repeating itself. It's bound to end badly again. It's no good . . ."

"But, Nigel," I said, leading him down a winding path toward the baby lions. "I love you. I've been crazy in love with you since I met you. We can make sure history doesn't repeat itself if you give me a quick history lesson."

"No, it's all too eerie. I mean, even your hair . . ."

"So I'll get a haircut. I'll become a blonde, and I'll go to one of those image consultants and wear tight clingy clothes and stiletto heels," I joked, though there was nothing at all funny about the offer. Why was I demeaning myself like this? What man could be worth such debasement? *What had Lisa just said to me about self-respect?*

"Look, Nigel, seriously, we've never even given this a chance. I haven't got a clue as to who you really are, or what it is that haunts you. Why don't you talk to me? I mean, whatever it is, it can't be that bad," I insisted without much confidence. "Sometimes it's better to just get it off your chest."

"That's true, and that's why I've written it all down. I've been incorporating it into my play, you see. And that's been cathartic.

And your dad has been very helpful, too. I want you to come to the play. And after the production, I've made the decision to move to Miami," he said.

I felt a drop of rain and hoped Nigel didn't notice. His rain thing, aside from being bizarre, was disruptive.

"I'll come with you," I offered recklessly. "Miami might be just the antidote," I said, continuing to surprise myself. "I could finish up my dissertation lying on the beach, and just sort of fax it off to New York. Or Fed Ex it or something—"

"That's absurd, Ella. There's nothing for you in Miami."

"I'll find something. I'll teach aerobics. I'll learn to surf. I'll have your baby." I hated myself for saying such stupid things.

Nigel laughed but he didn't smile. "I think we should just let this go, Ella. It was an interlude. When I met you, I thought briefly about stopping here. But like I said, this is history repeating itself."

It began to rain heavily all at once, and Nigel cursed the Weather Channel for having failed to predict precipitation. Then he ran ahead, darting through a group of little Cub Scouts.

I hobbled along, but quickly lost sight of him and began to wander through the pouring rain, calling his name, clutching the soggy toucan.

It was a long walk to the aviary, where I knew he'd be. He was sitting on a bench in the simulated rain forest. I limped in and sat on the bench beside him. The warmth of the rain forest felt good, but my hair was already starting to frizz.

"This is not an interlude to me," I said, though I was full of self-doubt and actually sort of embarrassed by these grandiose metaphors. Surely I deserved better. Someone who talked to me, who shared my interests, who was at least curious about my hopes and dreams.

"No, Ella," he said, reaching for my hand. "It's my fault. I've got to move on. You're getting all tangled up in this relationship. You're looking for deep meaning all over the place. There's nothing here. Well, there's something, of course. We've had a nice few weeks and you're really special and we've had some good times . . ."

A family of macaws screeched so loudly I could barely hear him. I said that this was confusing for me and it would be helpful if we could occasionally have important conversations in quiet locations.

"Isn't it a pity they don't have any bowerbirds in this rain forest?" he asked.

I said yes. It was a pity. And all at once my gloom turned to wonder. I realized I had just witnessed the full extent of Nigel's range. He was done emoting now and had gone back to the birds, the only place he was really comfortable.

"Did I tell you about the bowerbirds of the Vogelkop Peninsula?" he asked.

I told him that he had. Several times.

He said he was leaving town next week and would be by to collect his things in a few days.

"Aren't you going to even feed me the line about let's be friends?" I asked, eerily calm. I felt completely numb. I was studying him now, like any other animal in the zoo. Perhaps this was typical of his mating habits.

When he failed to answer, I stood up and walked out of the rain forest, taking the stuffed toucan and slam-dunking it into the trash on the way out.

We never did see the baby lions.

The half brother. Engels, at seventy, was still going strong. "Even the doctors won't believe me when I tell them I'm in my seventieth year," he was fond of boasting, "saying I look ten to fifteen years younger."

He still had the stamina for an all-night birthday party, even if he was not in a celebratory mood. His elegant row house was packed tight with friends; not only was Engels a beloved and respected comrade, but he had an established reputation for putting on a good spread.

As always, champagne and claret flowed freely. At 3:30 A.M., twelve dozen oysters appeared on silver trays. Congratulatory telegrams poured in from all over the world, and a cast of drunken guests read them aloud.

"So you see," he said later, "I did my best to show that I was alive and still kicking."

Which was actually something of a feat, given the circumstances: Helene Demuth had died three weeks before. She had lived with him for seven years, and her death not only left a gaping hole in Engels's daily life, but marked the end of an era of sorts.

Within the year Engels had developed cancer of the esophagus and larynx. He waited until the bitter end, however, to tend to his last piece of unfinished business. He wanted to die with a clear conscience, and that meant breaking some painful news to Eleanor.

He could no longer speak, and besides, he couldn't bear to look at Eleanor when she heard the news. Instead he dispatched a mutual friend to Eleanor's house, with instructions to deliver the truth about Freddy Demuth.

Engels was not the father, he said. Freddy Demuth was Karl Marx's son. Which made Freddy Demuth Eleanor's half brother.

She put on her coat and ran to Regent's Park Road, where she banged her fists on the door, hysterical. She demanded an immediate retraction. She insisted her father would never tell a lie. Engels could only shrug his shoulders weakly.

Eleanor demanded that he write the truth, and a

chalkboard was produced. Engels, with all the strength left in his ravaged body, confirmed the news, leaving Eleanor a new fact with which to wrestle:

Karl Marx had never acknowledged the existence of his only son to live to adulthood. And he had disowned him in order to preserve the integrity of his own bourgeois family life.

Chapter 13

"They're all over the lawn, like ants," said the Colonel. "It's horrible. You simply can't imagine."

He was wrong. I was capable of imagining just about anything given the number of painkillers I had ingested after my trip to the hospital.

I had, in fact, been in a semidelirious dream state when the phone rang, and I imagined that Louis Schwartz had called to congratulate me on my big speech in front of the institute. "Who would have thought that of all my many high-strung, chain-smoking students, you would have been the one to succeed?" he had asked, and then we kissed. His mouth had tasted like burned rubber.

"What ants?" I glanced at the clock. It was late afternoon, and my mouth tasted less like burned rubber than dirty socks. I tried to wiggle my toes, which were barely visible at the bottom of the removable walking cast.

After leaving Nigel in the aviary, I'd stumbled out into the street only to meet the bottom of a pothole. A compassionate group of Swedish tourists scooped me up outside the zoo and stuffed me into a cab with a ten-dollar bill and instructions to head toward the nearest emergency room.

It was mostly a blur to me, but I had the very vague and horrifying recollection of having told everyone, from the Swedish tourists to the turbaned taxi driver to the team of attending doctors and nurses to the receptionist who handed me a very large bill, that Nigel had just dumped me. I think I may have been sobbing all the while.

"Where are you?" I asked the Colonel, gathering the pieces of my dissertation that were scattered across the bed. I could hear him rustling something in the background that sounded like venetian blinds.

"I'm in my bedroom. In the big chair by the window," he replied matter-of-factly. "You know, the plush brown chair with the tan afghan. My grandmother knit it herself."

"Oh." This was slightly more detail than I had anticipated.

"But the point, you see, Ella, is that the camera crews are pounding on the front door, and they're all over the lawn, like ants. Not actual ants, of course. The ants are simply a metaphor. Do you understand?"

"A simile," I said groggily, trying to envision the Colonel in a plush brown armchair, ants swarming around him. "They were there yesterday, too," I explained. "I spoke to them. But instead of getting rid of them, I must have caused them to multiply. I still really don't understand this, though."

"It's a disaster" was all he said. "I need you to help me. Can you come right away?" I could have sworn I heard him mutter something under his breath.

Something like *the horror, the horror.*

The horror, indeed. The Colonel had not been kidding. Now dozens of local television stations and several of the networks had sent reporters. Vans sprouting large antennas littered the lawn. I pushed my way through the throng, muttering something about being family, but one of them recognized me from my moment of infamy.

"There she is," he yelled. "She's the Marxist! "

Suddenly the ants began to swarm, like they were coming in for the kill. I screamed and began swatting at them with a crutch while pushing my way toward the door.

"No," I heard another reporter yell. "She's the wrong one. We want that other woman. You know, the one who looks like Natasha on *Bullwinkle.*"

As I got closer to the house I could see the Colonel peering through an upstairs window. After a moment he appeared at the door and pulled me through, turning the bolts behind him.

"Oh Ella," he said. "It's so awful." He put his head on my shoulder and I could feel his body shake. "What happened to your foot?" he asked, looking down.

This was all very confusing, having him this close and this needy wearing only flannel boxer shorts and fuzzy slippers.

"First I slipped on some defrosted shrimp, and then I was in an automobile accident, and after that I fell in a pothole," I said truthfully.

He seemed perfectly satisfied with my answer. I patted him on the back awkwardly, while glancing around. His house was eerily quiet, and I realized that although the place was still in shambles, the workmen were nowhere in sight.

"Come," he said, taking my hand and pulling me through a side hallway. "We can talk in here."

We entered a plush sitting room that I had never seen before, which was a haven of chintz serenity given the state of the rest of his house. The walls were lined with bookshelves, and books and papers and empty glasses were strewn about as though he had been entertaining, which seemed peculiar; the last thing I knew, he had been as good as arrested by the British Airways crew.

"Were you having a party?" I asked.

He looked confused, but then he rallied. "Oh that," he said, waving a hand toward the table of empty wine bottles. "Well, yes, I had already scheduled my *Magic Mountain* discussion group before all of this other business began. I couldn't get out of it, though my heart wasn't really in it, I must confess. They all left rather abruptly when the ants appeared," he explained, opening the curtain for a moment to demonstrate. A toothless bearded man had his faced pressed to the window and was licking the glass. The Colonel grimaced and quickly pulled the curtain back.

"A *Magic Mountain* discussion group? You have an entire group devoted to discussing *The Magic Mountain?*"

"Yes. It's quite interesting, actually. We have an English professor from Georgetown who tutors us."

"How long have you been studying the book?"

"Going on a year, now," he said reflectively. "Though I confess to having supplemented my own reading with Cliff Notes," he said, clearing his throat. "We're at the part where winter sets in, and there is much talk of the outside temperature, as opposed to the daily fluctuations of Hans's body temperature. But I suppose that's not relevant just now."

"No," I agreed. "I wish you would tell me what's going on outside your house. I feel like I'm missing something kind of important."

"Let us sit," he said. "But not in here. I've changed my mind." I followed him down the hall into yet another wing of the house. We entered a recreation room the size of a high school gymnasium. But instead of a basketball court there were several televisions piled one on top of the other, all tuned to MTV. We sat on opposite ends of a metallic-framed couch, staring dumbly at a multitude of Britney Spears videos.

"I don't know where to begin, Ella," he said when the network switched to a Gap commercial.

"Well, begin somewhere, please." I had to shout to be heard over the ad. "Do you think we could turn the sound down?"

"Sorry," said the Colonel, brandishing several remotes and hitting the mute buttons.

"What happened at the airport, anyway?" I asked, finally able to hear myself speak.

"The airport. Right. Well, at the airport I was reminded that it is not legal in the United Kingdom to offer money to government officials. . . . I find it easier to travel in the developing world. They are much less fussy about these sorts of things. Don't you find that to be true?"

"Whoa. Back up here, please. Why did you offer them money?"

"It was awful," he said, pacing around the room.

He paused at the bar in the corner, complete with leather stools and an overhead wine rack, and poured himself a vodka tonic. I declined a drink, explaining that I had already loaded up on prescription painkillers.

"They took me from the plane into a little office and asked me question after question," he continued. "It was like being tortured, you know. In fact I'm quite certain that physical torture was going to be the next step. So I offered them money."

"You offered money to the police?"

"I was desperate. You know how it is. I said that I was a very important man in America and that they could not get away with this and why didn't I just pay a small gratuity and get this over with now."

"And what happened next?"

He stirred a piece of lime around in his glass with his pinkie, but he didn't answer. "I like your slippers," I told him.

"Thank you. They said I had made a really big mistake offering them money, and had just transformed an otherwise minor incident—unruly people are escorted off airplanes fairly routinely, apparently—into a criminal offense."

"So are they going to press charges?"

"Well, no. But they might have if it hadn't been for Veronica. You see, I had a little trouble controlling my temper."

"You didn't . . ."

He nodded. "I did. I couldn't help it. That policeman was so rude, Ella. And there was this lovely little model of a Boeing 747 sitting on the desk. It looked quite light, really. I mean who would have thought it could fly right through a window?"

"So then what happened?" I asked, not sure I really wanted to hear the rest of the story.

"Could you envision being married to me?" he asked instead. It sounded like more of a hypothetical question than an actual proposal. "You could join my *Magic Mountain* book group. Two is better than one, don't you think?"

Two marriage proposals in the space of two months. I was on a streak, though not necessarily such a good one. I couldn't think of anything to say. My mind was spectacularly empty. I felt light and free and could actually visualize the inner space between my ears: it was a deep purple and blue, like a Mark Rothko painting, I thought, wondering whether it was, in fact, Mark Rothko who painted those big abstracts. Hey, wasn't it Mark Rothko who slit his wrists over the sink so he wouldn't make a mess? I was feeling kindly toward Mark Rothko for being so considerate, and kindly toward the painkillers, and wondered how many I had left, and how long I could sustain this blissful state.

"Ella?"

"Oh, sorry. So what happened next?"

"I have quite a large house, you see. We could just stay in this wing until Veronica comes back with the money so that I can complete the renovation. It gets quite lonely here."

Oh why not marry him? Then again, maybe I should wait until my head was not full of abstract paintings to respond to his query. Would it be too crude to ask how quickly I could get on his health insurance plan, and whether his plan might retroactively cover my hospital visit? This was not entirely without interest. A relationship with an eccentric, albeit temporarily bankrupt, millionaire might not be the worst thing in the world.

"So how did you get out of Heathrow?" I asked, changing the subject. "Given what happened, I'm surprised they let you go."

"Yes, me too. But Veronica managed to sort it all out with a phone call. I had no idea these NUTS people were so well connected."

"Whom did she call?"

"No idea. They spoke in Russian for a while. Then she handed the phone to the policeman. Then he glared at me and told me to go home quietly."

"And where is Veronica now?"

"She had to leave quite suddenly. It was all very strange. A man came to the door looking for her this morning, and when I went into the kitchen to get her she was gone. . . . She didn't even have her coffee. . . . Probably she just went to the bank."

"And did you and Veronica . . . did you . . . hold hands and stuff?" The question was pathetic, but I needed to know.

"It was just business. She had been so helpful, and it seemed the least I could do was be friendly . . ."

He picked up the remote controls and scrambled the channels so that two televisions were playing silent music videos while one showed *The Simpsons,* and the other C-Span.

"I'm going to have to get home now," I lied, glancing at my watch. I was beginning to feel dizzy and nauseated and overwhelmed, and more than a little depressed. "Is there anything you need?"

"There is, in fact. Pizza," he said. "I need a pizza."

"With what on top?" I asked.

"Vegetarian. I'm a vegetarian," he said, pouring yet another drink. "I decided to become a vegetarian back in 1989, when I was staying on a farm in a small village in Bangladesh. I was living with a family of goat farmers . . ."

While pretending to listen, I called Dominoes. By the time the delivery man arrived and made his way through the crowd, however, the Colonel had passed out on the couch.

I shut off the bank of televisions, wrapped a couple of slices of pizza in a paper towel, and stuffed them in my bag to eat later. I paused to tidy up the room, gathering magazines and collecting empty glasses. I noticed a bottle of Windex sitting on the bar and began to spray randomly, wiping things clean. Carmen was not giving this room her all, I thought. I then put the rest of the pizza on the coffee table and covered the Colonel with a blanket. I was having fun playing house and thinking about the amazing ease of life while under the influence of Vicodan.

I let myself out the front door, fielding disappointed shouts that I was not the particular Marxist that the journalists had in mind—they seemed to want the Bullwinkle woman. I managed to push through the crowd, feeling no pain whatsoever when my crutch hit an exposed tree root and I fell into a thorny bush of roses.

The Unraveling. One unforeseen benefit of Eleanor's rather large inheritance from Engels was that Edward was suddenly around again, his disappearances less frequent for a while.

With her share of the money Eleanor decided to buy a house. It was not so much the desire to become a property owner that set her off house hunting, but rather the gamble that if she and Edward set up a real home together, he might see fit to stick around.

After weeks of searching, Eleanor and Edward settled on a modest suburban house at No. 7 Jew's Walk, in Lewisham, which they nicknamed "The Den."

Eleanor embarked on her domestic venture with optimism and wrote letters outlining her plans to cultivate her garden, and to buy pigeons, and to live happily ever after with Edward.

Before painting or planting seeds or shopping for furniture, she first threw herself at the task of sorting through the latest influx of her father's papers.

And though she and Edward continued to work together well—quite the revolutionary team, he quipped time and again—Eleanor knew that the deed on the house had failed to change the crux of things. They were still childless, and Edward continued to come and go as he pleased.

He showed enough tenderness to coax Eleanor through the rough spots, to keep her from throwing him out entirely. But the discordance took its toll: Eleanor was sick most of that winter, she couldn't seem to shake off the flu. She ate next to nothing and grew dangerously thin.

By their second Christmas in the house, the garden grew untended, and visitors commented that the house looked, if not unkempt, then unloved. During one of her more feverish nights spent alone with the flu she wrote to her sister Lavra that there was no point in having a home without children.

It was a blessing in disguise, thought Eleanor, when Edward hobbled home late one night, clutching his side. It was his kidney, the doctors said. He would need surgery—if he could afford it—followed by a long period of recuperation.

Eleanor offered to pay all of his bills, and to demonstrate her unending love she made Edward the sole benefactor of her will, leaving him not only all of her money—the bulk of which Edward had already spent—but her father's papers, as well as her personal possessions.

For weeks after the operation she tended to him, cleaning and bandaging his wound and spoon-feeding him. She wrote to a friend that he was a mere skeleton and could barely walk a few yards. But one day Edward proved her wrong and announced that a week by the sea—a week by the sea, alone—would do him good. Eleanor protested. She told him he was crazy; he couldn't possibly go anywhere. He could hardly stand!

But he went all the same, and came back with pneumonia.

No sooner did he recover then he staggered out of bed again. Off to the doctor in London, he announced, insisting on going alone. He borrowed more money from Eleanor and took a flat in London, explaining that he needed a place to recuperate between doctors' visits. Once, he was gone a month.

When Eleanor decided to refuse him a loan of money, gambling on the idea that maybe he would stay closer to home, things took an ugly turn. He began to blackmail Eleanor, threatening to disclose the truth about Freddy's paternity.

Eleanor was devastated, and turned to Freddy for solace. What she didn't realize at the time was that exposure of her father as a philanderer was really the least of her problems.

Chapter 14

After working for a while, I remembered the pizza in my pocketbook, which I then gave to Bob. I felt too queasy from the painkillers to eat, but Bob seemed to enjoy his meal; he was partial to the crust. We chatted amiably for a while about his being a pretty bird. It was a pleasant enough exchange, particularly given that he was about the best I could hope for in the way of company that night.

Bob sat on my shoulder awhile and shredded his meal into fine crumbs that stuck in my hair. Then he flew over to the desk, where he began to gnaw on my dog-eared copy of the *Marx-Engels Reader.*

The radio droned in the background as I made a specious attempt to clean up the apartment; the place still looked like a hurricane had blown through it, wreaking havoc and strewing consumer goods in its wake. The apartment even smelled like a hurricane, with several pounds of defrosted sea life having washed up on shore.

Bob screamed "Hi, Bob" some more in his charming British accent and I asked him politely to shut up so that I could listen to the news: a busload of tourists massacred in the Middle East; talk of hiking the minimum wage; cuts in education spending; film reviews; pesticides. It was pesticides that caught my attention. A new study . . . the repeated exposure to a group of commonly used pesticides caused a peculiar but consistent reaction in a group of little rhesus monkeys . . . the little rhesus monkeys kept repeating their mistakes. No matter how obvious the error, they could not correct their behavior. The little rhesus monkeys were stuck, destined to repeat their stupid mistakes for a lifetime.

I thought about that for a minute, and then I picked up the phone to call my father. I half hoped he wouldn't be home; voice mail was my preferred mode of communication, particularly when I was calling to ask for money.

Nigel answered the phone. It took me a couple of minutes to register the fact that Nigel was hanging out at my parents' house, eating a variety of teriyakied dinners, while I sat in my increasingly squalid apartment, dining with his bird.

He was polite but blunt. He said he was busy putting the finishing touches on his play for the premiere the next night.

"May I please speak to my father?" Just hearing his voice broke my heart all over again, a fact which I tried to disguise by sounding businesslike.

"See you then?" he asked. "You will come, won't you? I think it will really help explain things."

"Yeah, sure. Whatever. Can I speak to my dad, please?" I heard him summon my father. They were old friends already; he called him Morty.

"Hey, Dad," I said, shaken.

"Hello, Ella," he replied without much affection, and I instantly regretted having made the call. I began to fantasize about being a little girl in diapers, plunked down in the pesticide-ridden garden, chewing on a blade of grass.

"I'll come straight to the point, Dad. I need money."

"Ha! You need money? She needs money!" he shouted to my mother, and presumably to Nigel. "You need money again? Why don't you get a job?"

"Well, Dad," I said slowly, determined to control my temper, "as I think you must know, I *do* have a job, but my boss is kind of having cash-flow problems. And he never quite got around to giving me the health insurance forms to sign," I lied, "and now, well, I've broken my foot. I have a few hospital bills to pay—"

"Why can't you just get a real job, for god's sake?"

"What's a real job, Dad?" Despite my best efforts I could hear my voice dwindling into fourth-grade-like whining. "Is working at Value Giant the only real job in this world?"

"What's wrong with Value Giant, Ella? Value Giant has clothed you, fed you, and allowed you to attend some of the finest educational institutions this country has to offer. I'd say your sarcasm is misplaced."

Eeyore crawled onto my lap and began to purr and I stroked his neck.

"I'm not trying to be sarcastic, Dad. I'm just in a bind. Look . . . I'm almost done with my dissertation, and then . . . then I'm sure I'll get a real job. I'll pay you back, even. I just need you to help me with the hospital bills and give me enough money to fix my car. I'll take it from there."

Bob flew into the room and landed on my head, and he began to preen my hair. I realized I had forgotten to put him back into his cage, which usually involved bribing him in with a pretzel. Eeyore hissed, and I tried to keep an eye on the situation as Bob flew to the window, climbed up the venetian blinds, and hung upside down.

"To be perfectly frank, Ella, I was a bit put off by this Arthurdale business. I can't tell you how stunned I was to see you on the evening news. This nonsense has to stop. I'm a prominent businessman. I need a pinko daughter walking around talking about the evils of capitalism like I need a hole in the foot."

"In the head, Dad, I think is the expression. Listen, I was just trying to make a point about freedom of thought. I believe in America! I'm a registered Democrat . . . I voted for Bill Clinton, even."

"Let's not get started on *that*," he practically shouted. "Listen, I've gotta run . . . Nigel's calling me. We'll see you at Value Giant tomorrow night. I'll think about the money in the meantime. I'll try and come up with a loan plan."

Nigel needs him? I thought, puzzled. A loan plan? Would he charge me interest? Had alliances shifted this quickly that Nigel and my parents now formed the coherent unit of "we," with me cast in the role of an outside pronoun? I felt rejected in more ways than that. I had entertained visions of being involved with Nigel and his play. I had pictured us sitting up in bed late at night, drinking wine and discussing in great detail the character development of his protagonist and how to twist the plot just so. I had even entertained fantasies about a leading role. I thought I could be his muse.

I had admittedly entertained these fantasies at the same time that I had doubted his ability to complete a project of any sort whatsoever. But he had got on all right without me, it seemed.

I stared at my dissertation, but my head felt too foggy to do any further work, and my foot was beginning to throb again. I thought about ingesting another batch of painkillers—maybe even two batches, just for good measure—and climbing back into bed to sleep for a few days.

I hobbled into the kitchen to get the pills, but the phone rang before I could pry the childproof cap off the bottle.

The caller identified himself as Eddie, Jr. "I was beginning to think I'd never reach you at home," he said gruffly. "I've been trying you for about a week now."

"Yeah, well, I've been busy," I said in the belligerent tone he seemed to invite. "How did you find me? I mean, how do you even know who I am?"

"You're a public figure now," he said. "You've been on television. And besides, *mi amiga* Carmen over at the Institute of Thought, she said I could reach you at this number."

"Yeah, but you called here before my speech on TV," I said, spooked. "And besides, how did you know I was the person who you met on the Internet?"

"Don't tell me you're one of those quaint people who still believe there's anything like privacy left in this world."

I thought about that for a minute and replied that I supposed I was.

"We should get together," said Eddie Jr. "In person. I know something you might find interesting."

"Why don't you just tell me on the phone. I mean, it's awfully late to meet."

"No. It's personal, you see. Why don't I just come over?"

"No . . . no . . . that's not a good idea. My place is a mess. Let's meet tomorrow at . . ." I tried to think of a nice public place should he turn out to be the total lunatic that he probably was. "How about Java Books? The one near Georgetown. Meet me in the coffee shop around one o'clock."

Eddie Jr. agreed, and I hung up the phone and contemplated the bottle of pills for a minute before setting it back on the shelf. Just then I heard a horrendous shrieking noise coming from the bedroom.

It was as bad as I'd feared. Eeyore lay curled by the window with bits of feathers pasted to his mouth.

I decided to splurge and order something fancy, finally deciding on chai, which tasted pretty good even if it felt intuitively stupid to pay $3.95 to sit in a trendy café and sip Indian tea. Particularly when I only had ten borrowed dollars in my wallet.

I had nearly finished my drink and was beginning to give up on Eddie Jr. when he appeared, twenty minutes late.

He looked like a man who had forgotten to take his medication. Or then again, he might have been a man suffering the debilitating side effects of medication, e.g., the spittle accumulating on the side of his mouth.

"What happened to your foot?" he asked.

I launched into my convoluted story about potholes and shrimp and Swedish tourists and he nodded his head knowingly, as if he was thoroughly familiar with such personal calamities.

"So, you're Eddie Jr.," I said after an awkward pause. I extended my hand to shake his, but he pulled away and explained in slightly slurred speech that he "didn't do shakes." Which actually suited me just fine, as he seemed to be covered in a spotty rash. "I heard you were just a netmyth, but here you are, the man himself, in the flesh."

"I prefer to think of myself as an icon," he said. "Rather than as a man or a myth."

"Oh," I said. I tried to picture him as an icon; did he fancy himself a human icon, or something more abstract? Something you worship, or something you double-click on? I wasn't sure how to frame the question, so I did not try.

"So, like, how exactly did you come to be Eddie Jr.?" I finally asked. "Or rather, the icon of Eddie Jr.?" This seemed so clearly to be a joke that I felt relieved of all pretense of professionalism. As I stared at this sad specimen of an Eddie Jr., I started to wonder if, in fact, this was not some sort of premeditated, highly orchestrated prank put on by Lisa, or by the Colonel, or by my father, even, to demonstrate that I was in way over my head.

"My great-grandmother was, like, um, Eleanor Marx. You know, Eleanor Marx Aveling. I was named after Edward."

"So Edward was your great-grandfather. Which seems a little odd, since most historians believe that he never had any children, even with all of his philandering. . . . And besides, wouldn't that make you Eddie Jr. . . . Jr. . . . Jr.? I mean, wait a minute . . ." I pulled a pen from my bag and began to draw a family tree on a napkin. "I'm not very good at this, this is too much like math . . . but her son would have been Eddie Jr. and then his son—which is your father, right?—would be Eddie Jr. Jr. What is that, Eddie Sr.? Sorry . . . And then I'm assuming that the original Eddie Jr.'s offspring was a male, as well, which is pretty sexist of me, isn't it . . ."

Eddie Jr. mercifully cut me off. "I never said that I was Edward's son," said Eddie Jr., reaching for a napkin to mop up the bits of spittle that had sprayed onto the table.

"You never said what?" I tried. The café was filling up quickly, and I was half looking around for the prankster, or the hidden camera that would record the film footage that would later appear on *America's Funniest Home Videos of Failed Ph.D. Candidates.*

"I never said that my grandfather, my great-grandfather I mean, was Edward Aveling."

"I'm sorry," I said, "but I don't really get this. Who exactly was your great-grandfather, then?"

"Freddy."

"Freddy?"

"You know. Freddy Demuth."

"Couldn't be. Freddy Demuth was Eleanor's half brother."

"Well, you know how close they became in the end. She knew Edward was screwing around on her. And she and Freddy became . . . how shall I say . . . *very close.*"

"So," I said, leaning forward so as not to miss any piece of this fabulously weird story, "why are you called *Eddie* Jr., as opposed to, say, *Freddy* Jr.?"

"Eleanor didn't want Edward to know she was sleeping with Freddy, of course. So she named the baby after him."

"And why does this little piece of information not appear in any history books?"

"Well, we all know how manipulative Edward was. He knew the baby wasn't his, and he forced Eleanor to give it away. That added to her depression in the end, you see. *No one ever gets that fact,*" he practically shouted. "I mean, what the hell do people think made her so depressed in the end?"

I stared at him, trying to process this bizarre information. Eleanor was often depressed, it seemed to me. And she had plenty of reason to be.

"*She was postpartum!*" Eddie said, banging his fist on the

table. People turned and stared at us. I was almost getting used to causing scenes in public places by now. *"She was totally motherfucking depressed. They took that little baby away from her. It was the only thing she had left."* His eyes welled up with tears.

Was this plausible? I mean, she did seem overly moody and melodramatic in the end.

I felt particularly stupid sitting there as Eddie Jr. began to sob.

While his story was in part corroborated by his potentially inbred condition, I felt the overwhelming need to get away from him. I felt like he was some sort of blinking neon message—he looked the way I felt.

Still, I didn't want to cut him off completely. What if his story were somehow true? The Colonel would be ecstatic: it really could put the Institute of Thought on the map. On the other hand, it was pretty scary to realize that I had stooped to this level of thought. I was as nuts as the character sitting across from me. I was as nuts as NUTS.

"Listen," I lied, "I've got to go just now, but it's been really delightful getting to know you. I'd love to talk further. Is there some way of contacting you, other than on the Internet?"

Eddie Jr. said he was sure that he had a telephone number and an address somewhere, and began to rummage through his briefcase. He piled onto the table several bottles of pills and a bunch of used tissues. Eventually he located a crumpled business card.

· EDWARD AVINGTON III
ADJUNCT PROFESSOR OF MARXIST ECONOMICS
GEORGE WASHINGTON UNIVERSITY

"You're a professor at GW?" I nearly screamed.

"I was. Now I'm not."

"Why not?"

"They closed the department several years ago."

"Oh," I said. I knew how he felt. Marx was a dead man in more ways than one, and he was dragging those few of us who bothered to retain any interest in him into the cold dark ground, too.

I took another look at the card and had a thought.

"Let me ask you something," I tried. "Were you drawn to the saga of Edward Aveling because of your similarities in names?"

"Well, actually," said Eddie Jr., suddenly animated and articulate and less drooly, "it's funny you should ask. It was in college that I came across a reference to Aveling, and I started to dig deeper, and then I became fascinated and then totally obsessed. . . . *He had a voice like a euphonium*—that's what they used to say about him, you know. Someone once said that to me."

I felt my cheeks flush, thinking about being not unlovely. "And at what point did you discover you *were* actually Eddie Jr.?" I asked delicately.

"It was shortly after I lost my job," he replied, confirming my suspicions.

"Does that cast come off?" he asked quite suddenly.

I looked down at my foot, surprised. "Yes. It sort of snaps off at the side, so that I can shower. Why?"

"You should soak it."

"Soak what? The cast?"

"No, your foot. Go stick it in a hot tub or something. It will really help."

I thanked Eddie Jr. for the medical advice and said that I would call him, and we would keep in touch. I meant what I said. We were kindred spirits. Which was a pretty sad thing to have to admit—even to myself.

I had some time to kill before venturing off to Rockville for some theater of the absurd. I didn't particularly want to go home, where Bob's empty cage served as a painful reminder of the state of my relations with his former owner. And in my podiatrically challenged condition simply wandering around Georgetown, or even browsing in Java Books, threatened to be both painful and impractical.

Like a dog heading home to the master who beats him, I made my way into the institute and inconspicuously slid down the stairs to the basement. The Colonel's house may have been only moments away from official condemnation, but at least the computer still worked, so far as I knew.

Bitter Almonds. Eleanor slowly shed responsibilities, like a bird molting feathers for the spring. First, she resigned from several of the political organizations with which she was affiliated; then she cleared her desk of the bits and pieces of remaining literary projects. She began to turn down social invitations without explanation. She grew even thinner.

Edward returned again after a few weeks. He had managed to recover from each scrape with mortality, but was visibly weaker. His pale skin was nearly translucent, his hair long and stringy, and although he could walk, he was nearly bent double in pain much of the time.

Eleanor joked to friends that she and Edward had simply gone into hibernation for the winter. Spring was on the way, she said. Soon they would emerge, refreshed. But the postman brought a letter before the flowers began to bloom.

The morning began in typical fashion: the maid, Gertrude Gentry, brought them tea and toast and a stack of newspapers, and the couple chatted amiably about the weather—chilly but clear—and the latest political developments. They discussed their plans for the day, which consisted of little other than Edward's trip into London to visit with doctors.

As usual, Eleanor insisted on coming with Edward. Edward refused her company. Gertrude returned to the room with a fresh pot of tea and the morning post. She handed Eleanor a letter and watched her mistress begin to tremble.

Edward rose from the table as if in slow motion and demanded Eleanor hand him the envelope. Eleanor refused. She tucked it into the folds of her dress and ran out into the garden. Gertrude later claimed she had heard her scream.

Eleanor, it seemed, was among the last to know: Edward had gone and got married about a year ago, and his new wife was growing impatient.

Eva Frye thought she should introduce herself to Eleanor by way of post, since she half suspected Edward had neglected to tell her himself.

Who is she? Eleanor demanded, screaming.

Nobody special. Just an actress, Edward said. She had been in one of his plays, recently. She means nothing to me, he insisted, grabbing hold of Eleanor's hand. She was one of those prim and proper types. Wouldn't sleep with him until they were married.

But what about his wife? What about Belle? Eleanor asked. Her entire body was shaking, and Edward tried to pull her close. She backed away from him, bumping into the garden wall.

Belle had died a while back, he confessed. He was sure he must have told her.

It doesn't mean a thing, he insisted. I didn't even use my real name on the marriage certificate. I said I was Alec Nelson, I lied about my name and my father's name and my address. I even shaved a few years off my age, he said, laughing. So you see, it doesn't mean a thing. I'm sure it can be nullified.

What does she want? Why is she writing to me?

She wants money, Edward explained. She wants money and then she won't say a thing about this to anyone.

Eleanor said he could have all of her money then. She didn't need it anymore. Life was not worth living. Edward didn't argue.

He called for Gertrude, who was clearing up their dishes. He handed her one of his calling cards and scribbled a note on the back before sending her off to the chemist.

Tell the chemist I'll come round to pay him later, Edward instructed.

Dr. Aveling had always been very kind to her, Gertrude would later tell the coroner. Sometimes she almost thought he fancied her. Curiosity got the better of her and she read the note: "Please give bearer chloroform and small quantity prussic acid for the dog, E.A." Gertrude wondered about that for a minute; the dog hadn't seemed particularly unwell, but what did she know about animals? Besides, her reading wasn't so good. Perhaps she simply didn't understand the message.

Edward dressed and then went off to London to his appointment. Or was he gone already when Gertrude returned from the chemist? She couldn't really remember. It hadn't seemed important at the time.

She returned to her round of morning duties, and by the time she opened Eleanor's door to make up her room and collect her washing, it was too late. Her face was a pale blue. The room smelled peculiar, not unlike bitter almonds, she later said.

Chapter 15

Friday night, rush hour, strip malls galore, the neon sign for Value Giant beckoned like a tease several gridlocked blocks ahead. I rolled my heap of crunched metal and shattered glass down Rockvillee Pike, ignoring the pitiful stares of fellow motorists. For lack of a better solution, I had retrieved my car from the body shop that afternoon. It might have looked like hell, but once they fixed the radiator it ran well enough to get me where I needed to go, and besides, the likelihood of scraping together a couple thousand dollars for the repair bill any time soon seemed doubtful.

The wind began to blow, violent and sudden and totally out of the blue on an otherwise magnificent evening, and I prayed for a hurricane, or a tornado, or even an earthquake, to relieve me of the night ahead.

I was all for the idea of bringing culture to the people. Puppet shows at the playground were good. Rock concerts in the rat-infested stairwells of the New York City subway stations could sometimes be uplifting. Once-famous violinists from the Moscow Philharmonic reduced to peddling for handouts on the street corner I could comprehend. But the idea of staging a play at Value Giant? Bringing art to this vast land of discount merchandising struck me as a contradiction in terms. But maybe I was wrong; behind the curve, once again. Shopping, after all, was said to be entertainment. So perhaps theater-in-the-discount-department-store was, in fact, the next new thing..

In any event, I felt the need to go. I longed to see Nigel, if only to further my dispassionate study of the man. I planned to disguise myself as just another detached member of the audience, suppressing the fact that I had had an epiphany of sorts: I had come to the realization that our falling out was all my fault. I shouldn't have nagged him so much about his wedding ring, or his sloppiness, or his elusiveness, or his many other totally inconsequential character flaws. And I should not have gone on about these absurd Eleanor Marx and Edward Aveling parallels. I was a shrew who had driven away the man I loved by thinking too hard.

This had occurred to me as I sat with paper and pencil, trying to solve the new equation: Bowerbirds + Wife + Rain - Dalmatian + Logger = ? I hadn't figured out the answer, but instead had recalled how sweet he had been with our pets, which had convinced me he would make a wonderful father. And I also remembered how cute he was in that stupid winter coat of his, and how sexy he looked in the morning, wrapped in a towel, shaving (on occasion), and then I began to cry again.

Although I desperately wanted to tell him these things, I had resolved to muster some self-respect and assume the attitude of a person who did not care. Plus, I had to confess to reading something into the ominous foreshadowing and profound symbolism of the bird-swallowed-by-the-cat business. Still, as I sucked the mess of bones and beak up the plastic vacuum hose while Eeyore stared at me curiously, I tried to shrug it off as a mere coincidence.

My father greeted me coolly, my mother lukewarmly. We stood awkwardly in the luggage department, near where the stage had been assembled. They obviously believed that the breakup with

Nigel had been my fault, and their collective mood was not unlike the time they had set me up with David Vanderbilt IV, who was nominally related to Gloria and was poised to inherit the yacht club that my parents belonged to. I had said truthfully after an expensive dinner that we hadn't clicked. What, was I too good for him, my mother had asked accusingly.

My mood began to shift subtly, and I wanted to explain that I was not entirely at fault here. That they ought to at least consider the possibility that Nigel might have contributed to the problem. But I kept silent.

I excused myself politely, surprised to have spotted Lisa in the crowd.

She was arm in arm with Paul, and she introduced us to each other. I was sort of surprised by her latest choice in man. He looked manufactured: his teeth were too white and his hair was too black and he wore a heavy gold chain around his neck. I couldn't understand the attraction.

"What are you doing here?" I asked in disbelief.

"Are you kidding? They were advertising this on the back of every bus in town. It was written up in the Style section this morning. I wouldn't have missed it for the world. They're already saying this is going to be the twenty-first century's answer to Shakespeare in the Park."

"That's kind of a depressing thought," I mumbled, staring at a giant banner overhead that heralded a half-price sale on bath towels. "How are you feeling?" I glanced inadvertently at her rounded stomach. Lisa took my question as an opportunity to bring me up to date on her love life. She and Paul had just spent the weekend in Paris, she explained. While walking through the Louvre hand in hand they had decided that this was the real thing; they planned to move in together next month. They would have five children between them once the baby was born, she continued, and naturally, they wanted a few of their own. The only glitch was that Paul's wife was threatening to kill them both. She had, in fact, just purchased a small firearm. She sent Lisa nasty postcards in the mail each day. One had arrived that morning. It contained several uppercase letters cut out from a magazine and pasted together to form the word WHORE. Hayden saw the card lying around and asked what w-h-o-r-e spelled and she said it was just an advertisement for a new perfume. Their respective lawyers were trying to work things out, seeking restraining orders and injunctions and counter restraining orders and counter injunctions. She said all of this quite matter-of-factly, though Paul seemed to be a bit tense. All in all the conversation did nothing to revise my thinking of Lisa as my ex–best friend.

I looked around for Nigel, but was informed that the distinguished playwright was not available to greet his estranged fiancée, as he was currently busy with photographers and reporters from the Rockville *Gazette*.

Someone thrust a glass of cheap Chilean wine in my hand and I drank it eagerly, mildly worried about the interaction with the painkillers, but hoping for a higher state of clarity. Santiago sauvignon, the label boasted. The vintage had been conspicuously etched out.

How had this happened so quickly? Just a few weeks ago he was an unemployed ornithologist with the secret ambition to write a play. Now, at his very first production, he had a full house and his own, albeit local, paparazzi.

I found my father again and, after much prodding and threatening and harassing, he finally confessed that he had hired his mega public relations firm to coordinate this opening night extravaganza. They had sent press releases to every major news organization claiming that this was an historical tie-in between bulk discounting and deep theater.

"Why?" I asked.

Because Nigel was the most charming man he had ever met, was his simple reply.

"But this isn't fair," I quite literally screamed. "You're willing to fund this gala event, but you're still jerking me around financially, when all I want is money to pay my hospital bills and get my degree. Plus my car is a bit messed up," I added, lowering my voice.

"Calm down," my father instructed as he pulled me into an isolated corner stocked with thousands of cans of dog food. His naturally ruddy face was even more red. Had he been a cartoon character, steam would have been pouring through his ears.

"You're embarrassing me in front of my employees. Look, Ella, I'm not going to walk away from you and your problems . . . it's just that your needs become overwhelming sometimes what with all of these graduate school bills pouring in. I'm going to help you, but let me be clear that it won't be another free ride. Just give me some time to work out the kinks. And pull yourself together," he scolded.

My initial urge was not to pull myself together, but to let myself go entirely. To throw a temper tantrum. I imagined how satisfying it would be to lie down on the floor and start kicking cans off the shelves. But even when my father had reduced me to the emotional age of two, I understood intellectually that such a response was neither dignified nor demonstrative of self-respect.

So I wandered off in search of another glass of Santiago sauvignon, instead. I was no longer aiming for clarity, but looking instead for total inebriation.

The first act was as advertised: the play was about birds. There were white birds and gray birds and large birds and small birds. Mostly the birds flew across the stage, eliciting oohs and aahs from the audience while a single violin played in the background. Personally I thought it was kind of stupid.

My epiphany stood itself upside down somewhere toward the beginning of the second act, however, when the mellifluous voice of my ex-boyfriend began to narrate the tale of doomed love while the birds continued to fly around overhead. I was no longer sure that I wanted to offer apologies as much as bolt onto the stage and strangle the man. That was just about the time the birds disappeared, and were replaced by an actor and an actress and something became disturbingly clear: *he was writing about us.*

The female lead was a brilliant but neurotic scholar of classical Marxism who fell in love with an evasive ornithologist. Together they roamed the aisles of Value Giant, looking for good deals on major household appliances, including a new coffeemaker.

I could tell from a variety of largely meaningless incidents that had occurred in the course of our brief relationship (e.g., my breakdown over the pressed duck Santa Fe) that he was not making a single thing up, except for the fact that we had never visited a Value Giant together.

He had not been busy scribbling late into the night so much as running a tape recorder.

I couldn't help but observe that the female lead was not very attractive. In fact it was hard to understand the attraction at all. Her hair was positively atrocious. I was not quite *that* unlovely, I wanted to protest. I weighed at least ten pounds less, at any rate.

She was constantly badgering the ornithologist about his past. Overanalyzing the mating habits of birds. Always trying to read his mind. And reading things into things. She drove everyone around her crazy.

And yet if I could totally set aside my ego (which I was not at all sure I could), I had to admit that bits of the play—the commentary on shopping anyway—were pretty funny.

Yes, Nigel seemed to be saying, this was our culture and it was god-awful and pathetic and noisy and devoid of any spirituality and yet who were we to judge? Looking for a good bargain was a legitimate pursuit, as meaningful a way to pass the time as reciting poetry on a picnic blanket. Sort of.

But then the plot began to twist and turn and a dozen green

birds, all of whom looked like Bob, flew on to the stage. I groped my way to the back of the room and grabbed yet another glass of wine, attempting to siphon off the bits of stray cork floating around in the liquid. I had the sudden, absurd idea that if I could manage to catch one of these green birds, I could take it home and stick it in Bob's cage.

"Never thought he had it in him," said the woman next to me.

"Yeah, me neither," I said reflexively. I wasn't really paying attention, but instead was wondering if a bird could survive an hour or so inside my pocketbook. I caught a glimpse of the woman and did a double take. She looked like me. Clearly she must have thought that I looked like her, 'cause our eyes locked and I felt something like tangible and instant hostility and I knew she was Lily before she told me as much.

"Weird coincidence, isn't it?" she said, extending her hand. "Lily Lark."

I shook her hand even though I really wanted to pull her hair out in what must have been some sort of primal, biological, uncontrollable, instinctual, Darwinian preservation of the nuclear family mating kind of thing. Because, under other circumstances, she looked like someone I would like to go have coffee with.

"He's a real drain on emotional resources," she said by way of breaking the ice. "I'd leave while you can. Leave him before it gets ugly."

"What do you mean?" I asked, stunned by this blunt pronouncement. The woman on my other side put her finger to her lips suggesting I be quiet. "What happened with you guys?" I whispered. But the other woman glared at me again, and we both turned and watched the play for a while.

Things were not as they seemed, it seemed, to quote my new friend, Eddie Jr. Jr. Jr. The not so brilliant young scholar of classical Marxism was always picking on him and quizzing him about the past and forcing him to engage in small talk. He explained all this to the clerk at Value Giant when he came back a few weeks later to return the gas barbecue grill he and his fiancée had purchased. (Where would we have put a gas barbecue grill, I wondered? On the balcony of our one-room apartment facing onto Connecticut Avenue?)

"Did something really tragic happen with you two?" I whispered, pulling her toward the back of the room.

"Define tragic," said Lily.

"I don't know . . . he just seems so shattered. I kind of thought maybe you two had been in an accident or something. Or . . . I don't know . . . lost a baby or survived a tidal wave or—"

"No. I just couldn't take it anymore. It was like he was there but not there. Five years and all he ever talked about were birds. I paid our rent and I bought his clothes and beyond that there was this huge disconnect. He was in bird land all the time. He turned our backyard in London into a goddamned rain forest. I'm not sure he even knew what I did to earn a living. . . . I tolerated it, justified it, until we got to New Guinea, and this thing happened with Bud."

"Bud?" Nigel was right in one respect, with a character named Bud, this was definitely not Romeo and Juliet.

"Yeah. Bud was a logger from New Zealand. It was stupid and meaningless and in retrospect it was a mistake, but I thought maybe I'd get his attention."

"And?"

"He went insane. I mean really. It kind of took me by surprise, 'cause I didn't think he'd even care. He went over to the northern part of the island and found Bud and punched him in some stupid macho gesture. I don't think Bud would have hurt him, but some of the other loggers saw this and they thought it was funny—you know, Nigel, all lanky, trying to beat up on a two-hundred-pound logger. They roughed him up kind of badly. . . .

"Apparently he wandered out of their camp and sat down under a tree and started going on about birds and monogamy and rattling off statistics. This is what Bud told me, anyway. I was back in our cabin, down the hill, packing."

I couldn't believe what I was hearing; this was such an incredibly sad story and I felt so bad for poor Nigel. I winced at the image of him being tortured by beefy loggers, especially after suffering the knowledge that his wife was sleeping with Bud.

"So what about the rain?" I asked, needing to create a clearer picture.

"Does he still have that rain phobia thing? It happened to be raining. That's all. He sat down under a tree and he was pretty badly beaten up and it rained. It poured, I guess, and he simply freaked out. . . . It was about twenty-four hours until they got a medic to him. . . . I mean, it was awful, and I was responsible, but it seemed to be where we were headed all along. He said he'd give me another chance, but I couldn't go back there, you know?

"When we got back to England, I served him with divorce papers, but he apparently tore them up. I've been trying to serve this guy papers for almost a year, but every time I find him, he tears them up and moves again. Just about two months ago I tracked him down in Georgetown, but by the time I got the papers there, they told me he was gone again. It doesn't matter anymore, though. The divorce is official, despite his best efforts."

"You're divorced?" I asked excitedly. I was still looking for the bright side.

"Officially as of a month ago, but I hadn't been able to find him to tell him the news. Like I said, he just keeps moving. Then I saw this advertised on the metro."

"What do you do anyway?"

"I'm a veterinary surgeon."

"Wow. You're a veterinary surgeon," I repeated, wondering how a woman smart enough to get through vet school could put up with Nigel for five years.

The play meandered along as we spoke, but I wasn't paying too much attention until the end, when the couple had a confrontation in the rain forest. While they argued about his being aloof, a bowerbird wove a piece of rope around a twig. The wife had shouted to him one last time that she was leaving, that she was taking a walk, heading north, toward the logger station up the hill. The ornithologist had shouted in return that she really should come look; the bird had found a couple of gold bangles—they looked like hers, in fact—and had hung them on a branch.

I jangled my wrist and Lily looked at my bangles with amusement.

"Keep them," she said. "I'm not that sentimental."

I drank another glass of wine, but was still unable to achieve the level of alcohol poisoning required to get me through the end of this evening. I glanced at the bottle. It contained only one percent alcohol. I would have to drink an entire case just to get a small buzz.

The play ended with a single violin playing in the background as the playwright walked through the revolving doors of the department store, laden with shopping bags and lessons of modern life and the meaninglessness thereof. He was, apparently, moving on to Miami.

The sound of heavy sobbing filled the room as the makeshift curtain went up and a wave of unending applause began. There were several ovations, during which time I decided to drink the wine directly from the bottle while I watched the reporters mob Nigel. It looked like his fifteen minutes of fame were bound to be more promising than mine had been.

I tried to push my way backstage. I wanted to tell Nigel that I understood. Or that I thought I understood, though I could not really articulate what, exactly, there was to understand. He thought he was a bird? A monogamous bird, with a monogamous bird wife? Wasn't there a word for that—something like anthropomorphism? Or. . . . I had come to understand that he was a repressed, sort of disturbed man? Or, I understood that his great tragedy was that his wife had an affair with a logger named Bud?

Whatever it was I was supposed to understand, I wanted to tell him that I could help him through this, that we could definitely marry now that he was officially divorced. But I saw him surrounded by photographers and by my family and by his mother, even, and he was smiling hugely and laughing, like a load had been lifted off his shoulders.

I was leaning on the emergency exit of Value Giant smoking the cigarette I had bummed from a cashier in the sporting goods department when the Colonel appeared, looking dapper but tipsy.

"Quite a good performance," he said. "Did you notice that the lead character looked a bit like you? And she was a political theorist, too. What a strange coincidence!"

"Indeed," I said, coughing on the smoke, that the wind had blown back in my face. "I'm surprised to see you up and about. No offense, but you were kind of a wreck when I saw you last."

"Yes, well, things did not go exactly as planned with this NUTS thing, as you might have guessed. It threw me for a loop, financially as well as psychologically. I needed a drink or two to get through it."

I gave him a skeptical look that said that I didn't buy his excuse—he needed a drink or two to get through daily life, at this point.

"Veronica has been arrested," he continued, nearly whispering. "They may want to charge me as an accessory, but I've retained a lawyer—well, my nephew agreed to take me on pro bono, actually—and he seems confident I can claim to have had no prior knowledge."

"Prior knowledge of what?" I asked, holding tight to my scarf so it wouldn't blow away.

"Knowledge that NUTS was just a front. Their money was tainted. Mafia money, apparently. Which my lawyer says shouldn't really affect me, since I never saw a penny of it."

"Nor did I," I couldn't help but add.

He ignored me and continued. "This whole catalogue idea, it was just a scam, Ella. It was a front for some Slavic prostitution ring they seemed to have going. They just needed to generate some hard currency. Veronica was some sort of infamous madam. . . . They were also dealing a bit in arms, on the side. They had no interest in putting a new face on Karl Marx. . . . I just can't believe I was so stupid. . . . and now my house, it's a total disaster and I don't have the money to finish it. . . . And it's not just my house. The whole institute . . ."

I tried to think of something positive to say, to be a glass half full kind of person. "It's not a complete failure," I offered. "You still have the Kyrgyz, don't you?"

"Well I suppose that's true," he said, brightening a bit. "And I suppose we could always see if we can't get the Kyrgyz to recommend us to their friends. We could build on what we have. There's still hope, isn't there?"

"Of course there is," I lied.

He pulled the flask from his pocket and I took him by the arm and led him toward my wreck of a car.

"Come, I'll drive you home," I said, completely sober despite my best efforts. "You can pick up your car in the morning."

Mrs. Warren's Profession. Eleanor's history gets unearthed from time to time, often for the oddest of reasons. After an interview with Marx's great-grandson, M. Robert Jean Longuet, ran in the *New Yorker* magazine some forty years ago, one reader wrote a letter to the editor explaining his own obsession with Eleanor Marx's story, which was sparked by the following lines in Bernard Shaw's play *Mrs. Warren's Profession:*

"Where are you going to?" Frank calls after her. "Where shall we find you?"

"At Honoria Fraser's chambers, 67, Chancery Lane, for the rest of my life," Vivie replies.

Number 67, Chancery Lane happened to be the address of one highly inquisitive man named Felix Barker, who, after pondering this coincidence for a while, decided to write George Bernard Shaw a letter, seeking enlightenment. Shaw wrote back, explaining that he had chosen that address because Karl Marx's daughter Eleanor had once lived there with Edward Aveling, and that she had "suicided" there when she found out he had married another woman.

Mr. Barker wrote to *The New Yorker* that he began to imagine his room peopled with the ghosts of a variety of famous figures, including Aveling and William Morris and Keir Hardie. He envisioned Eleanor moving about the room, pouring strong coffee.

And so he began to dig, and thereby unearthed Eleanor's saga, stringing it together for a brief publication in the Department of Amplification.

He was to learn that his interest was purely the result of a fluke. Eleanor had not, in fact, ever lived at 67 Chancery Lane, but rather at 65 Chancery Lane, and Mr. Barker writes that he had to readjust his fantasy now to pretending that he could see Eleanor in her flat just outside his window.

Shaw had gotten one more small fact wrong. Eleanor's suicide had taken place at The Den, and not at Chancery Lane.

But it hardly matters. The details get muddled with the passage of time even if, as they say, God is in them.

Epilogue

When I arrived home, I took every pill left in the bottle of Vicodan, but that only amounted to three, and all I learned was that I had a startlingly high tolerance for painkillers. For days, I contemplated starving myself to death but could hardly make it from meal to meal as it was, and my moody and tragic dreams about Nigel were increasingly punctuated by more compelling dreams about food, such as the one about a bean and cheese burrito smothered in sour cream.

Still, having a breakdown seemed like the thing one ought to do after my convergent and humiliating debacles. It was what Eleanor would have done. It was what I tried to do, but it was just not so easy to arrange.

Spending my days sitting on a pile of wood-chip mulch, staring at the empty birdcage and weeping not only proved unproductive, but boring, so after a couple of weeks of self-pity I did the only thing I could think of to break my miserable spell: I packed up my bags, threw Eeyore in the car, and headed back up the turnpike, toward New York.

My return proved altogether less traumatic than anticipated. Ira and his wife were surprisingly understanding about my train wreck of a thesis. While unqualifiedly rejecting the paper, he did note that I had indeed made Eleanor's life political, yet in the end,

I had made it personal again via my emotive dissertation. I had come full circle, he said. Despite his upbeat tone, I understood this to be a backhanded compliment: what he was really saying was that I had come full circle and ended up precisely where I began. Nowhere. Or to be more descriptive: in New York, broke, without my degree.

Still, Ira and I have reached a sort of détente: we have an appointment to go over new ideas for dissertation topics, and his wife has even volunteered to make us dinner when we meet next week.

The staff at Julio's seemed happy to see me, which was truly touching. Working the night shift, which is generally pretty quiet, gives me plenty of time to contemplate topics. One idea is to further pursue the Eddie Jr. Jr. Jr. story, which seems to me a pretty good vehicle for describing the human toll of the decline of Marxism in the twenty-first century. Another thought is to write something about the exploitation of waitresses in America. Perhaps there is an international angle to consider, though that could require a bit of travel.

Yes, I do sometimes consider the possibility of giving up on my quest for a Ph.D. I would certainly not be the first person in the course of human history to have quit in the middle of something, and besides, I could argue that it is possibly more productive to cut my losses now, sort of like walking away from the craps table when you are down to your last two chips.

It is only when my father calls to remind me of his proposal—he will forgive my accumulated debts and throw in a new car to boot if I will simply enroll in the management training program at Value Giant—that I recall my burning passion for political theory and redouble my efforts to come up with a groundbreaking topic.

I have not heard from Nigel since the night of his performance, but my parents report that he is indeed at Parrot Jungle, where he has convinced the owners to let him stage his play on weekends, with a trial run through the summer.

And the Colonel is doing reasonably well, given the circumstances. Carmen called to report that a giant oak tree fell on his roof during the windstorm on the night of the Value Giant perfor-mance, which she described as a blessing in disguise. The insur-ance money had proven enough to restore the institute to its former state of damp grace, and the Colonel, who had sustained minor injuries while asleep in his bed, had been thrown into a pri-vate detox center by his estranged wife, who technically owned the house and had therefore been summoned by the police.

We speak often, the Colonel and I. Now that he is sober he seems to have no recollection of the fact that he expressed a ro-mantic interest in me just a few short weeks ago. I'm assuming this is because he is more inhibited when sober. This is better than thinking that he proposed to me only because he was very drunk. In any event, he is warm and kind, and frequently urges me to re-turn to work for him, or at least to come visit. I still have my health club membership, and we could sit in the Jacuzzi and soak my foot, he says. His invitation is not without appeal.

I had not heard from Lisa until the day she showed up at my door, unannounced. She had her newborn strapped to her chest in some newfangled baby carrier, and she was crying. I took her in my arms and tried to console her, concerned yet secretly pleased to learn that even Lisa experienced occasional moments of weakness.

I invited her in and urged her to let me hold the baby, whom she had named Jayne.

"She's absolutely beautiful . . . and I'm so glad to see you." I meant both things sincerely. There was a way in which my es-trangement from Lisa had cut even deeper than other painful recent events. "How is Hayden dealing with his sister?" I asked, suddenly feeling a surge of genuine affection for the dreaded toddler.

"Not bad," she explained, "but the whole thing with Roger and Paul has been sort of difficult for him. He's been a little demand-ing." A little *more* demanding, I silently corrected.

"Well, what's the status of the whole Roger/Paul thing?" I asked, petting Eeyore, who had crawled onto my lap to get a better view of Jayne. I wasn't sure Eeyore had ever seen such a tiny baby before and hoped he would be more sympathetic to it than he had been to a certain other unmentionable small creature.

Lisa began to cry again, and I went running about in search of Kleenex, to no avail. I returned with a roll of toilet paper. "Didn't you hear?" she asked, sniffling.

"Hear what?"

"That Paul was sleeping with half the neighborhood?"

Suddenly I was glad to be living in my own shabby, crime-ridden building where neighbors did not even greet each other in the stairwell, never mind sleep together. "What do you mean?" I asked stupidly.

She blew her nose loudly, and looked like a wreck, with a red nose and streaky mascara. "I mean he was sleeping with half the neighborhood. He was having affairs with two other women in the playgroup."

I refrained from pointing out that two women was not exactly half the neighborhood. I was frankly stunned that any man would even consider two-timing Lisa; she seemed to me like the ultimate catch with her beauty and her brains and her self-respect and all the other stuff she had that I did not.

"God, Ella. How could I be so stupid?" she asked, perhaps rhetorically, bursting into a fresh round of tears.

Jayne began to fuss, responding instinctively to the sound of her mother's distress, and I stood up and began to pace around the room, swaying Jayne gently in my arms until she fell back to sleep. She was lovely and I fantasized about telling Lisa to leave her with me while she pulled herself together. Emboldened by these maternal stirrings I felt, for once, like I could see things clearly.

"Listen, Lisa," I said with unprecedented confidence, "we all have our different areas of strength. Sometimes very smart women fall for men who are bad for them. And perhaps the reverse might be true. Maybe women who are not so smart in areas of important things . . . like, for example, postmodern analyses of popular television programs or . . . or the deconstruction of marginal historical figures . . . maybe they are the women who are smart when it comes to things like relationships!

"Besides," I continued, "being in love is overrated. Being in love is a form of mental illness. It's like drinking too much. You lose your perspective."

I was so excited to be on the other end of this that I rambled on for a while longer, wondering if there might be a thesis topic lurking about. Somewhere along the way I mentioned that in a few weeks, when my nieces were out of school for the summer, I was planning to take them to Florida and perhaps she would like to join us.

"My sister and her husband are going to Europe and they offered to foot the bill if I took the kids on vacation. Can you believe, that of all the places in the world, they want to go to Parrot Jungle?" I asked.

Lisa stopped crying and looked at me strangely.

"Oh don't worry, I don't have any interest in seeing Nigel," I insisted. "I just thought it would be fun to see the birds."

"I never should have brought you to Washington, Ella," Lisa said, sounding quite grave. She walked over and embraced me and patted me on the back for a long time, like I was a rattled puppy, or perhaps a mental patient who needed to be talked down from a ledge during a psychotic episode. "That really was a huge error of judgment on my part."

"No, no," I insisted. "It was a good experience," I lied. "And I learned a lot. It was a good beginning . . . *That every beginning is difficult holds in all sciences,*" I said aloud, wondering who had said that.

Maybe it had been Louis Schwartz.

Notes and Acknowledgments

The historical portions of the novel—those presented as the fragments of Ella's dissertation—are a blend of fact and fiction. While I have attempted to present a largely accurate picture of Eleanor's life, many scenes and details have been invented, as has the interpretation of certain events. All passages that appear in quotation marks, as well as all excerpts from letters, are taken from historical records and are documented in the notes that follow.

Several sources proved invaluable, especially two meticulously detailed, out-of-print biographies: Yvonne Kapp's two-volume biography of Eleanor Marx—*Volume I, Family Life 1855–1883,* and *Volume II, The Crowded Years, 1884–1898*—and Chushichi Tsuzuki's *The Life of Eleanor Marx, 1855–1898, A Socialist Tragedy.* Frank E. Manuel's *A Requiem for Karl Marx* similarly provided a wealth of historical material as well as an inspired analysis of Marx's life—and of his carbuncles.

Many thanks to Jean Heilprin, Pooh Shapiro, Karen Deans, and Addison Ullrich for suffering through early drafts of this manuscript. Also to Melanie Jackson for believing in this book, and to Marysue Rucci, who has been both an inspiring editor and a pleasure to work with. My husband, Steve Coll, offered always patient advice and encouragement for which I am grateful. And thanks to my parents, Marian and Joseph Keselenko. I hope my father would have laughed.

Section Notes

Epigraph From *The Eighteenth Brumaire of Louis Bonaparte,* as reprinted in *The Marx-Engels Reader,* edited by Robert C. Tucker. W. W. Norton & Co., Inc., New York, 1972, p. 436.

Prologue Passage from *Capital,* Volume. I, Chapter X, The Working-Day, as reprinted in *The Marx-Engels Reader,* edited by Robert C. Tucker, p. 249.

Karl's Carbuncles "My illness always comes from my head . . .": letter from Karl Marx to Friedrich Engels written October 19, 1867, as printed in *A Requiem for Karl Marx,* Frank E. Manuel. Harvard University Press, Cambridge, Massachusetts, and London, England, 1995, p. 86; "Never, I think . . .": *Eleanor Marx, Volume I, Family Life 1855–1883,* Yvonne Kapp. Lawrence and Wishart, 1972, London, p. 36; "This is a perfidious . . .": *A Requiem for Karl Marx,* Manuel, p. 81–82.

Birds and New Guinea *Ornithology,* Frank B. Gill, W. H. Freeman & Co., 1990; *New Guinea, an Island Apart,* Neil Nightengale, BBC Books, 1992; *The Lives of Birds: Birds of the World and their Behavior,* Lester L. Short, Henry Holt & Co., 1993; *The Minds of Birds,* Alexander Skutch, Texas A&M University Press, 1996.

A Few Impressions of Edward Aveling "Though no woman . . .": *Bernard Shaw, Volume I, 1856–1898, The Search for Love,* edited by Michael Holroyd, Random House, 1988, p. 154; "Shut up your purse, tight . . .": *Bernard Shaw Collected Letters, 1898–1910,* edited by Dan H. Laurence, Dodd Mead & Co., 1972, p. 7; "a little lizard . . .": *Eleanor Marx, Volume I,* Kapp, p. 264; "I have a fear . . .": *The Life of Eleanor Marx, 1855–1898, A Socialist Tragedy,* Chushichi Tsuzuki, Clarendon Press, 1967, p. 107;

the worse the reputation . . . .: This was actually the observation of a family friend, Wilhelm Liebknecht. *The Life of Eleanor Marx,* Tsuzuki, p. 99.

Hampstead Heath Eleanor's "confession": *The Life of Eleanor Marx,* Tsuzuki, p. 17; "Jenny is most like me . . .": *The Life of Elenor Marx,* Tsuzuki, p. 63.

Arthurdale Material on Arthurdale from *Eleanor and Franklin,* Joseph P. Lash, Konecky and Konecky, 1971, chapter 37.

Madame Bovary "Now her chest began to heave . . .": *Madame Bovary,* Gustave Flaubert. Translated by Geoffrey Wall, Penguin Books, 1992, p. 266; "You see I'm not clever enough . . .": *The Daughters of Karl Marx, Family Correspondence 1866–1898,* commentary and notes by Olga Meier, Harcourt Brace Jovanovich, 1979, p. 148.

Eleanor, Observed "She was the gayest creature . . .": description by Eleanor's friend Marian Skinner, as reprinted in *Eleanor Marx, Volume I,* Kapp, p. 205; "A lively young girl . . .": *Eleanor Marx, Volume II,* Kapp, p. 206; "A broad, low . . .": *The Life of Eleanor Marx,* Tsuzuki, pp. 54–55; "A German-looking lady. . . .": *Eleanor Marx, Volume II,* Kapp, p. 140.

The Honeymoon "*Morally* as free . . . *Eleanor Marx, Volume II,* Kapp, p. 18.

Divorce and Remarriage "I am very lonely . . .": *Eleanor Marx, Volume II,* Kapp, p. 21.

A Not Unlovely Oval Face Description of labor movement in America from *Labor's Untold Story,* Richard O. Boyer and Herbert M. Morais, United Electrical, Radio and Machine Workers of America, New York, 1955; the *Chicago Tribune* quote appears on page 91 of *Labor's Untold Story;* "The man wore a grey . . ."; *The Life of Eleanor Marx,* Tsuzuki, p. 135. Additional descriptions of the American journey provided by *Eleanor Marx, Volume II,* Kapp.

Ella's notes on airplane from *Labor's Untold Story,* Boyer and

Morals, *Eleanor Marx, Volume II,* Kapp, and *The Life of Eleanor Marx,* Tsuzuki, pp. 138–139.

Unpaid Bills "AVELING'S UNPAID LABOR . . .": *Eleanor Marx, Volume II,* Kapp, pp. 171–74; "Altogether, delivering lectures . . .": *The Life of Eleanor Marx,* Tsuzuki, p. 143.

Freddy Demuth "The usual round . . .": *The Daughters of Karl Marx,* Meiers p. 199.

The Half Brother: "Even the doctors . . .": *Eleanor Marx, Volume II,* Kapp, p. 424; Description of party: *Eleanor Marx, Volume II,* Kapp, pp. 425–26; "So you see . . .": *Eleanor Marx, Volume II,* Kapp, p. 425.

Bitter Almonds "Please give bearer . . .": *The Life of Eleanor Marx,* Tsuzuki, p. 317.

Mrs. Warren's Profession Felix Barker's letter to the New Yorker appeared on November 27, 1954.

About the Author

Susan Coll was born in Manhattan and has lived in Los Angeles, New Delhi, and London. She has worked as a travel and feature writer and has contributed to the International Herald Tribune and the Asian Wall Street Journal. She currently lives in Bethesda, Maryland. This is her first novel.